THE SUNFLOWER AND THE SPARROW

FRED SIMPSON

To my brother and sister, Anthony and Margaret, with love.

CONTENTS

PART I

CAROL

The years had drawn her mouth into a purse. Each demand, each command, every slight and dismissal – every sting of humiliation – had served to tighten the strings, so that her mouth, one sensed, would not open, even to eat, without considerable effort. The purse looked to be fashioned from leather, old and unoiled, and her lips were weathered folds of the same. One could surmise, even from across a dining room table, that a condensate of Carol would taste bitter – so bitter, in fact, that it could be incorporated into the fight against malaria. Men might say that her mouth was too bitter to kiss, but it was men – one man in particular – who were responsible for turning her blood into bile.

It was in the day when women were expected to marry that Carol first met Kevin, and it was with a sense of relief – triumph even – when they 'got together'. She had been raised in a rural village in Taranaki, primary-schooled there, high-schooled as a boarder in New Plymouth, before making the natural progression into an office job at the local farmers' co-op store. Come the week-end, she did what everyone in the district did after work on a Friday: head to the club for happy hour, in her case with her parents. The club was the centre of all that offered hope in the world, and it was inevitable that it was at the club, on a Friday night, at that very hour, that he first materialised. The club, like countless others, offered a rugby/cricket field, a couple of hard tennis courts, and, most importantly, a bar with darts and discounted beer prices. It was in the day when only men were allowed into bars, because they swore, and so Carol sat where she always did, just outside of swearing range, in one of the many green metal chairs that decked the ladies' lounge. Children were permitted to play in the ladies' lounge.

Her mother sat with Carol, and above them hung the honours board. Her father's name featured, chiselled into the wooden panel in gold lettering, as club RUGBY CAPTAIN 1955, and club CHAIRMAN 1961. It was 1965, as she recalled, and the board, because it also had to accommodate tennis captains, cricket captains, as well as the recipients of greater district honours, was starting to warp under the weight of lettering. Netball did not feature in those days – probably because there were not enough tall women.

Her father had brought them each a drink from the bar – more specifically one beer, two lemonades and two glasses, so that they could share shandies. Carol had waited for this, for adulthood, all her life, and her time had finally come. Club rules, strictly enforced by the committee, stipulated that ladies had to be over eighteen years of age before they could drink alcohol in the ladies' lounge, and Carol, elevated by a brief speech and the customary round of drinks from her father, had followed the quaint tradition of coming of age, in this self-same lounge, just two months prior. What remained unspoken, but widely understood, was that the lounge offered unattached men and women the ideal setting to make contact, to spark, as it were, an attachment; and this is what was achieved between Kevin and Carol.

Men came filing out of the bar clutching jugs of beer, prompted by the announcement of the much-anticipated meat raffle. Those who were married had seats reserved for them by their wives, and those who were not married, stood … except for one man who Carol had not seen before. He sauntered over to a vacant chair at their table, acknowledged her mother and her with a faint nod, and then scanned the room like a surveillance camera. His lips, she noticed, were like pencil lines, and they, linked to his unblinking eyes, hinted at mockery – at a suggestion of the merest sneer. She kept him in focus throughout the excitement of the draw. The treasurer of the entertainment committee was called upon to blindly select, then scrupulously verify, the pairings of the sheep carcass cuts to ticket holders. It was a merry time of predictable protestations and harmless ribbing; but Kevin remained impassive – inscrutable – and Carol's interest was aroused. This was a man outside of the mould, someone who was self-confident, mature – a man out of the movies – a man who could raise one up.

On the completion of the happy hour draw, her father, who sat to her right, engaged him in conversation. She desperately wanted to hear what was being said, but the room was noisy, and she did not want to appear foolish. Besides, for the life of her, she could not think of anything important to say. She thought of Mt Egmont, or Mt Taranaki – the name that the young were encouraged to use – because everyone living in Taranaki thought of Mt Egmont. The mountain, with its major and minor heads, was visible on a clear day from everywhere in Taranaki, because it was 8261 feet tall, she remembered, and it looked like Mt Fuji in Japan. It also killed people every year. There were other facts about the volcano that she could have told the stranger, but she would not have told him about that special day with her father when they walked the contour to Dawson Falls and the wood pigeon, the kereru, led them. It had snowed the night before, and small drifts of the fresh powder had collected alongside their path and on the boughs of the giant trees. She remembered the silence that listened to the crunch of their boots, and she remembered the occasional exposure to the peak, high above them; but mainly she remembered the fwu-fwu-fwu of the kereru's wings. Her father signalled for her to stop, to stand absolutely still – and they waited, thrilled, until the next fwu-fwu-fwu exposed its large body and small head – fleetingly. There was just a flash of belly-white and green wing; but the magical thing, the thing that bonded her father and her in enduring memory, was that the bird led them, led them to the falls over the next hour and a half. It didn't stay, the bird, to receive their thanks, but simply disappeared. They were left to look across at the long spout of silver that was moving but was not – at the backdrop of rock and lichen – and eat their boiled eggs and biscuits. She wept some years later when she sneaked out to watch the film *Camelot*, and the opening scene had Richard Harris and Vanessa Redgrave meeting, unexpectedly, in the same crisp forest of snow.

But, although Carol could not talk, she could observe, and glances ostensibly directed beyond Kevin confirmed that he was indeed old – at least twenty-six or twenty-seven – and that his left ring finger remained unadorned. She found out later from her father that he was an agricultural salesman from Hamilton with a three-month posting to rural Taranaki. Carol remembered sitting up in her room that night, until late, and coming to the realisation that this was her opportunity. If ever she was going to fulfil her dream of having children and her own home in a big city, Kevin was her chance. Even his name thrilled her! She realised too, however, that she would have to be extraordinarily lucky to win his heart.

As luck would have it, they were married at the club six months later. Her parents, quick to recognise his potential, invited Kevin to dinner soon after the first meeting. They had lamb shanks – he was plated two – as well as baked custard for dessert. The recipe for the baked custard was one that had been handed down through maternal generations, and it was made clear to Kevin that Carol was linked to that lineage. Their relationship was able to further advance because Kevin's job offered him the opportunity to call into Carol's co-op three or four times a week, on business. He managed to maintain a perception of professional divide when he called and did not make obvious his intentions, but she could feel a current connecting them, and, from her kiosk, she fed on his confidence and steely charm. She became privy to his selling style: "Selling ... selling. The first rule of selling is that you never mention the word," he would say, and, thrillingly, she became party, as a witness, to 'the transfer of ownership' of many a plough. Each transaction that went through (and some, let me tell you, were big ticket) added to her certainty that this was a man with a future.

And, blessedly, with regard to their own transactions, one thing led to another, and another, and, because it was in the day when it was customary to marry if illicit intimacy bore fruit, nuptials were brought forward.

Carol's father, being a former chairman and current life-member of the club, was able to secure its facilities for the reception – with the proviso that all catering would be carried out by the catering committee. This was not a problem because Carol's mother was the secretary of the catering committee, and her fellow members were only too willing to oblige. Carol's mother told them not to skimp, and they did not skimp. Even concerns around guest numbers were satisfactorily settled without having to create lifelong enemies, because Kevin had so few people that he wanted to invite. His father he considered dead (more about that later), but his mother and sister were invited, as well as his boss and best man, who had to travel all the way from Hamilton.

One could not say, if one was truthful, that 'the town' was particularly happy with Carol's happiness though – too many of its other sons and daughters remained unattached – but it was generous enough to try to hide its envy in celebratory brandy, sherry and beer (this preceded the time of wine, you understand); and the sheer fact that rumours of an undisclosed 'other' turned out to be true, was a God-sent salve to all. Her parents, indeed, could be justifiably proud of the send-off that they had provided, even though it took them at least a decade to financially recover. They were not prepared – perhaps they were too tired – to follow up on reports of bottles of whisky being whisked away – the day was too precious for that.

So, there she was, on the threshold of bliss, about to set off to the Raglan Hotel for a three-day honeymoon after a first night in Inglewood. Her happiness was almost complete. The only dampener, and it was inexplicable at the time, was that a part of her – possibly the part involved in swallowing – felt sore, constricted, and caused her to choke. She had sensed the impact of finality, of never again, and the disappearing image of her parents holding hands – something that they seldom did – caused a stab, just a stab, of doubt.

It was only later that bitterness set in, later, when there was enough space in her head to gain perspective, but at the time Carol had no option other than to waste her youth. Kevin had rules, and Carol obeyed them, because it was easier that way. They were laid down, he explained, to make her a better wife. He had prerequisites for approval, and the first was to have his loose-leaf tea, brewed in a pre-heated pot and poured with milk and one sugar, ready for sipping when he sat down for breakfast. But it was his egg, or eggs, that he was most particular about. They had to be fried in salted farm butter and basted to ensure vertical consistency, while the white – this was important – had to be solidified in an even radius from their yolk centres. Carol learned too that the utmost care had to be taken in the transfer of egg from pan to plate, as any puncture or spill would be flung onto the dining room floor.

Kevin worked hard, Carol was made to understand, and he would not have her waste a penny. He was a man of lists as well as rules, and the list that he most frequently referred to was the one dealing with waste – heating the house above nineteen degrees in winter, for example, was the equivalent of 'savings incineration', a term, the expression of which, his graphite lips were particularly adept at annunciating. But their budget meetings were the most telling for Carol, partly because every penny (or cent after the introduction of decimalisation) had to be accounted for, but also because they took place every Wednesday after he returned from golf. The golf, and the two beers at the nineteenth hole, he would point out, were not carried out for pleasure – for fun – but for networking – for putting food on the table. It was damned hard work, and he would not countenance her going over budget – even for staples. After the meeting was over, however, and 'general business' had been concluded, he would relax and allow Carol a sherry before dinner, while he himself would 'pop another top', before telling her about his difficult day – in Morrinsville, or Matamata – while she rubbed his feet. But the third beer, she found, had the effect of sharpening his sarcasm, as well as his insistence on carrying out unorthodox conjugal manoeuvres; and she would have preferred to have moved the meetings to Thursday.

Her pregnancies, children's births (two, and two years apart), as well as their early upbringing, were barely remembered by Carol.

She couldn't recall, for example, the vomiting or the near-psychotic fatigue – she couldn't even recall the experience of searing labour pain that her friends spoke of with trembling voices – but, on reflection, it was the effective disappearance of the self that she had earlier started to formalise, as well as the shock that this loss caused, that resulted in her near total amnesia. The years between eighteen and twenty-five are meant to consolidate the self, to complete the portrait of adulthood – seven years to detach, then reattach to parents; seven years to reform the concept of home; seven years to dodge catastrophe and emerge with purpose and direction – but Carol spent those years as an automaton. Small children, as those of you who are parents will endorse, are all-consuming. They have the tendency to both diminish and expand the self, depending upon how long they sleep, or how often they are sick, or smile, but in order for their infancy to be recalled in any affectionate way, it needs to be remembered in the context of a couple's loving battle with doubt and inadequacy. Each needs to give his, or her, all – photographs are not enough; but Kevin's only offering was a firm 'hands off' approach. Not only did this include the quaint male aversion to nappy change and rising in the night, but also, and more tellingly for Carol, his complete emotional sterility. He was immune to the enormity of his task, even as an adjunct, and she had no one to turn to.

Her parents visited when they could, but they were not welcomed. Even during and immediately after her labours, when her mother's instincts overrode humiliation, she was not allowed much time alone with her. Kevin went back to Taranaki just twice in those seven years, to her old home, for long weekends, and she wished that he had not. She herself was permitted to visit her parents for a week each year, with the children. Her father would come and fetch them. She would try to plan the visit in summer, so that they could use the new pool that had been built at the club. She would also use the peace to sleep. Little of her life in Hamilton was spoken about, apart from the activities of the children, but the children, in their own way, told it all.

They had started out their married life living with Kevin's mother and sister in Dinsdale, on the Whatawhata road. They had their own room but shared the house's single bathroom and toilet. It was to be an interim arrangement until they could save for a deposit for their own place. Kevin was energised, as much as Kevin could be energised, by the opportunity that this provided for them to financially advance. It would also, he explained, provide Carol with an effectively free apprenticeship in housekeeping, with his mother acting as her foreman.

What was clearest in her memory of those times, however, was her mother-in-law's fixation with radio, and, in particular, with daily serials. Nothing, not even her son, could come between her and her serials. The telephone was not to be answered, the door was not to be opened, and woe betide Carol if little Evan, her first-born, let out a yell at the very moment when a murder was being committed or the name of a secret lover was being revealed. She learned that it was preferable to take him outside, anywhere, regardless of the weather, rather than remain confined, and it was at this early time that she got to know the river.

Hamilton is a peculiar city, in that it has turned its back on its soul – its river – a river banked by massive ferns, flax, and trees that live precariously. You can walk the main streets of Hamilton and not know that its artery is just out of sight and sound and smell – that ducks are teaching their young to find food in the eddies on the inside of bends. They run south to north, the streets, and parallel to the river, but their commercial buildings form a buffer. Some claim that it was Kiwi modesty on the part of early town planners, to hide the jewel, to make it appear unlovely, some that it was mere stupidity, but for Carol it was a personal gift. Even the river paths in the late sixties were rudimentary, but they offered an escape, a sanctuary of peace where she could make her own determination on where to walk, or when to stop to watch the mood and movement of water. Carol had never heard of Heraclitus, but she would have subscribed to his observation that 'you could not step twice into the same river; for other waters are ever flowing on to you'. It was often misty in winter in Hamilton, especially along the river, and that enhanced its mystery, but, more importantly, the mist granted Carol her wish, at least for an hour or two, to be rendered incognito. It enabled her to evaporate from sight, so that she could connect, unmolested, with a broken, floating bough, and accompany it on its journey to Port Waikato and the sea beyond.

Evan was born while they were still living with Christine, her mother-in-law, but, by the time that Stewart came along, they had moved to Hillcrest. Hillcrest was an expensive suburb, even then, because of its university, schools and elevation, but Kevin had got wind of an acrimonious divorce through a client, and he made an offer on the couple's house before it was even listed, and the price, he proudly announced, was 'a steal'. He even had the couple's wood supply included in the chattels. The three of them moved across town before the ink was dry. Having her own home was what Carol had always wanted, but she had anticipated a weatherboard house fenced in rose-draped white picket, with a tree on the lawn for the children's swing, as well as rhododendrons (a New Plymouth speciality), exploding with colour in spring.

When she was first shown the house it was a disappointment: not because it was built square, of clinker brick; not because there were no annuals bordering the lawn; not even because its only tree was a messy loquat; but because it did not feel like home – not her home. But the move away from Christine and Ethel, Kevin's sister, was, she had to admit, a huge relief, and Hillcrest offered access to the river's other bank. It was a little further to walk to, and the walk back, especially when she had to push and carry two children up the long hill, was taxing, but the Hamilton Botanical Gardens that adjoined the river reminded her of Pukekura Park in New Plymouth – her favourite place in the whole world. In fact, Kevin himself would accompany her to the gardens with the children occasionally, if he wasn't playing golf, and the flowers seemed to sweeten him. At times like these, eating ice cream at the café by the pond with old people smiling at the children as they passed, Carol felt a hint of optimism that she was hesitant to hold on to.

Kevin had a company car. He joked that it was his office, and that he spent more time in the car, driving around greater Waikato, than he spent with his wife. Private use was permitted, provided it was logged, and so he saw no need for a second car, even an old and ugly one, for Carol to use. She had two good legs, he would say when the subject came up, and everything that she could wish for was within walking distance. He was infuriated, therefore, when he discovered that Carmel, a friend she met at Evan's kindergarten, had started taking Carol out of town – to Cambridge, Te Awamutu, even Te Aroha – in her Hillman. They would drop their older children off at the kindergarten, and then head out for afternoon tea. Winding down the windows 'to smell the silage', they would strain their voices attempting songs as different as Canned Heat's 'On the Road Again', 'When a Man Loves a Woman' by sexpot Percy Sledge, and 'Penny Lane', the sweet, sweet song by the new rock group sensation, The Beatles. Carmel's favourite, though, was 'A Whiter Shade of Pale', by the band with a funny name, Procol Harum; but when she tried to sing the upper notes they would simply disappear, picked up (with some alarm, one imagines) by animals with a greater frequency range than humans, out herding the sheep. They also, on their drives, made it compulsory to stop, at least once on each outing, when colour caught their eye – sometimes this was a bed of mixed annuals, sometimes a blossom-laden trellis, sometimes even a glistening perched high in a poplar; but Carol's all-time favourite was a stand of deep-yellow, father-tall sunflowers, bending west, towards her, on a farm near Mt Maungatautari.

Her Stewart and Carmel's Beryl were quiet as whispers in the back, always, and it was as close to carefree that Carol ever got in those early days in Hamilton.

Carol's friendship was the first that she had formed since school, but it was, she could feel, reaching a depth that other friendships had never approached – a depth that risked self-disclosure. She looked forward to being with Carmel, not only because she was fun and funny, but because Carmel wanted to be with her. For four years Carol's conversations had been guarded and measured, linked to 'getting ahead', but with Carmel she talked about music, film, how to be a good mother – and more and more about her parents and Taranaki. Kevin she never mentioned, other than to say that he worked very hard. Carmel, though, was effusive about her husband: "Jim's a honey, an absolute honey. His job is to bath the kids, and dress them, but by the time they've finished with him he looks like a drenched sheep. And the mess!" She paused, with half a daylight moon beyond her shoulder, before continuing, "I just love that time of day. I can get on and cook the dinner with Barbra Streisand while they have their rough and tumble on the carpet; then we feed them, put them to bed – no nonsense – before sitting down to eat ourselves. Jim pours me a sweet wine – you can get them in casks now – and he has his beer. Heaven! Pure heaven!" And then, the awkward next step, "You've got to come over for a barbie this weekend. Make it lunch. Jim is dying for some man company."

"I'll check with Kevin, Carmel. Thank you. He's so busy, you know."

"Nonsense! No excuse. We'll see you Saturday – and bring nothing but your records."

What Carol couldn't bring herself to say, however, was that she didn't own records. Kevin wouldn't allow her to buy them – "Too pricey", and "What's wrong with your radio?" She also couldn't voice her nagging concern that Kevin might destroy their friendship – a friendship that she had kept secret. Her small contribution to petrol costs, as well as the odd scone for afternoon tea, could not be hidden in the 'miscellaneous' column for ever, and Carol quivered at what would ensue when he found out – and she was not wrong!

Their Wednesday night budget meeting had been successfully negotiated – only just! Her extra spending had been accounted for under 'kindergarten incidentals', and they had moved onto the pleasantries of Kevin's hard day, when Carol casually mentioned the invitation to Jim and Carmel's.

"Who?" he asked in surprise – the third beer starting to take effect.

"Carmel – a woman whose son goes to the same kindergarten as Evan."

"And Jim?"

"Her husband, dear."

"How do you know this woman?"

"Well, we talk, Kevin, about the kids."

Just then, as his father's eyes began to swivel, Evan entered the conversation. "Mummy goes for rides with her, in her car."

"A car? She has a car? You go for *rides* with her?"

"Just to the shops, Kevin, or down to the river."

"Mummy drives the car, too," Evan added.

"*What?*"

"Well," Carol's mouth was drying, and the pitch of her voice was altered by the stickiness, "I haven't driven since leaving Taranaki, and, and Carmel kindly suggested that I take over the wheel occasionally – just for practice."

"Are you completely stupid?" It was a rhetorical question. "You are stupid – more stupid than I thought. *Say it!*" he shouted.

"Kevin, I …"

"Say it." He was speaking quietly now, and the lines comprising his lips were curling, menacingly.

There was silence, apart from a sniffle from Evan. Carol was too frightened to cry. "I, I'm stupid."

"Again, louder."

"I'm stupid."

Kevin slowly released his grip on her arm – she hadn't been aware that he had hold of it – but fixed his eyes on hers. "Don't you ever drive a car again without my permission. Don't you ever."

"Yes, Kevin," she whispered.

"And tell them to get stuffed. What's she after anyway? A foursome?"

Later, after a silent dinner and a fourth beer, he interrogated her further. It was then that the enormity of her wider excursions was fully exposed. He wanted to know where she had been, when, and what she had spent his money on. In particular, he wanted to know how often she had driven Carmel's car. This had to be elaborated on, over and over again. For some reason her driving 'without permission' raised the fury of infidelity in him. A curfew was established before the night was out, and yet tighter reins were imposed on her allowance. I won't go into what happened after they went to bed, but suffice to say she didn't sleep, at all, and by noon on the never-to-be-forgotten Thursday that followed, she was cried out. When her father died five years later, her tear glands failed to respond.

You might wonder why Carol didn't leave Kevin there and then, but it was in the time when divorce for a young woman with two small children and no means of independent income was unthinkable; but change was effected, and should have been plain to see. Humiliation is never forgotten or forgiven, not by individuals, nor by nations. It is branded into the consciousness of both like a burning iron and waits to take its revenge – to replicate the humiliation and harm. The wait may take decades for the individual, as it did for Carol, or centuries, as it did in the Balkans – with the poison of bitterness acting as its smouldering fuel. Kevin might have been forewarned had he read Herodotus – 'Do not humiliate people, because they will thereafter subsist on dreams of revenge' – but he had not.

His father left home when Kevin was thirteen, when the farm went bankrupt. He moved to Oregon, of all places, and gradually lost touch. Ethel kept in contact with her father, and even visited him, but Kevin refused to look at her pictures of giant trees. Kevin grew up seeking approval from his father, but found only contempt. He was not good at rugby, he hated camping, and he could not be trusted to close a farm gate. Their life after the bankruptcy, in a state house in Hamilton, was sustained by crushing frugality, and his mother became a shrew; but Kevin decided upon a different path. He would make money, he would move to Hillcrest – he might even own a boat that he would race around Lake Karapiro ahead of others – he would, in effect, win.

Success does not come easily, however. As a teenager he learned to use fabrication to enhance self-confidence, and he parted his hair in the middle; but experience is what teaches us most, and, as we have learned, those linked to humiliation are the ones most likely to endure. Kevin had his share of them at school, and they taught him, in effect, never to leave his underbelly exposed – never to lose control. One such incident occurred when he lashed out angrily and impetuously at a boy younger than himself, who had pushed in front of him at the tuck shop; but the boy was stronger than him, and Kevin was quickly wrestled to the ground and his mouth stuffed with soil. And girls, he realised, posed an even greater risk of fragility. It perplexed Kevin that he could be irritated by their silliness and sulks yet find alluring the smell of chlorine on their skin after swimming. After one particularly clumsy advance and rejection, he decided that he was done with them; but then, in early adulthood, when the imperative for a wife became more pressing, he devised a strategy, a pose, that he was sure would succeed. He would offer aloofness as his bait and wait for someone like his mother to bite.

It was no wonder then that complacency set in, that he was smug in the knowledge that he had regained control of his wife. He had long forgotten to look for kindness in eyes – not even in the eyes of dogs – and so he had never noticed the kindness leave Carol's. He had never noticed either that her mouth was starting to pucker, that it was taking on the appearance of a sphincter, a sphincter designed more for continence than kissing. Kevin was able to detect weakness – hesitation, 'soft spots' in body language, and he was successful at their exploitation, but Carol could hold his hand with hatred, and he never guessed.

And so, the years went by. Kevin sold more farm implements, and his firm gave him season tickets to the rugby, where he could mix and mingle. He was so successful that, for a brief period, he became the chief salesman for the whole of the central North Island – in charge and overseer of a substantial team that covered the Waikato, King Country, Taranaki, Taupo and Bay of Plenty districts. After two years the huge area that he controlled was substantially downsized, however, following a series of complaints – even resignations – by employees over his 'management style'. He was angry – of course he was angry – but he never accepted this as a demotion – never elucidated the extent of territory loss to

Carol. He accounted for the reduction in 'away trips' by saying that he'd had enough of them, and that he had negotiated for others, underlings, to traverse the wider region. He was sick of carrying the weight of the whole company, he told her, and it was time to get a load off his back.

But the load shifted from his back to his belly and detonated a cold fury that would simmer unabated until it caused the next calamity.

In the interim, meanwhile, he continued to prosper in the only way that he knew how. He sold their first house in Hillcrest and purchased another. It was substantially larger and had views over to Mt Pirongia, which the setting sun caught in silhouette. Then came the boat, after the boys left home. He bought it at the Boat Show, as a package, complete with trailer and winch. One problem was that he couldn't use his company car to tow the boat (the fitting of a tow bar would have been a giveaway), and so he had to buy one of the new Japanese utility vehicles so fashionable at that time. It had 3.5 litres of power packed under its bonnet, he told his boss, and could have pulled a train. Carol had the job of guiding him as he reversed the trailer down into the water at their first outing. She stuffed it up, as she did everything, and caused him to jackknife, repeatedly. Her hands were all over the place, but the more he shouted, the more she flapped. People, the same people, started to gather at the boat ramp every time that he tried to launch after that and snigger. Eventually, when fury could no longer be sustained, he finally lost control of his tongue and lashed out at them most viciously. As a consequence, he and his boat were banned by the lake committee for a minimum period of three calendar months. It was, in effect, the end of his boating career. The boat was stored in his third garage until the following summer, when he sold it at a profit.

Whereas Carol was able to recall very little of the first five to seven years of her marriage, the 'excursion incident' effected a reboot in the region of her brain's hippocampus, which became obsessively receptive to each and every spouse-related slight that came its way. Noxious sensory impulses synapsed to Kevin would immediately be soaked in concrete and left to set. Her friendship with Carmel had not been able to survive his scrutiny, but she had used the related hurt to fashion a permanent smile. His refusal to allow her to work, to use a hairdryer when he was home, to swim unchaperoned at the municipal pools, to watch afternoon television, to buy winter clothes before the spring winter sales, to arrange extra maths lessons for Stewart: all of these indignities, and so many more, added sinew to the suspenders that supported her facade. A camera, filming in infrared, might have caught her face off-guard, might have detected a flicker of murderous intent; but Kevin could be forgiven for believing that he had fashioned the perfect wife. His confidence was tested, however, when he got sick.

For years, for financial reasons and because he found them smug, Kevin had avoided doctors, and he had doused the gnawing fire in his upper belly with antacids and aspirin. First, he had used teaspoonfuls of baking soda before bed, then the more convenient Quick-Eze that he bought by the boxful at filling stations, but when he was woken one night by the expulsion of bright-red vomitus, he panicked.

"Carol, Carol!" he bellowed. *"Look at this. Carol."*

Roused from the authenticity of dream, it took her some thirty seconds to register and raise the angles of her mouth to replicate her aforesaid smile. She turned then, languidly, to look at him in the weak, bedside light. He looked ridiculous, holding his mouth open for her to see the blood, eyes watering, and snot hanging from his nose. His white, stained sleeping vest, one that she particularly despised, was wet through with sticky red. She stared at him, and him at her, and then he heaved, and heaved again, choking as a giant clot slopped out.

'What if I just watch,' she thought to herself. 'There's so much blood. There can't be much left.'

"Call them. C...call them quickly," he stammered. "The pain is terrible."

"Do you know their number, my love?"

"You know their number, you fool – 111."

He heaved again, as she reached for the phone, and plugged in the numbers. "Yes, yes, it's Mrs Burton. I have an emergency. I have a husband who is dying … about to die. Would you send an ambulance? My address – of course, it's …"

Kevin survived the night, but he never recovered his confidence. At the hospital he had to be transfused with a pint or more of blood, and an emergency gastroscopy revealed the erosion of a large duodenal ulcer. He was on a drip and unable to eat for three days. Results of biopsies taken during the operation were blessedly benign, but he was advised to take large doses of oral medication 'for the foreseeable future, to prevent the development of malignancy in the lower part of your swallowing tube'. He was reassured that he didn't have a *Helicobacter pylori* infection – whatever that was! It was all very bewildering. Annual endoscopies, it was stressed, were imperative to monitor this, and he needed to contact his GP for their facilitation.

Kevin, unaware of the change in GP demographics, assumed that most were male, and he was startled, but subsequently relieved, when told on arrival that an appointment Carol had made for him with her own doctor, Edith Liddle, had had to be shifted to Dr Frank Edge. Dr Liddle, the receptionist explained, had been summoned to the morgue.

His relief was initially replaced with awkwardness, however, when he was confronted by a number of introductory questions from the doctor related to his social habits, his occupation, his 'level of activity', and, especially, about his family history; and he found it both comforting and annoying when Carol tried to answer certain questions for him. Dr Edge, or Frank, the name that he referenced on their arrival, thanked Carol for her input, but suggested that he would rather the responses came directly from Kevin himself. After completing his history, Frank checked Kevin's height, weight, pulse, and blood pressure. His heart and lungs were auscultated, and his tummy prodded.

"Have you had your prostate checked yet, Kevin?" he asked, while he had him lying supine on the bed. "It's not something that we need to do today, right now, but it is important at your age. Any flow difficulties? Any problem sustaining an erection?"

He made a faint effort to shake his head, happy that the curtain was closed. The prostate did worry him. The men at work were always on about it. "Haven't had it checked," he whispered.

"Okay." Frank motioned for him to lie on his left side with knees flexed, placed a sheet over his middle, and, within a minute, it was over. "Good. Thank you, Kevin. All fine. Nice and normal. Please hop down and get dressed."

Frank gave him a script, as well as a form for blood tests, "to check cholesterol and sugar, et cetera", and he was free to go.

Carol was disappointed that it had all been too easy, that she had been unable to press her advantage, and she regretted having not delayed the appointment until her own doctor, Edith, was back. Edith was one of the few people who was aware of his true nature, and she would, Carol was certain, have made his consultation far more uncomfortable.

Carol's disclosure to Edith had come about without prior intention during a routine blood pressure review, but it was the subject of weight which had provided the prompt.

"Just don't know what else to do, Edith. I garden and walk, I stopped white bread and Coke, cut down on potatoes, and I only keep biscuits for my husband."

There was a pause at that point, and Carol was waiting for Edith to repeat her sermon about 'energy in and energy out', but instead she asked, "Are you unhappy, Carol?" This was not the first time that Edith had posed the question.

"Of course not. I've told you before, …"

"I know, Carol, but I suspect that you are."

Carol stared at Edith, aware that her cheeks were burning. "What do you mean?"

"It's just something that I sense."

"Sense?"

"Yes, something that I've sensed for some time." She paused again, before continuing, "You appear to me to be shielding your-self – wearing armour. What are you trying to protect yourself from? Hurt?"

Carol looked down at her flat shoes. "Maybe," she whispered.

"Would you like to talk about it – to me, or to a counsellor?"

There had been a further long pause before Carol whispered again. "It's him. I hate him."

"Your husband?"

Carol nodded.

"That's not good," Edith answered quietly. "That's not healthy for you. Does he hit you?" Carol shook her head. "Does he bully you in other ways?"

"Yes."

"Would you like to see someone who could help?" Carol shook her head. "Okay, Carol, the door is always open. You can make contact by phone too – any time, but you can't afford to bury this. Something has to be done."

But her secret of hate was what sustained her. It offered the only thrill. She saw herself as a double agent – someone who was other than she appeared. Unhappy? Maybe not. Carol could warm Kevin's slippers and smile sweetly as she slid them over his feet, then turn sedately towards her dining room mirror to inaudibly mouth revulsion. The mirror bore witness too to her mimicry, and those accustomed to her leathery expressions during guarded times would have been astonished by what it reflected. After Kevin's company car had driven him away in the morning, she would don her props (horn-rimmed reading glasses and fake moustache), and her collagen would ignite. Because Kevin's lips were thin, the grey fur above them obscured what little flesh they contained, and her prop, the mirror delighted in observing, replicated in parody the aperture that he spoke through.

It is likely that this covert entertainment would have sufficed had Kevin's health not deteriorated further, but a heart attack afforded her the opportunity to do real harm. Just a few months after the stomach bleed, he started to feel discomfort in his left arm when he mowed their front lawn. It troubled him too after a large meal. Carol reassured Kevin that it was tennis (or was it golfer's?) elbow; but early one morning he was woken by a weight on his chest that made it difficult for him to breathe – a weight that squeezed cold sweat out of his pores.

To Carol's credit an ambulance was summoned, and, before the day was done, two of his coronary arteries had been stented and death had been averted. But the shock was like nothing that Kevin had ever previously experienced. His bleed he could see, taste – it made sense to him – but part of his heart dying! It was terrifying. To compound this, he was given several more pills – 'for secondary prevention' – and his activity levels were curtailed. For Carol, though, it was a godsend! Her husband had been rendered dependent and demoralised! Furthermore, for at least a month or two, he could not drive, and, because she was not permitted to use the company car (company policy), and because Kevin had got rid of their utility after the boat was sold, he was forced to give her the okay, as well as the cash, to buy a small second-hand car. She chose a yellow one, because he preferred white.

He was off work for three long months. Carol survived (some might say thrived) by taking advantage of his dilapidation. Her vehicle was used to ferry him to and from appointments, but also to disappear for periods of the day – returning just a little later than anticipated. "The traffic, Kevin. The traffic! Hamilton's becoming another Auckland." Remonstrations were demurely deflected with a "I'm only doing this for you, my sweet. Just sit and watch the golf." And then she would add, with the hint of a twinkle in her eye, "You deserve it."

The following six years, right up until the day that Kevin had his stroke, Carol was able to savour her bitterness and roll it around on her tongue, licking when the opportunity arose. He was still working, albeit in a lesser capacity, and he was not yet an invalid, but he had developed diabetes as well as gout in that period, and, because he could not cook, Kevin had to rely on his wife for meals. She put a stop to his butter, bacon, chocolate and pink lamingtons (a particular favourite), but felt disinclined to begrudge him his beer and anchovy toast. They, her reading of *Wikipedia* suggested, were the ingredients most likely to inflame the joints of his left big toe. An audit of her activities as a dutiful wife would have unearthed nothing untoward, however. In fact it would have resulted in the highest possible commendation – especially after a perusal of Carol's meticulous compilation of lists, coded in green, red, and amber, which outlined Kevin's dos, don'ts and maybes. They pertained to diet and driving, of course, but also to the potentially detrimental effects of excitement.

Intimacy, for example, coded as a sub-category, had its effective limits determined by her monitoring of Kevin's carotid. As soon as he signalled intent she would reach for his neck with her right hand while holding a luminous watch with the other, and count. An agreed precautionary threshold was set at a pulse of 140, and any rate higher would trigger alarm and recoil.

One could look back on this period as Carol's purple patch, as a time when comparative power was recalibrated and poison gave pleasure; but it was a pity, one could argue, that she spent so little of it at the river – so little time with her adult sons. It would have been easy with Evan, as he had married and lived close by, but Stewart, accumulating assets in Australia, would have required more effort. He did return home, though, briefly, when his father had a stroke, and a family reunification of sorts was achieved.

Kevin lost his ability to express himself, to speak, although this, they were assured, would improve. "But the hemiparesis – the weakness down one side – is dense, I'm afraid, and your husband is very unlikely to walk again, unaided."

"And his mind?" Carol queried. "Has he lost his mind?"

"You mean his intellect – his ability to think? Loss of cognition is difficult to quantify at this point, but your husband has demonstrated a reasonable level of recognition – understanding – and he is beginning to co-operate. He's expressing his emotions too, by crying a lot, and this is a good thing. We can be hopeful that cognitive damage is limited, but we cannot be certain."

"What can we do?" asked Evan.

"You can talk to him, touch him – show him that he is not alone."

Carol had long hoped for a calamity to befall Kevin, and death would have been her preference. Another heart attack, perhaps? Or cancer of the lung? Even an accident? But, although the stroke happened in an instant and left him contorted, it offered no end point. There had been no time for her to fashion a response – a strategy – and she was, quite frankly, shaken by how much she had been shaken. He was completely helpless, and the crying – the crying with the crooked face – the one lid open to a bulging, terrified eye! Could this be the same beast who had ruined her life? Could she possibly make what was left of his life more miserable?

Carol could not think beyond the immediate, and it was Evan and Angela, his wife, who arranged for Kevin to move from the hospital's rehabilitation ward to a rest home – as an interim arrangement. It offered the best option for him at that juncture but was not sustainable in the longer term because of cost. Kevin had built up a sizable nest egg and his wife was capable of caring, and so the state would not fund his stay. Over the following few months another option was settled upon. They would keep the large house, but reconfigure and renovate – build ramp access, widen doors, fit a stool to the shower floor – but, more significantly, internally subdivide, so that Evan and Angela, a trained nurse, could move in as adjacent supports. Angela was heavily pregnant and expected to deliver before the move eventuated, and one could be forgiven for assuming that the anticipated arrangement offered each the ideal; but the question remained, despite (and arguably because of) Kevin's infirmity, was cohabitation feasible, or safe?

FRANK

There are not many who are totally in command of his or her field of expertise – people whose sleep is more likely to be disturbed by snoring than by doubt – but Cynthia was one. Her field was defined and delineated by the variable dimensions of the human mouth, but primarily focused on the bone and enamel that comprised teeth, as well as by the substrate into which they were so precariously embedded. "Teeth is what we're about, Frank," she explained, "but remember, teeth are nothing without gums – nothing. Like nails without toes." She looked out – or rather pretended to look out, because there was no window as such – before reinforcing her wisdom with a further, "Like nails without toes." Frank blinked to signal his comprehension but could do little else. He was lying semi-supine (which wasn't the preferred position for his back), with his mouth wide open to accommodate a loud sucking apparatus, and he simply couldn't see. Cynthia's nurse had removed his spectacles and replaced them with goggles. This, it was explained in a preamble, was a precaution to prevent self-contamination; but he was, to be honest, more concerned about the possibility of having his tongue shredded.

Armed with the pithy but grammatically correctable phrase 'bacteria is your enemy', Cynthia held nothing back when it came to dental hygiene. Her fingers, which reminded Frank of well-endowed parsnips, were applying significant angular force to a variety of hooks and probes in the exploratory phase of her assessment, and the implements were creating all manner of sickening sounds, the worst of which reminded him of aluminium scraping on ice. He could, he was certain, taste blood.

Phase two – the treatment phase – involved the gymnastic application of shrieking drills as well as instruments of medieval torture to scarify tartar from every crack and crevice that offered it a home. The effect was to impose physics-defying demands upon the elasticity of Frank's cheeks and lips, effectively transforming him into a reincarnation of Jerry Lewis. Frank felt a momentary wave of sympathy pass over him for the last of the imperilled periodontal bacteria cowering behind pillars of plaque, aware that they were soon to be dislodged and swirled without ceremony down a blood-tinged spittoon.

"Problems, Frank." Cynthia liked to be frank. "There are two that you won't hold on to. Too much shrinkage. Bone loss too. One probe went beyond seven mil. No going back from that."

"So, so ..."

"You use electric?"

"Yes."

"For long?"

"Well, since you told me to two years ago."

"Should have started long before that, but good – and Piksters? What size do you use?"

"Piksters?"

"The little coloured brushes. I gave you sizes one and two last time – purple and white," she added somewhat impatiently.

"Oh, yes. Yes, I used them for a while."

"You need to use them *all – the – time*, Frank. You know that.

Your teeth are only as healthy as your gums, you know? Bacteria is your enemy."

"I know, Cynthia. Sorry. Can I buy some more from you?"

"Of course you can, Frank," and then she added, looking directly at him and with an expression of studied professionalism, "So this is what we'll do, we'll get a referral off to a specialist peri-odontist – could be a wait – so that you can be assessed for a peg."

"A peg?"

"Yes, Frank. As I was saying, two of your molars are as good as gone, and then what will you do?" She appeared to be waiting for an answer, and he was about to reply, when she added, "If you were half-glass-full you'd be a happy man," adding after a dramatic pause and a brief chortle, "two less to brush. But seriously, Frank," resuming her professional demeanour, "what about mastication? You can't put all the onus on incisors."

"No, no, absolutely – so you'll make the referral?"

"Of course, I will, Frank. See you in six months. Don't forget your Piksters."

"No."

Frank paid for his twenty-minute half-hour appointment (discounted for age) and calculated that her hourly rate was triple his own.

Blame it on fluoride deprivation in the fifties or blame it on the import of cheap Fijian sugar, blame it on hard brushing if you will, but don't blame it on Cynthia. It is true that her diligence placed unprecedented demand upon specialist dental services in the greater Waikato region, thereby contributing to an inordinately long waiting time for first appointments, but a breach in enamel is a breach in enamel! Be that as it may, Frank was informed via Cynthia's receptionist that he would need to accept an appointment in an affluent Auckland suburban clinic if he wished to avoid the dental deterioration that time delay would cause. He accepted, and, after completion of a pre-appointment questionnaire guaranteeing payment as well as error absolution, he found himself in four short weeks back in a semi-supine position being cheerfully probed and prodded while he responded to the commands of "Open, please", "A little wider", "Now bite – up and down – side to side – again – thank you." He was then whisked off to a side room where his chin was positioned onto a cushioned bar covered by disposable plastic. The bar was in the middle of a white machine and a brief image of Anne Boleyn entered his head as it was manoeuvred, neck craned, into position. The operator then flicked a switch, and the machine was off – humming like a transformer as it slowly circumnavigated Frank's cranium.

After a wait of just five minutes he was invited back onto the specialist's electric chair and shown impressive 3D images of his molars and their accoutrements. It was a "Where are we?" session, in which his teeth were graded into 'hopeless', 'at risk', 'fair', and 'good'; followed by a "What shall we do?" session, detailing the need for one extraction, one gum flap/reset, one cap levelling, and one peg. The "What it will cost?" session was deferred and would follow in the post. It was all a little bewildering for a doctor who'd never been a patient, but Frank was confident that all would be revealed as the weeks rolled by.

After a month he telephoned the periodontist's office to find out when the therapy would begin and was told that a letter outlining treatment recommendations would soon be in the post. That afternoon, instead of the expected letter, he received a copy of the 'Beam Cone CT' report. It indicated that he had a stone in his right salivary gland, but, of greater concern, it also described a significant degree of calcification involving his left internal carotid artery. Frank was aware that a brain was not worth much without a patent left internal carotid artery, and the possibility that his was blocking did not sit comfortably with him.

After forty years of GP practice he had encountered virtually every ailment, accident and disease that could be afflicted upon *Homo sapiens*, but he had encountered these afflictions from afar, a chair away, and the impact on him personally had been limited. They had largely, and mercifully, passed him by. But inherent in this letter was something disquieting – something to upset his equilibrium: he had, at seventy, entered that stage in his life when all bets were off. Anything could happen, and would, whether it be gum recession or stroke, and he had to decide how he would deal with this absurdity. Frank had opened the letter during his tea break, and, for the rest of the afternoon, had functioned on two levels. On one he had continued to operate as an effective doctor, but on the other he had become Prospero, with every third thought on his grave.

After he had said goodbye to the last patient of the day, Frank subsided into his seat and stared directly ahead. He was puzzled, but what puzzled him was not that the possibility of age-related disease of a potentially serious nature was unexpected, but rather that 'he had taken it this way!' All his professional life Frank had instinctively connected with people receiving bad news – had comprehended the extent of their turmoil, and, whether by silence, touch – putting on the kettle – he had managed to provide a conduit through which their bewilderment could subside. Yet here he was, as inept as anyone, with a mind that had lost perspective. It was ridiculous. He tried to read the report again, as if it were not his own, but he kept getting stuck on 'calcification', 'carotid', 'consider MRI', and could not stop catastrophising.

Just then Eleanor walked in. "Frank, I thought that you'd left for home already?"

He put down the paper quickly and smiled. "Hi, El, no. Just finishing up here."

"Are you all right, Frank? A long day?"

"Yes – not too bad – just a bit tired."

"Sure you're okay?" He hesitated just long enough for her to continue, "What is it, a difficult patient?"

"No, no," he countered, smiling, "I'm the difficult one."

"What do you mean?"

"Oh, it's nothing really, just my carotid." She sat down next to him. "No, honestly, El. I'm just overreacting."

"What is it?" He handed her the letter, and Eleanor took several minutes to read through it, before turning to face him. "It's probably normal for your age, Frank. Most people over sixty have ..."

"I know, I really am being silly. I, of all people, should know ..."

"Know what, Frank? Know that everything's fine? It may well be fine – probably is – but you don't know for sure, and that's unsettling."

"But it's my reaction," he said, looking directly at her. "My reaction is over the top. I really can't think straight."

"Nonsense, Frank. It's normal. How else is anyone with insight supposed to react?" She placed her hand on his shoulder. "I'll give the neurologists a ring in the morning and get their advice. You probably need an MRI or MRA, or both for clarification, and then you'll know where you stand. Does Milly know?"

"No, but I don't want to worry her."

Eleanor smiled. "She'll worry more if you don't tell her. Your face is a give-away." And then she added, "Would you like me to pop home with you, for a drink?"

"No, thanks, and what about Harry? Won't he be home alone?"

"No, my mother picks him up from school."

"Of course. Is it working out okay?"

"Early days yet, but yes. She's a great help, and the arrangement has been good for both."

"I'm so pleased, and ... thank you, El."

"You'll be okay, Frank."

"I know."

———

Frank's mind was much, much clearer when he stopped his scooter next to the lemon tree and Emma came out to meet him. She had the habit, no matter how many times he drove in each day, to stand next to the car or scooter as it stopped, and howl. He would then get out or off, pat her, and watch as she galloped up and down the driveway, howling all the while. Emma was a good eleven years old now, and her gallop was not as fluid as before; but her eyes still danced with the same delight, just as they did when she was a pup.

Milly opened the front door, laughing. "About time, mister, she was starting to put on 'that face'."

"Just got held up a bit. How was your day?"

"Fine. The presentation went well."

"Of course, I forgot about that."

"Too busy thinking about your beloved patients?"

He kissed her, and then said, "No, not really. More about myself."

"Yourself?"

"It's nothing – probably nothing – but I'll have to look into it."

"What, Frank? You have me worried now."

He proceeded to tell Milly about the letter, and about his reaction to it, and then he talked about Eleanor's help in putting the whole thing into perspective. "I'm not too worried, Mil – really. Everyone our age has wear and tear, and if my carotids are corroding, I can get on and do something about them." He could see in her eyes that she was not convinced. Ah, those eyes! He had never been sure of the colour, even at their first encounter when he had looked up and into them in the university library. Their colour was altered, enhanced, and diminished by mood as well as by light,

and age had added opacity; but, fundamentally, they were his
constant. He touched her cheek with his as Emma nudged his
pants with her wet nose.

"Come on, girls," he said, pulling away, "time for a wine under
the walnut tree." After a dry spell it had rained that day, and the
busy lizzies were sparkling. The couple moved their seats to face
them and the lavender beyond. Bumblebees worked like heli-
copters carrying monsoon buckets, their legs laden with pollen. 'I
would hate to have my smell go,' he thought, 'as much as my sight.'

That night he slept but did not sleep. Milly, too, was restless, and
even Emma had nightmares. It was as if he had cast a tarpaulin of
unease over their beautiful home and kept in the cold. His mind,
aroused by the piercing truth but irrationality of half-dream,
perseverated on and on about disablement and death, and, by four
o'clock when lucidity returned, he had come to terms with the
possibility of retirement. Over the past several years he had been
disturbed by the increasing number of lifelong colleagues and
contemporaries who were terminating their careers. Some were
able to choose the timing of their retirement, while others were
not so fortunate. Frank himself vacillated: after a day in which he
was spooked by a number of desperately sad or complicated cases
– after a day in which he felt right out of his depth and old – he
would come home and surreptitiously scratch an asterisk into the
thirty-first December box on his calendar; but on other days –
most days really, when he was telling old ladies that they were
pregnant – or pretending not to know where children's ears were
– or when asked by Eleanor and Edith for clinical advice – he
would leap onto his scooter like a schoolboy, and ride home with a
head full of joy.

Now, he realised, the decision could be made for him.

Eleanor emailed Frank's limited CT scan report to the neurologist the next morning, and a time was set up for a call during the lunch break.

"Everyone's carotid walls are calcified at seventy, Frank, but the scan does appear to show that the process is quite advanced on the left."

"Oh!"

"Doesn't necessarily point to significant pathology though." They were both quiet for a few seconds, before Keith continued, "An MRI of your brain, as well an MRA with contrast of your neck, would elucidate this."

"In terms of stenosis?"

"Yes – but we don't recommend endarterectomy, even with a critical stenosis, unless there's been an event."

"An event? A TIA, or stroke?"

"Yes."

"So, what would I do – if it is closing up?"

"Simple measures, Frank. Stuff that you've told your patients for years – stop smoking, moderate drinking, low fat and sugar diet, monitor blood pressure, cholesterol, and so on. I would probably add aspirin, as well as a statin. The target LDL is 1.8."

"Thanks, Keith. So, I should go ahead with those investigations?"

"I would recommend them, Frank – but bear in mind that they are comprehensive … detailed … and they may show up something that you don't expect."

"Of course. I understand. Thank you, Keith."

"It's likely to be okay."

"I know. Thank you." There was a pause, and then Frank added, "Would you mind getting the referral off?"

"Of course, and we'll talk later."

"Thank you."

Frank sat sipping his coffee quietly. He tried to keep Larkin's terrifying poem, 'Aubade', out of his mind, but the words, 'Flashes afresh to hold and horrify'. Or, 'The sure extinction that we travel to'. Even, or especially, the final line, 'Postmen like doctors go from house to house'. The brutal honesty of the poem epitomised the mood behind a call that a colleague, Rob, had received from a terminally ill patient at two o'clock in the morning the previous week.

"The phone drilled into a confusing dream that I was having, and when a woman's voice asked if it was me, I wasn't sure; but then I realised that it was Katherine, Hugh's wife. She was apologetic, but concerned: 'It's Hugh,' she said, 'he can't sleep.' I asked to speak with him, and there was a pause. Finally, he came on – his voice was strangled. 'Rob,' he whispered, 'I can't sleep.' 'What is it, Hugh? Is it pain?' 'No,' he answered, 'no pain.' 'What is it then, Hugh?' There was a longer pause and I could hear him shift, but, finally, he said, 'Will I die if I go to sleep?' I was taken aback, and my mind raced. It took a full minute before I could answer. 'You won't die, Hugh, not tonight – not for a while yet. You need your sleep – Katherine does too.' 'Thank you, Rob. Goodnight.' 'Goodnight, Hugh.'"

Frank looked up at his wall, at the laminated infant pictures that his daughter Jane had drawn thirty years before. Their colour was not as vivid now, but patients still thought that they were those of his grandchildren. Occasionally one would tilt, inexplicably, and he would put it straight. On another wall, above his desk, hung a painting of a very sad clown – inappropriate, perhaps, in a place dedicated to raising spirits – but it was the work of his older sister, completed when he was a young man, and it had intrigued him ever since.

He thought of Keith's kind words, and advice. 'I have so few risk factors,' he mused, 'I am fairly active, hardly fat … no diabetes, hypertension … my cholesterol is reasonable … never smoked …' But then, for some reason, he thought of Rome. He and Milly had taken the train into central Rome from the airport and were pulling their cases through the streets towards their hotel. They were excited but tired, when suddenly and quite unexpectedly, he was overcome by a powerful feeling that his father, long dead, was nearby. He swung around to look, nearly knocking over a pedestrian as he did so. Milly was startled. "What is it, Frank? Have you dropped something?"

"No, no, it's just this sensation – feeling – that came over me."

"What feeling, Frank? Frank? You're getting in people's way."

"Sorry," he replied, shifting his case onto the steps of a shop, "but I felt the presence of my father."

"Your father? Frank, you're frightening me. Are you okay?"

He stepped up into a shop doorway, and the sense of his father's presence intensified. He turned to look inside and realised why – a tobacconist! Shops dedicated to smoking had long since disappeared from New Zealand, and this most ancient of aromas had been subsumed – assumed forgotten – but here is was … effecting a paternal resurrection. His earliest memory was of his father, hot leather shoes discarded after returning from work, one stockinged foot resting on an opposing knee, allowing space for Frank to push up through the triangle and onto his lap. His father was always smoking – he never remembered him not to be – but it was the sweet oily feel and smell of the tobacco that it was his job to draw out of his father's pouch that he loved most. Frank would watch intently as his father ceremoniously packed the bowl of his Dr Plumb pipe, lit the top leaves until they crinkled, and then pressed them down with his black thumb, as he sucked and puffed. Then would come the inestimable joy of being held by a warm arm with a smallpox scar, as columns of smoke curled up and out of his father's nose and mouth. There was never a birthday or a Christmas when his father was given anything other than a pipe, or cigars, or tobacco, as his gift; and it was in shops such as this one in Rome, where they could be found. Nicotine brought him such joy! In fact, the only photo that he still had of his father as a young man reflected this. It was one taken in North Africa, during the Second World War. His father was sitting on the side of a camp bed, in a tent, apparently alone in his early morning reverie, smoking a pipe. He appeared to be unaware of the black and white photographer – of the war.

'Everyone' smoked in those days, and what struck him now, as he waited for his first patient after lunch to arrive, was that he had of course smoked himself … certainly throughout his early life. Houses, cars, shops, cinemas – even the doctor's surgery – almost every internal space would have fumigated his lungs during that period. It was no wonder then, that his arteries had been tarnished too!

Frank was early for everything, and everything, inevitably, was late. His scan was no exception, but it gave him time to complete a lengthy questionnaire. (No, he did not have metal in his eye, nor, as far as he could recall, in any other organ; No, he had never reacted to dye; No, he was not especially claustrophobic.) It also gave him time to flick through two pointless magazines; to study ubiquitous waiting room art; and, finally, to focus on the nervous discomfort of a much younger man who had arrived without his insurance number. The man called home with a voice that projected beyond the river: no, he hadn't gone in yet – no, they hadn't told him what was wrong – no, his head was still 'funny'. After providing the receptionist with his insurance number he returned to his seat – a couch, in fact – but the act of sitting looked unnatural – more like that of a circus bear perched on a stool.

Some patients returned from brain MRIs vowing that they would never have another. "It's like being buried alive." But Frank was determined to relax and chose 'classical' as his preferred headphone music. He decided to listen intently, and was able, in the quieter intervals that magnetic readjustment allowed, to discern a Mozart horn concerto – he could never differentiate one from another – sweetening his brain … sweetening his brain, even as its secrets were being elucidated. What if the magnets could draw out his memories and align them like tacks? Would first love, first hurt, first shame be exposed, and point south? And the smell of his father's smoke? Would it cause a distortion in the size or shape of his olfactory lobes? Would they think he was a fish?

His reverie was broken by an announcement through his headphones, "We are about to inject the dye into your vein, Frank. Are you ready for that?"

"Yes."

"It will send a cold feeling up your arm but won't hurt."

"Thank you."

The horn, which had been silenced by the announcement, resumed its lament, but just momentarily – just while the unpleasant flush of cold shot headwards – then the magnets sprang into action one last time, and Mozart was subsumed. This was the MRA (Magnetic Resonance Angiogram) phase of the investigation, and Frank knew that it would be the most telling – it would determine whether the arterial feeders to his brain were up to scratch, or not.

As he was led out of the procedure room Frank touched the shoulder of the young man who was prepped and ready to enter, but the gesture appeared to startle rather than comfort him.

The radiologist's report took only three days to appear, and three minutes to read. Frank arrived early to work, as he always did, and he was alone when he opened the mail bar on his computer. There were twenty-nine results, tabulated by patient name in alphabetical order, and his mind was focused on their processing. His own name on that list, therefore, struck him initially and fleetingly as incongruent. The order and framing of the lettering were primordial in their familiarity, yet they appeared misplaced; but there was a thrill too – this could change everything?

Frank opened the report and went straight to the conclusion: 'This is a normal MRI of the brain. Normal cerebral and carotid/vertebral vessels. Normal contrast-enhanced MRA of the carotid and vertebral arteries in the neck – including the great vessel origins.'

Everything was normal! What was all the fuss about?

Frank sent a message to Milly, then sat back in his chair. One of Jane's pictures was askew – the one featuring Rapunzel – and he stood up to straighten it. He then balanced himself on his left leg, for a full minute, before moving onto his right. A medical article had claimed that this proprioceptive exercise was better for the brain than jogging. 'Stuff it,' he muttered, as he settled back onto his chair, 'you've had enough pampering for one week. Back to work.'

The first patient on his busy list was Quince.

QUINCE

Quince got his name from the fruit, the prototype of pears and apples that could have been the cause of Adam's lapse – the fruit that, despite its pink blossom, was displaced from hillside orchards and relegated to the rear where it could bear its bitter fruit unseen, but still be added, or added to, and offered up in silver spoons as jam or jelly … or marmalade. Yes, 'marmelada', Portuguese for quince (marmalade was once made exclusively from the yellow flesh), is lifted to the irresistible when the fruit is added to its mix. But what of our own Quince, was he much the same? Did he too hide tang beneath a banal exterior? Did he too contain a similar, essential essence that often went unnoticed, even by himself? Was he the saffron in the soup?

Mary thought so, and she considered him as indispensable as music at her dinner parties. His contribution was difficult to define, but it was easy to quantify. Add Quince to the mix of her influential band of guests and they would relax and lose their inhibitions – dance even – but leave him out, and the evening dragged. The paradox was not lost on her: here was a man who, by every modern measure, had failed – a man who hadn't moved on – but, but! He had to be there.

The name, however? How did the name arise? We will leave that for his mother to explain. It was her story, and she told it often enough!

"I was forty-one weeks pregnant and standing over the stove, stirring. My belly was so big that I had to stretch out my arms to reach the pot. The smell of sweet had me heaving, and the two little ones were pulling at my puffy feet.

"Wally walked in off the farm, his socks dropping grass. He picked Pansy up off the floor, and asked, yet again, 'Any thoughts, love? It could happen this afternoon.' Wally, my mum, everyone was pestering me about the name. I lifted my eyes wearily and looked out of the back window. Our quince tree was still laden – more yellow than green. I had jellied, stewed, jammed – even distilled them in brandy – but the fruit kept coming, Wally-picked. I couldn't win! Peeled quince was piled on a board to my left, unpeeled was in a basket to my right – the pot was filled to its lid with yellow. It was nauseating.

"I put down the ladle, swivelled slowly, lifted Rose, looked squarely at Wally, and announced, 'Quince'.

"'Quince?' he queried.

"'Quince,' I replied. 'We have two flowers – the next one is going to be a fruit. Boy, girl – something in between – it's going to be Quince.'

"And that was that. He was delivered at home that night."

"Just as well you hadn't planted a persimmon in its place, Wally," was the witty comment that Uncle Arnold always followed up with, "or we'd have a 'Percy' in the family – God forbid!"

As a small boy the retelling of the story made him feel unique, as if he had been born on his mother's birthday, and he loved to press against her shoulder as she repeated herself, over and over again. But, with time, he became aware of disinterest, even hostility and ridicule, in the feigned laughter of her friends. He also began to notice that his sisters, as well as his father, would drop their heads when she launched forth. For years he thought that they were jealous, but it was only when he was older that he realised the story was a mockery, and he displayed perversity by telling the story too, to everyone who queried his name.

Childhood had been easy rather than happy, and it was difficult to remember much that was worth remembering from that time. 'I was raised on a farm', he would say, dreamily, by way of yet another introduction. It implied that he was of good breeding stock, dependable, an early riser and reader of the weather. It worked, but only for a month or so, because it simply wasn't true. He had been pampered by his sisters (the older of whom inherited the farm), and he had voluntarily disengaged from his father when physical strength no longer impressed him; but his mother – his mother was the one person in his youth whom he wanted to connect with, but never did. It was as if she had always had the measure of him – knew that he had chosen avoidance and become a fraud. Her contempt was never verbalised, not even when she was dying, but Quince had come to believe that his mother had instinctually anticipated that her unborn child would be an unambitious quince, and an unambitious quince was what he had become. He saw it as predetermined that he would be a disappointment to her, that he would never have the courage to search for, develop, and reveal qualities that lay hidden; but when he was laid low, when his veneer of complacency was shattered, it was his doctor who startled him into action with an alternative view on why he was the way he was, and what he could become.

At the age of forty-five, and soon after Thelma walked out, Quince suffered a crisis – a crisis of self-recognition. It was triggered by an encounter with the bathroom mirror just two days after he had negotiated his birthday. It was his custom to glance at himself after emerging from the shower, and then to glance again, and because this had been a daily habit throughout adulthood, he had seldom noticed change. The mirror's and his own eyes would meet, briefly and self-consciously, like those of people on opposing escalators, and then they would shift to shoulders, arms, belly and below, before meeting again, and lingering. But on this September morning something had changed. The man standing before him was barely recognisable. It was as if he had met up with a school acquaintance, someone he hadn't seen for twenty years – someone he struggled to reconcile with as the same person – someone plain and pathetic.

He dressed that morning as if he had never dressed before, in a deliberate, operose manner, as though the clothes were not his own – as though the clothes were those of a woman with buttons on the other side; and when he ran a comb through his thinning hair the teeth caught scales on his scalp. He walked into a lounge still recovering from revelry and wondered who he was – what he was. There was no substantive 'I' for evaluation.

For two to three months following this revelation Quince was at a loss. He had become what his mother believed he would – a nothing. Even reading was becoming difficult because he found it difficult to see, and he did love reading. He googled the symptoms of lethargy, fatigue, headache, constipation, insomnia and progressive blindness, and what he found was unsettling!

'I have diabetes, or something growing in my brain – or bowel,' he decided, and what was the other thing that men had – that his father had – a prostate? What did prostates do, anyway?

At first, he drank more, not excessively, but more, and because he lived alone, he seldom rinsed his glass. His garden, set on a hill with a partial view of Maungatautari, was neglected. He still mowed, but he didn't weed. Beds previously planted with colour that stopped cars in the valley below were neglected, and both dock and dandelion flourished. Whereas he had previously prided himself on his quirky cooking, his experimentation with flavours, he chose now to subsist on easy meals bought frozen. His weight increased and his morbid paranoia worsened. Pansy, ever patient, had had enough.

"Go and have a check-up, Q, from top to bottom. If they find something, they can cut it out, if they don't, you can stop moping around in your smelly clothes. You're brighter and more talented than Rose and I put together, yet you carry on as if the world owes you a living. A pity that you didn't have kids. They would have straightened you out!"

Pansy's directness shocked Quince. After she'd stamped out with angry tears in her eyes, he took another look in the mirror. The next day he cleaned up his house with a wet mop as well as a vacuum cleaner, cleaned himself, weeded two front beds, and made an appointment with his doctor in Hamilton.

He still 'knew' that he was ill – dying even – but he had come to the heroic conclusion that it was time to confront whatever it was – for his sister's sake – so that she could be left with proud memories after he had perished.

The doctor didn't appear overly concerned, however, even after Quince handed him a note listing his alarming symptoms.

"We will see what we can do," Frank said, "but first a few questions." Quince nodded. "Any cough, night sweats, loss of weight, double vision, blood in the poo?"

Quince was distracted, as the list was rattled off, by the doctor's untamed eyebrow and ear hairs. Each strand of hair was drained of pigment, and each appeared determined to encroach upon the territory of the other. There was also a disconcerting dark spot on Frank's left forehead.

Quince's silence was enough for the doctor to continue. "Good! How much alcohol are you consuming, Quince? As much as your late father?"

"Well. I ..."

"Good. Do you have difficulty going to sleep?"

"Yes."

"Wake early?"

"Yes, but ..."

"Good. We'll run a few tests and I'll see you next week. Still engaged with the opposite sex?" he added as an afterthought.

"Well, Thelma and I ..."

"I know. That's why I'm asking."

"Well, no. With my symptoms, et cetera ..."

"Okay then, Quince. Get these done, and we'll see what we can do."

"But what about X-rays, Frank, or ..." he hesitated briefly, "... a colonoscopy?"

"You want a colonoscopy?"

"I don't want a colonoscopy, but a friend said ... because of my constipation, and because an uncle died of it, I should have one."

"What was 'it'?"

"I don't know. Something down in the gut, or somewhere."

"No problem, Quince, a colonoscopy it will be. Let's throw in a chest X-ray too."

"Well, not if you ...?"

"No, no, I see that it will be therapeutic."

The doctor stood up, smiling – ushering Quince towards the door. "Sorry, Frank, just one more thing: should I have an MRI as well, of my brain ... just in case?" He wasn't sure why this request appeared to momentarily startle Frank, but, because Quince had the means, he had his blood and urine tests, chest X-ray, colonoscopy and brain MRI, all within ten days. The preparation for the colonoscopy he found the most physically demanding, but it was the MRI that gave him the creeps.

He felt especially sorry for himself when he presented, alone, for the MRI. "You are welcome to bring a support person with you if you want to, but it isn't necessary, and most people don't," was the answer that he received when he had telephoned the day before the appointment. On arrival a lady in green went through a daunting questionnaire with him, emphasising that 'accuracy' was of the utmost importance – "From both parties. We are entitled to understand where you are coming from, and you are entitled to understand where we are coming from. Are you with me? Are you happy that you know where we are coming from?" He sensed that he should nod in agreement, and so he did. "And now if you would complete our questionnaire, and sign in the space highlighted."

Are you claustrophobic?

'I have been' would have been the truthful answer, but instead he wrote 'No' – concerned that she might think less of him if he confessed.

Do you have any metal in your body?

He wasn't sure. Did he? Did fillings count? He remembered a girl in his primary school who had a plate in her head. He and his friends wondered how the surgeons found the space – even for a saucer. The girl's head wasn't that big! At least Quince didn't have to worry about head metal – the region that they were scanning was his head – but he did recollect being turned upside down by Dr Johnson after biting through a glass mercury thermometer as a child. It's likely that he would have swallowed some, because his mother always brought this up when his behaviour warranted it –

and mercury, he was clever enough to know, was a metal – and so he ventured to ask the lady if it was important.

"No," she said, and then added quickly, "What music do you like?"

"Music?" he queried.

"Yes."

"Why?" he asked, puzzled.

"Because it's loud."

"What?" he asked.

"The magnets."

"Oh, oh … any music, thank you," he whispered.

And then he was whisked into a white room and tied down like a prospective amputee in the American Civil War.

"Lie still," she said. "You can press this buzzer if it all becomes too much for you." Her meaning was clear.

After earphones were applied, she left the room, and he became aware of crackly tunes filtering through his brain – and then it all started! His bed thrust him backwards into the belly of the machine, and the magnets got going – rattling like rocks in a limestone crusher. He was too startled to move, and he didn't dare press the buzzer.

On his way home to Cambridge he absent-mindedly took a wrong turn and found himself near the university in Hillcrest. He was about to double back when colour caught his eye – giant sunflowers were peering at him from over a white picket fence. Without thinking, and without parking safely, he got out of his car so that he could take a closer look. He himself grew sunflowers – he always had – but that was out in the country and on a larger scale – but these heads, and one in particular, seemed to be beckoning him. He pushed closer, past a thorny shoot of banksia, and was about to place his face in the central whorl of seeds when a nervous cough startled him. Someone, a lady in her late sixties or early seventies, was bent over on the other side of the fence with a trowel and sunhat staring at him.

"Are you a burglar?" she asked hesitantly.

"No, no, I'm so sorry," he replied. "It was just your sunflowers – this one in particular – so lovely … I just had to take a closer look."

She continued to stare at him for a minute or two, and he wasn't sure whether or not to retreat. Finally, the lady said, "Do you want it?"

"Pardon?"

"Do you want it – the sunflower?"

Quince was taken aback. "No, I couldn't really. I just wanted a closer look. I …"

Before he could say another word, she had cut the long stem and passed him the swinging head over the fence. "Do you live close by?"

"No, yes … in Cambridge."

"I'll get some wet tissue and a plastic bag."

"No, really …"

"Won't be a sec." And with that she walked briskly towards her house and into the conservatory to its right. The house was well-positioned on a rise and had an unobstructed view, he noticed, of Pirongia. He had climbed the mountain once, from the east, with a girlfriend who played hockey, and ever since its outline rekindled images of the girl's muscular, competitive, and sexless legs powering up the scree and away from him. His focus was still on the corrugated silhouette and the images that it provoked when the lady reappeared with the sunflower stem wrapped in wet newspaper and plastic.

"How lovely of you! You're very kind. Thank you." Pink tinted her cheeks as he added, "I'm Quince."

"Carol."

"Thank you again, Carol."

"Any time."

"Bye."

"Bye."

Quince was calm as he waited next to a frail lady and opposite two dripping infants, for Frank to call him in. Pansy had offered to accompany him, but he wanted, he said, to face the music alone. She placed herself on standby, however, in case he was too upset to drive himself home.

"Hello, Quince, sorry I'm late again. Come on in." Frank appeared especially jovial today, cracking an in-house joke with a nurse as they approached his consulting room. "Take a seat, take a seat. How're you feeling, Quince? Any better?"

"Well, no, not really." He hesitated, and then added, "The tests, Frank, and the, the procedures."

"All normal, old chap, all normal."

"Normal?"

"Yes."

"And the scan, the magnet thing that I went into?"

"Oh, that. Don't think I have that back yet. I'll give them a call. Hold on a minute, Quince. What date did you have it?"

"The sixth."

"Should be back by now. Should be back." Quince felt his palate beginning to warp. "Hello, hello, is that Results? Good, good. Dr Edge, GP, here. Could I have a report on a brain MRI? Yes. No. Patient's number is YQB648. No, no, 'B'. 'B' for butter. Yes, yes, that's his name. No, no, it's not a nickname." Hesitation. "Good, good, you've found it? Yes, yes, send it through the wires. Yes, now, please. Patient's waiting. Okay, okay. Thank you." Putting down the phone Dr Edge turned back to Quince. "It'll be through in a minute. So, what are you up to? Still living on the farm?"

Quince nodded. He didn't trust his voice. The doctor turned back to his screen, humming. The humming had always irritated Quince. "There she blows," he exclaimed, before spending a few minutes peering over his glasses as he read the report.

"What does it say, Frank?" Quince asked weakly.

"All good, all good."

"No tumour?"

"Of course not. I didn't need this to know that," he said, smiling. Frank then leaned forward and looked kindly but directly at Quince. "You've been worried, haven't you, Quince?" Quince nodded. "Well, I've been worried too."

Quince looked up sharply. "Why?" he asked.

"Not about this stuff," he said, waving his hand across the screen, "but about your head."

"My head? You mean the blindness."

"No, no, not the blindness," he laughed. "A cheap pair of reading glasses from The Warehouse will fix that. No, it's your head, your brain. It's bored stiff."

"Why?"

"Because, at forty-odd, you haven't tried to fly – never risked falling. You've spent your life paddling in the shallow end and your brain has had enough." Quince stared at him. "Your mother, bless her soul, didn't do you any favours. She placed you in a box, and you're yet to jump out."

Quince, perplexed by the plethora of metaphors, murmured, "What do you mean?"

Frank looked directly at him. "Your mother was tired when you were born, Quince. She was tired before you were born – a bright woman with nothing to look forward to but feeding and wiping, and I'm not sure how to say this ... she resented you."

"What?"

"She wanted to live in a city – Auckland – anywhere. She wanted to be young in her youth, travel … and when she fell pregnant with you – with two young daughters to care for already – well, she saw another twenty years and knew it would be too late. It wasn't your fault," he went on gently, "of course it wasn't your fault, and of course she knew that – but her resentment never quite subsided."

"But …"

"She loved you, Quince, but it was a love tainted by bitterness." Frank paused again, before continuing, "And so she applied the brakes – made sure, without ever admitting it to herself, that your potential was never encouraged. Your mediocrity, you see, legitimised her ambivalence."

"Do you mean that she didn't want me to be a success?"

"If success is to challenge life in order to discover who you are and what it offers, then yes."

"How do you know this?"

"I arrived here soon after you were born. Your parents chose to travel to Hamilton for doctor stuff, from Cambridge – not sure why – and I spent a lot of time speaking with them individually – to both of them."

"My father too?"

"Yes, your father too. He was no fool. He was shut out, just as you were, and damaged by the war."

"But what do I do now, Frank? You say that I am well?"

"You are well, but you haven't grown up."

"But I'm comfortable, Frank. I have everything."

"Comfortable! Comfortable! That's just it. That's what I'm trying to say to you. Comfort's the problem! Take risks. Go to jail. Get out of Cambridge. Even your relationships were safe, Quince. That's why they couldn't last. Did you mourn when Thelma left? Julie?" Quince shook his head. "Well, go and find someone you can't do without, someone who could break your big, beautiful heart. Take on the world, Quince. It's in a mess."

"Should I take a break?"

"You've taken a break all your life. Take on a challenge. Are you going deaf, too?"

Quince had been encouraged and cajoled by his sisters in the past, but this was brutal. The shock must have registered in his face in the pause that followed, because there was a softening in Frank's tone as he added, "I'm sorry, Quince, but it's up to you."

Quince had intended driving back through Hillcrest again on his way home, but he was preoccupied by what Frank had said – the revelations about his mother – his safe life. It was true. When Pansy inherited the family farm, Quince, and his sister Rose, had been more than fairly treated. Each was given a one-third share of the farm's capital value, as a cash transfer, and the amount had been substantial. Consequently, there had been no imperative for Quince to establish a career. He had worked, of course he had worked, in various jobs, but not with any real commitment. He had (his term) 'willingly participated in the workforce', but, if the truth be told, this participation was largely aimed at staving off accusations of slothfulness as much as earning income! He even limited himself to work that was within easy driving range of the elevated patch of land perched on a corner of the family farm that he had purchased for a song from his sister. It was the fashioning of this land into a terraced jumble of colour and contrast that formed the substantial, and some would say the only, part of his legacy. But, as he approached his long driveway and looked up, he realised, to his burning shame, that even this had been neglected, and he was in no mood for interrogation when he walked through the door.

Pansy, and her setter, Bill, were waiting for him. Pound, his own dog, had the good sense to stay outside. "What happened, Q? What did he find? You look terrible!"

"Nothing," he mumbled.

"Nothing?" Quince walked past her, irritably withdrew his hand from the licking dog, and threw his coat over the couch. "Nothing?" There was a pause. "I don't want to talk about it. Not now."

"But …"

"Not now, Pans. Please. I'm fine. Just leave me alone."

Pansy turned sharply on her heels. "Good! Come on, Bill. We have better things to do than watch Mr Misery wallow!"

Quince sighed and placed his feet on the coffee table. One foot disturbed a note – it was the note that he had hastily scribbled down when Mary phoned to invite him to dinner. The dinner was imminent, and he'd forgotten to make an excuse.

ELEANOR

Based on the argument that tourists had to go somewhere and everywhere else was a war zone, projections for arrivals and departures at Auckland Airport had gone through the roof. In order to accommodate these, as well as to maximise their spending while in transit, renovations were under way, and, as a result, airport noise and announcement volumes were exceptional – even for an airport! But the paradox for Eleanor was that they facilitated detachment and effected calm, allowing her to lean back and reflect. Harry was happy (he could be seen paging through children's books from where she was sitting), while she, in Frank's words, was 'spent'.

How, Eleanor mused, had she arrived at this juncture? Eight years had passed. Only eight? Was a lifetime that little? She smiled as she recalled the awful kerfuffle with Security that had preceded the odyssey, and how it had unsettled her. Eleanor's former patient, Ted, had bequeathed her the unenviable task of lugging what she believed to be his burnt remains all the way to Africa, for delivery to his boyhood friend, Alec, a doctor who worked in the small southern village of Portland. It was the urn that had caused all the official consternation, but, eventually, and after much embarrassment, Eleanor had been able to hand it to Alec. What she had not envisaged, however, was that she would return to New Zealand after just a two-week stay in the state of Bwazi both smitten and pregnant – her lover the adopted son of Alec and his wife Leah, an Ndebele whose parents had been murdered by the forces of the incumbent president.

The realisation that she and her son Harry must get away became obvious to her after a single consultation at work when she found that she had, quite simply, lost interest. It had always been her fear that she would lose control and laugh (as only Eleanor could) during a consultation, but this was not the case. A patient, familiar to her as manipulative, self-absorbed, selfish and insufferably boring – someone who had sucked and sucked the marrow out of her for the past year – returned, yet again, with unreasonable demands. Among the most pressing was a renewed request for a sickness benefit. Eleanor was well aware that this was inappropriate, illegal even, and certainly not in the patient's best interest; but she felt a wave of negative empowerment come over her, and simply demurred. What did it matter? She felt nothing: no irritation; no anger; no guilt. Eleanor was past caring.

Frank looked directly into Eleanor's eyes after she had described her detachment and relief while they were having tea, and then offered this advice:

"Go, Eleanor. Take Harry out of school and bugger off."

"Do you think so, Frank?"

"Yes."

"But I've only been working here for a year!"

"So what? I'm the boss."

"No, really, Frank, it wouldn't be fair."

"I want you to last, Eleanor, and you won't unless you take stock."

"Take stock?"

"Of what you want, and where you're going."

Eleanor was silent for a minute: "Would you and Edith be able to cope – for a few weeks?"

"Of course."

There was a further pause. "We could visit Peter again, in Queensland. Harry loves being with him."

"Visiting Peter is not enough. Peter is a wonderful brother and uncle, but he's as helpless and worried as I am."

"What do you mean?"

"You're in trouble, Eleanor. You're existing for Harry, and nothing more. It's unhealthy."

"Has Peter been in contact with you?"

"Yes, several times – but this is my suggestion."

"But what about work? Harry's schooling? My mother? The animals?"

"All surmountable."

Eleanor's eyes filled with tears when she recalled that conversation with Frank. The advice had shocked her into action. What Frank did not anticipate, however, was quite how drastically his advice would change her life – that she would act again on impulse.

"What's the matter, Ma?" She looked up and into those dark, soft eyes that she adored. They were so much like his father's. "We gotta go to Gate 23."

"We do indeed, young man. You lead the way."

Five months prior, Mary had phoned inviting her to dinner – again. She and Joe were having friends stay, and they wondered whether Eleanor would like to join them. This time, however, Mary was ready for the excuses: "Harry is welcome to come along if his grandmother can't look after him." "No, Eleanor, we are all tired." "No … no, there is always work to do, and work can wait." "I don't care if Harry has a cold. Everyone has a cold."

Eventually Eleanor agreed, but with the greatest reluctance. She could think of nothing better on a Saturday night than curling up on the sofa to watch General Audience movies with Harry, her mother and Whitey (their West Highland terrier). If it was cold, they might even have the privilege of Cedric (the cat) hopping up onto one of their laps. But it was mainly the effort that Eleanor dreaded, having to dress up smartly (when she kept so few smart dresses), having to apply make-up (a narcissistic exercise); but mainly she dreaded the monumental effort that was required for her to get through an evening of small talk.

Mary was a good friend – she had known her for many years, had met her at university – and she liked Joe. They had gone out of their way to include Eleanor and Harry in their family outings since they'd moved from Taupo: to the botanical gardens in Hamilton, to Karapiro for picnics by the lake, to Raglan beach where the dogs ran wild – but dinner was a step too far. They would try to 'balance the numbers' by inviting a solo male, usually a professional divorcé deemed incapable of cooking for himself, and Eleanor found that awkward – even insulting. And it wasn't just Mary and Joe who did this, others did the same. There were the introductions over white wine, with Eleanor's pedigree as a GP mentioned (followed by the inevitable quip, "I'd better cut out the cream"); there were the over-polite comments about the hosts' garden (barely visible); and of course there was the customary peering at children's photographs: "And what's Ruby doing now?" "Is she still keen on photography?" "She's so pretty! Obviously doesn't take after her father."

Other guests appeared to settle easily into conversation. They chatted naturally and authoritatively about their holidays, their work, Donald Trump, North Korea, the housing crisis in Auckland, and of course their children, but even they found the subject of Harry awkward. They were aware that he was a fatherless African love child, but detail eluded them. "How's your little boy?" "Has he settled into his new school?" "Is he a good runner?" Eleanor found it excruciating, but, after they had been seated and she had had a couple of wines, she would silently observe the men and women trying so hard to enjoy themselves, and her cynicism would subside and be replaced by tenderness and pity.

Eleanor was at the end of her first trimester – estimated at twelve weeks by scan – when Aaron disappeared. His flight was booked, his visitor's visa arranged, and he was due to arrive in New Zealand early in the New Year. It was just after Christmas, a Christmas which was as happy as any that she could remember as an adult. Her brother Peter and his partner Sophie had come over from Australia for two weeks, and it was all fun and games. Peter was so much more at ease with their parents than she was, and they responded by shedding their preoccupation with age. Peter particularly loved fishing and music, and, whenever the weather permitted, he had his father out on Lake Taupo with their boat bobbing to the beat of Bob Marley. And when they got back, he had his father smoke their trout ("No one else is allowed to touch it, Dad"), while his mother made their favourite chive and butter sauce. It was a time when Eleanor really got to know and love Sophie. She was unpretentious, perceptive, smart, and full of mischief. The girls – Eleanor, her mother and Sophie – went to town together while the men were fishing, and even though Sophie was the foreigner amongst them, it was she who discovered the adult shop tucked away in one of the town's side roads. Its walls were painted the customary black and silver and its window display could best be described as enticing.

At first Eleanor thought that Sophie had mistaken it for a funky emporium. She tried frantically to gesticulate and warn her not to enter, but her gesticulations were ignored as Sophie steered the unsuspecting old lady through the tasselled entrance and up to the impressively arranged 'candle' counter.

"Any particular size interest you, Marion?" she asked casually in her Aussie twang.

"Size?" There was hesitation, before Marion continued, "But what are these objects?" She stared at one particularly bulky specimen, before reaching out to pick it up. "Is that a wick coming out of it?" she asked innocently.

"It is, Marion."

"But what is it for, Sophie?"

"For a variety of things really."

Marion turned the candle around in her hand and held it towards the minimalistic light. She hesitated and then spoke slowly. "It looks rather rude to me."

"It is, Marion," Sophie replied, maintaining her deadpan expression.

But her mother's face as she processed the unthinkable was too much for Eleanor. She rushed towards the door, exploding with laugher. Her flustered and perplexed mother followed, while Sophie sauntered out with only the faintest of twitches disturbing the corners of her mouth. "Should we find a place for a cup of tea?" she asked innocently.

That elevated Eleanor's shrieking, screaming laughter to another level. She was effectively immobilised by mirth and afraid to move. Pregnant bladders are pressurised as it is, and Eleanor's choking, spluttering and limb contortion simply added to the risk of leakage. Similar risk haunts the aged, and Mrs Hutton, who had not seen Eleanor laugh like this for months, started up as well – not as boisterously as Eleanor – but just as catastrophically. She too wept; she too pressed her knees together; she too let a drop slip.

And all the while Sophie held on to her nonchalant look – just the twitching giving her away.

"Tea, darlings?" she repeated, before swinging her handbag in the direction of the main street.

The dawning awareness of pregnancy was a revelation to Eleanor. The fact that it was a totally unanticipated outcome of a brief and surreal relationship with a man she barely knew, was, curiously, not the issue. The absurdity that she had not thought to take precautions, the fact that she had embarked upon an incomprehensible rush for intimacy (where she had been so hesitant in the past), were not what startled her. Rather, it was the wonder, the wonder that placed her on a different plane.

Having diagnosed and managed so many pregnancies in the past, Eleanor was perplexed that she had been oblivious to the thrilling edge that hormones added to emotional intelligence. There was an awareness, not only of tight and tingling skin that craved to be caressed, not only of fat redistribution and bowing of her lower back, but also of a general sharpness that delineated the intonation and pitch of a person's voice. An acquaintance would say one thing, but Eleanor would sense that she meant quite another. She became hypersensitive (like skin affected by prodromal shingles) to what Quince later called 'the insincerity of kindnesses' – the affectation of caring so common among those in the 'service industry'. This increased awareness accentuated her vulnerability, but it also brought a keenness to her appreciation when kindness and compassion were authentic. She recalled one Friday on her way home from work when her Chinese grocer had thrown an extra couple of onions into her basket, and this had provoked a greater outpouring of tears than the onions did when she got to slice them. She had to write a note, translated into

Mandarin by one of her colleagues, to explain to the poor man that the reason for her tears was appreciation rather than insult.

But it was her unborn child that totally absorbed her.

With just ten days until Aaron was due to arrive in New Zealand, everything was in place. Eleanor would drive up to Auckland on her own to meet him. They would spend three nights in her favourite motel in Parnell, so that he could recover from jetlag (she had already booked the fourth floor double room that had its own balcony, and its own view over the city, the harbour, and the volcano of Rangitoto), and they would spend their two, lazy, summer days climbing Mt Eden, swimming at Cockle Bay, and drinking coffee in Vulcan Lane. Eleanor wanted to touch Aaron's skin, to caress his long, thin fingers; she wanted to hear him speak – to watch him speak – to marvel at the synchrony of eyes and accent. (Ah, those eyes! He didn't need to speak – his eyes spoke for him.) She wanted to connect, or reconnect, to assure herself that he was real and that she herself was not completely mad. Eleanor needed to reassure herself that it was more than animal instinct that had temporarily blinded her – that it was more than a hormonal imperative. She needed confirmation of love, not just reciprocal love, but love that incorporated – cupped – the smouldering warmth in her belly. She wanted Aaron to see her distended veins and flushed face, her fattened buttocks and filling breasts; she wanted him to place his cheek, his ear, above her pubis and face her. They could meet any challenge then: his reception from her family, friends, and colleagues in Taupo, as well as the 'practical' impediments and unresolved issues and decisions around immigration, work, and residence. Could Aaron stay? Would he want to? An African with a deep and abiding love for his failed country! Could he bear to leave behind his surrogate parents, Alec and Leah? Could he abandon his solemn and dangerous commitment to change Bwazi – to participate in the elimination of the corruption, cruelty and greed that had defiled it? She did not know, but their tripartite love was the only hope.

There was always the fear though that it would not happen – that he would not come. Eleanor was only too aware that Bwazi was a dangerous country for a dissenter. Not more than four months previously she had stayed there, in the city of Bulungani – in the village of Portland. For all of the intoxicating beauty of the country, for all of the generosity of its people, the menace was palpable, and the menace lay heavily on the shoulders of Aaron, Leah and Alec.

So, when the call came from Alec – his voice almost inaudible – she was not surprised.

"Eleanor, is that you?"

"Alec?"

"Are your parents with you? Your mother?"

"What is it, Alec? Your voice … it's hard to hear."

"It's Aaron, Eleanor … he hasn't come home."

"He hasn't what?"

"He hasn't come home."

"What do you mean? Is he lost?"

"We aren't sure, but we have to prepare ourselves."

Patients described feelings of nausea and dizziness – a drainage of visual colour – when they first received shocking news, but Eleanor felt herself detaching, separating from her body, and hovering above it – levitating, as it were. She watched her face mouth the words, "What do you mean?"

"Leah received word … this is so difficult, Eleanor. Leah received word through her contacts that Aaron might have been picked up near M'zunga."

"Picked up?"

"Apprehended by the Special Branch." Eleanor failed to

respond, and Alec continued, hesitantly, "That's not a good thing, Eleanor."

"Could he be in prison?" Her body was emitting pulsations of strobe light. "Could they be keeping him somewhere?"

"We have checked. We … I'm sorry, my dear … I will hand you over to Leah."

"Hello, Eleanor. This is Leah speaking." The body's face smiled. "Until we get confirmation there's always hope, but I'm afraid it does sound bad." Leah hesitated, and then added, "Most people simply disappear."

Aaron was never found. It was assumed that he was murdered and discarded, as so many others were at that time, in the Bwazian bush. Eleanor hoped that the bush was flush with the elegant msasa – *Brachystegia spiciformis* – the tree that Aaron loved so dearly, but this was unlikely. M'zunga, the area with pools that Alec and Ted had fished in as boys, was further south, in the Limpopo valley where it was lower and hotter. Msasa preferred the hills closer to Bulungani, where Aaron had gone to school, but M'zunga was mainly thorn and baobab country – rich in bird life. Eleanor was comforted by that. She had never met anyone who had had a greater affinity for birds than Aaron. He could identify them in flight, by feather – by the pitch of a single call. He knew by their beaks what each ate. He could distinguish whether a tree of red-billed quelea were squabbling or warning of a snake.

There was no possibility that she could visit and investigate, not in the early phase of pregnancy – not with the physical danger that a visit posed. As adopted parents of Aaron, Alec and Leah were targeted in the weeks and months that followed. They received direct as well as anonymous threats, and their calls were monitored. Alec had to cease carrying out his remote rural clinics with Jabu, his nurse, and very few patients were able to access their free service in the village of Portland itself. Eventually their son managed to get them out of Bwazi and had them join him and his wife in England. The couple left with nothing but sorrow.

Colleagues and friends alike were agreed, Eleanor's reaction to Aaron's disappearance was cause for concern. After her return from Africa, and in the early stages of her pregnancy, she was either laughing or crying. She was vulnerable, dreamy, took time off work when feeling unwell. Photos of Aaron, mainly taken by Leah, were everywhere: on her mantelpiece, next to her bed, in her purse, and they were readily brought out for showing. Compliments about his handsome dark eyes and ebony skin made her laugh out aloud. She was a lady in love.

But, after the phone call, it all changed. There were no more tears – no more laughter. She no longer admitted to fatigue – vomiting was carried out with the secrecy of a bulimic. Offers of help were abruptly rebuffed. Work became her refuge, and the foetus her obsession. Her obstetric knowledge was refreshed and updated, and every sensation of belly life noted. The fluttering at twenty weeks and the kicking at twenty-six were recorded, but never shared. There was a forbidding formality about Eleanor that had never been seen before. Patients were exempt, of course, and they continued to enjoy her full attention and care, but those close to her – even her parents – felt marginalised.

Betty, her colleague in Taupo, eventually had had enough, and questioned her directly about depression. "Are you feeling low, Eleanor? Are you sleeping poorly? Have you stopped socialising? You don't think that you need help? Medication? Julia? She's an excellent clinical psychologist."

Eleanor recognised the line of questioning, and she added

sarcastically, "You haven't asked the compulsory question, 'Any thoughts of self-harm?'"

"That's not fair, Eleanor. You know why I'm concerned."

"For the patients?"

"No, not for the patients, the patients are just fine. I'm concerned about you, and you know why."

Eleanor apologised, and thanked Betty, reassuring her that she would take her concerns seriously. Sarcasm and cynicism had never been part of her nature – never – and she was ashamed that they were surfacing now.

A unique combination of fear and excitement accompanies a first pregnancy. Only a mother would know that. It is primal, powerful, urgent, and linked to something beyond perception. Fear of never-before-experienced pain, the possibility of catastrophic loss – even of death – but also the anticipation of a fulfilment, a completion of an inexplicable imperative. "How will I cope as a mother?" is a question often asked. "How can I – me – do justice to this life miraculously created?" These fears, this excitement, can only be confronted with the passage of time. But to make them bearable, and to prevent them from becoming pathological, they need to be shared through trust – trust of midwife, doctor, of loved ones like parents, but especially and essentially by the other in the making of the miracle. Expectant mothers need to know – to have no doubt – that the father is feeling something of the same fear and excitement that she, the mother, is – that he understands how high the stakes are – that he won't pull away when she places her cold feet behind his knees.

Initially Eleanor survived on blind anger, anger directed mainly at Aaron. Again, this was an emotion that had never previously lingered in Eleanor, but she could not stop her mind from stinging. Despite an awareness of his responsibility, despite his declaration of love and commitment, Aaron had put himself in harm's way. Was it possible that there was an intentional element to his death? Their futures really were irreconcilable after all. He couldn't have left Bwazi, and she couldn't have lived there! Could this have been his solution? Had he even loved her?

But she was also angry with herself: 'How could I have been so stupid?' and Ted, the deceased patient who was responsible for sending her on the ridiculous mission in the first place, he had to share the blame too! What maddened her even more was that she couldn't even legitimise grief: she hadn't known Aaron long enough!

After Betty's talk, however, a re-evaluation took place. Eleanor realised that her behaviour was unfair, selfish – cruel even – and that it was time to refocus. She suppressed her hurt, anger, bitterness and blame; made an effort to at least appear more cheerful; she invited her mother to come along to her next scan; she shared small talk with friends; she took time off to rest as term approached – but – but – the source of her strength never changed, it continued to stem from a solitary focus – a focus on her foetus, and the new life that it would deliver.

Betty was not fooled – she knew Eleanor only too well – and she was determined to remain vigilant.

Eleanor worked right up to the thirty-seventh week of her pregnancy, and she would have continued to work beyond that if her blood pressure hadn't started to rise and her feet to swell. Constipation and piles were troubling her, her back ached, and reflux forced her to sit up through the night, so bed rest with a modicum of shuffling were all that she could achieve in the final couple of weeks of her pregnancy. It was also the period when she finally dropped her guard and allowed her mother, and a few of her good friends, to 'fuss'. For all her medical knowledge, and probably because of it, Eleanor had to admit to moments of blind terror.

But when labour started, first with contractions, and then with spontaneous rupture of membranes, she felt a deep sense of relief. One way or the other it was going to be over, and she herself could do no more. She had chosen a midwife who was older, and one who was happy to follow the 'medical model' of care. Eleanor had seen too many 'natural' deliveries go horribly wrong, and she wanted everything that conventional medicine could throw at her. So there had been prior agreement, even before the rise in blood pressure, that she would deliver in Rotorua Hospital, with both an obstetrician and paediatrician in attendance. It was also agreed that both Eleanor's mother and Betty would be with her throughout. Her father would stay at home and man the phone.

As it turned out the labour proceeded as well as could be expected for a primigravida. Her first stage lasted for fifteen hours, and the hours passed with intermittent and then regular contractions, interspersed with comic repartee, back rubs and sips of cold green tea. The foetus was monitored throughout, and it was only as she entered second stage and started to push that the foetal heart dipped. What surprised Eleanor most from the experience was the calming role played by her mother. She had been invited to the delivery suite more out of kindness than with any expectation of her being useful, but Marion emerged as the prime helper – the essential one. Eleanor reached out to her mother, as we all do when we feel helpless (even after their death), because we retain the unremembered memory of being housed within them. Eleanor searched those ancient eyes for affirmation when the pain became unbearable that she herself would be capable of fulfilling the primordial role – and was comforted.

And then it was over, and they could rejoice. A long boy, with wet, brown skin and pink feet, was gently draped over her chest as his cord was severed. The infant's eyes were screwed shut, but he had one fist raised high above his head, in triumph.

Harry changed everything for Eleanor, but he also restored much of her former self. The uncharacteristically chilly, forbidding armour that had sustained her through her pregnancy was discarded, and its components of suppressed anger, sarcasm and bitterness dissolved. She re-emerged in colourful dresses with dishevelled hair – kind to a fault, and vaguely aware that she was not coping in her happy chaos. Her helpless infant was studied in minutia, but it was his father's eyes that entranced her, that replaced the umbilical link. They were slightly asymmetrical, as all eyes are, but it was their depth, their darkness, their accommodation to different light, that drew her in. They were mostly closed though, when he fed – when he nuzzled her breast – but this was arguably the most precious time of all for observation. It was his strength that surprised her, the hold that he had on her nipple. There was no letting go! And the sensation! The sensation of milk transfer through cotyledons, more like ripples in space-time than rivulet flow – straight into his warm mouth. She would watch, entranced, as he reached surfeit on her second breast, sucking less and less, until he subsided into sleep.

Those were the tranquil times, but many times were not! Like all babies, the volume and pitch of Harry's cry was disproportionate to his size, and when it persisted without a remediable cause Eleanor was as helpless and desperate as any mother. She would try further feeding, but he would not feed; she would try a dummy, but he would spit it out; she would try winding, rocking, walking, driving – anything that her exploding brain could think of – but he would scream on. She obtained prescriptions for antacid, omeprazole, ranitidine and paracetamol from her colleague, Ben, but all that really helped was time, and, as Ben kept reassuring her, "He's well, El, perfectly well."

And he was well. He remained in the 75th percentile for height, weight and head circumference throughout the neonatal period, and all his milestones were reached well within the prescribed limit. Eleanor was aware that it was her fatigue – exhaustion, Ben called it – that Harry was responding to. "They pick up on your stress, El, and let you have it. Have your parents take him for a few hours so that you can go out for coffee with a friend – so that you see there's life out there."

Eleanor knew this – she had given the same advice to many patients in a similar state of exhaustion in the past – but it was helpful and comforting coming from Ben. She was also very much aware that she could easily slip into an obsessive, even neurotic, relationship with Harry, and he didn't deserve that. He already stood out as different, and she didn't want him burdened further by an over-possessive mother! And so, she did take breaks – short ones initially, and then longer ones once she stopped breast-feeding. Both her mother and father, as well as Betty, even friends, were more than willing to help, and Harry seemed calmer with them.

But the biggest break of all came when she returned to work, tentatively at first, but work, nevertheless. It was the cake-and-condom present that she received from reception staff on her arrival; it was the challenge and stimulation that provoked her in her first consultation; it was the different level of fatigue that floored her when she arrived home with Harry … but most of all it was her sense of profound relief. Eleanor had regained direction, but it was the culture of her practice that had made this possible, a culture that had evolved by extension from the good people who owned it. Betty was one of the 'originals', and she, along with her now retired partners, had purposefully and unpretentiously nurtured a caring and supportive workplace where people felt valued and safe, where profit was never the prime focus. Testament to this was the fact that turnover of staff, over many years, had been negligible, and recruitment, like the recruitment of Eleanor, had been decided not by CV, reputation or formal interview, but rather by hearsay and first impression. Their tearoom, at any given time, exemplified this – it was a happy mess – but the casual establishment of an effective crèche to accommodate the infants of their young staff was what ensured enduring gratitude and loyalty. Eleanor was able to return to work – initially for two mornings a week – because she knew that Harry was happy and safe in a room just ten metres away.

The metamorphosis of Harry was observed then, and shared, not only by Eleanor and her parents and immediate friends, but also by those at the workplace, and, by the time that he had graduated to kindergarten, he had become well socialised. If he was sick in the night, Eleanor knew that she could phone in the morning to have her appointments shifted to another doctor. When kindergarten closed for the holidays, she was able to take leave.

And so, this life of mother and child progressed, with each 'stage' experienced as an unfolding miracle – the first steps, the first words confirmed, the increase in sophistication of play activities, tantrums, defiance – Eleanor marvelled at it all, and could not imagine a life without him.

But something else was emerging from the metamorphosis, something of his father, Aaron. It wasn't just the obvious physical features of darker skin and hair growth – these would be apparent in any child with Ndebele genes – it was more his mannerisms, the position that he slept in, or the expression that transformed his face when his thoughts were far away. It made Eleanor feel sad for what could have been, but it also made her more determined than ever to have him 'know' his father. Photographs helped, but also stories of Bwazi, Bulungani, and Portland in particular. She did not need to lionise the father in these stories – Aaron's intelligence, compassion, courage (yes, she could now admit that his final act was one of courage), and, above all, his gentle kindness, were extraordinary, and it was imperative that Harry grew up knowing this. It also made her more determined than ever to take him, one day, to visit Bwazi, so that he, like her, could experience the light and smell of Africa.

Eleanor had come to recognise a common awareness in her older patients of the stepwise progression of ageing. She had always thought of it as a continuum, but they changed her mind. A recognition of decline would be triggered by a challenge, they explained, a challenge that previously would have been met without hesitation, but which now caused difficulty and demanded caution – even avoidance. But in Harry, she realised, the steps went the other way. Eleanor would spend weeks unaware of an aspect of his maturation, and then he would do something, or say something, which jolted her. His graduations from daycare to kindergarten to school were obvious milestones to overcome and celebrate, but it was the progressive nuance in thought sophistication that unsettled and surprised her most. A character was emerging – personality traits – that would define him for the rest of his life. They would be modified and moulded by his experience, of course, but the essential Harry was showing himself. She recognised his father, others his mother, but it was his 'Harry' that was emerging.

Seven could be considered the perfect age for a child – thirty for a young adult perhaps, sixty-five for one older – but seven is the age when a child looks and acts like an angel. No longer helpless, but still innocent, trusting, eager and compliant, he is his parent's perfect companion.

But the year he turned seven circumstances changed – circumstances that drove their move from Taupo to Cambridge. Betty retired and the medical practice was sold to a corporate. This had the effect of ripping out its soul. In the same year Eleanor's father died after a short illness and left her mother bereft. Ben mentioned to Eleanor that his Uncle Frank, who worked as a GP in Hamilton, was looking for someone to join his practice. Would she be interested? Ben himself had decided to specialise in paediatrics. The meeting of Frank and Eleanor, with Harry in tow, resulted in an immediate and rare connection. No mention was made of salary or contract, and her curriculum vitae, she noticed, was barely glanced at. She, her mother, and Harry would move to Cambridge (a small town just south of Hamilton), without delay, and she would begin work as soon as she was settled.

Within six weeks her flat in Taupo was sold, and they had moved into a house in tree-lined Hall Street. The property had a separate garage and flatlet with a corrugated iron roof draped in wisteria, which would serve as Marion's 'own space'. Harry was enrolled in Cambridge East Primary School – just a few blocks away – and their new life began.

PART II

CAROL

arol's hopes were raised in the first few months following Kevin's stroke because he made little effective recovery. She was particularly buoyed by the apparent permanency of his 'expressive aphasia' – a product, it was explained, of 'a significant insult to his inferior frontal operculum, or Broca's area'. He retained his ability to receive and process information – to comprehend – but his ability to express, to search for and sensibly assemble words, did not return; and all that emerged from his twisted mouth when such a search was attempted, was spittle. At first these futile efforts would turn his face puce, and he would splutter, but he later learned, because he was no fool, to use his better hand to signal. Whether these signals were understood and acted upon depended on the receptivity of his communicant, whether she be a rest-home aid assisting him with feeding, or whether it be his wife, working out where to scratch.

Carol decided, after having had to overcome the disappointment that Kevin was not going to die, that the year ahead, the year of his internment while house renovations were carried out, was going to be her happiest. Kevin, after all, was at his most helpless, while she was a bird set free. She was determined that activities and possessions formerly forbidden be performed and purchased at the earliest opportunity, and, having taken control of both credit card and car, there was no stopping her.

Evan and his wife, Angela, were quiet and determined activists for bicycle lanes, for bus lanes, for eventual monorail, and for a phased-in requirement that the power propelling people from A to B in any vehicle other than the abovementioned, be sourced solely from sunlight, wind or biofuel. She understood their argument, and, with her grandchild about to arrive, supported it politically, but privately she simply could not resist her car. It was yellow, it was warm, it had Spotify linked to Bluetooth, and it went wherever its wheels were directed. It would stop for her to wind down a window and sniff if a storm was approaching; drop her at a matinee; drive her to The Base to buy underwear; find her country cafés where she could sip cappuccino and slip tidbits to sparrows; but, most tellingly in terms of reassurance, dutifully retrace the routes that she and Carmel had taken all those years ago. With the help of her precious little vehicle, she, herself, could decide whether to come or go, and the thrill was intoxicating. She wished that the year would never end.

Carol maintained the outward appearance of the dutiful wife and visited Kevin regularly, but not with the regularity that formed a pattern, and this left him guessing as to when she would arrive. Some days it was early, before he'd had his wash, some days at lunch time, when the smell of steamed food was nauseating – when he was seated with others, older, who could not hear – and some days she did not come at all. She brought him audiobooks on any dull subject that their library offered, as well as biscuits that should have been forbidden – sometimes soap or socks. She made him moderately comfortable by puffing up his pillows; she reset his television on something endless, like cricket; she dutifully informed and alarmed him when commodity prices were poised to plummet; and she would even, albeit rarely and when visiting with Evan, clip his talons. If the rest-home orderlies had been familiar with the word, they would have called her efforts agapistic. What Carol couldn't bring herself to do, however, was to authenticate her agapism by offering more than was publicly observed, and more than was perfunctory in terms of need. She found it impossible to 'touch' him with anything more than functional digits, couldn't soften her voice, her eyes, or the sinew that buckled her lips.

But on one visit well into the year she was surprised to find Frank Edge, Kevin's doctor, sitting on his bed. What surprised her was not that he was there, in the rest home – she knew that as her husband's designated doctor he was obliged to provide three-monthly reviews which she herself made a point of dutifully attending – no, it was more that he was actually sitting on the bed, that he was unaccompanied by the identifying accoutrement of every physician (the stethoscope), and that there was no nurse present.

"Hello, Carol."

"Dr Edge!"

"Frank, please."

"Any problem?"

"No, no medical problem really. Kevin and I were just about to have a chat."

"A chat?"

Frank stood up, smiled, and gestured for Carol to sit down in Kevin's armchair. "Come and join us. You don't mind, do you, Kevin?" Kevin looked down, but made no signal to register an objection, and, after Carol was seated, the doctor eased himself back down onto the bed. He placed his hand on Kevin's forearm, the useless one with the fat, bent wrist, and said nothing for at least two minutes, before continuing with an unexpected directness: "This isn't working, is it, Kevin? You're miserable. You must be. There's no progress. You have no life." There was no initial response from Kevin, and Carol's eyes remained fixed on the points of doctor-patient contact, wondering why they looked more natural than grotesque. Fine rain formed droplets on the window, coalesced, and then slipped down, blurring the blooms of a common pink camellia. Beyond that there was a bare silver birch. "It must have been devastating. You must have felt – you must feel – that everything was taken away from you by the stroke. Did you feel like that? Do you now?" Kevin's right eye was always wet, and it was left to his left to answer. "Does your sister visit?" No response. "Your son?" A slight nod. "That's lovely. He worries about you – like Carol," he added, startling her.

There was a longer pause now, just as there was a pause in the rain. "Going through the motions is not enough, Kevin – swallowing pills, swallowing mash, swallowing your pride. Wouldn't you like to walk again? Be able to tell people what you're thinking? Feel less frightened?" he asked quietly, and for the first time Kevin raised his head and looked directly at Frank – one eye as wet as the other – each wild and cornered. Frank tightened his grip on Kevin's arm. "We can do that, Kevin. I'm sure we can. You won't believe me, because you feel so down, so flat – so useless. Isn't that so?" Kevin nodded. "Well, I'm going to perk you up by asking you to swallow another pill," he smiled, "just trust me on that – but I need you to fight. You're the key here. It will be hard, there'll be ups and downs, but anything's better than this, don't you think?" Again, Kevin made a faint effort to nod. "You've got to get out of bed, Kevin – you've got to want to – out of your easy chair – out of here – out of this miserable old-age home. We need you in the Waikato. Farmers are always complaining – you know that – whether it's wet, dry, windy, or anything in-between, whether they grow heifers, horses or herbs, whether the dollar's up, down or sideways; and I've been told that you were a master at making them feel better ...", pause, "by selling them the moon."

Kevin was not an easy man to amuse, and smiling, for him, had always been more a calculated expression of mockery rather than of mirth, but the one corner of his mouth that curled up, just momentarily, following the quip, would not have had time for cynical preconception, and may well have registered Carol's first observance in him of verifiable jocundity.

What followed after a pause, however, was a sound that could only have had its origins in anguish, and it emerged distorted by nerve damage and secretions; but its message was clear, and, after it had subsided, Frank was confident that Kevin was indeed prepared to try, prepared to fight – prepared to revolt against helplessness. His confidence, furthermore, and quite understandably, was extrapolated to embrace Carol with the assumption that she would continue as a vital contributor to Kevin's transformation. Family doctors are at risk of coming to believe that their every insight and pronouncement strikes a chord, and one could forgive this one therefore, as he took his leave, for misinterpreting her feeble handshake as a fawning 'thank you', when in fact it was anything but.

Kevin had undergone intensive rehabilitation in the early post-stroke phase, as an adjunct to his admission, but it was in effect a time of bewilderment and humiliation in which he had felt back at school and bullied. He'd received no effective recovery treatment at the rest home either. It had served merely as a place of safe containment. But, although Frank's proposal of a further four to six weeks of hospital-based intensive rehabilitation appeared to offer more of the same, this time, Kevin sensed, it was going to be different – different because it was authenticated by someone whom he could trust. Since his father's betrayal he had scorned the very notion of trust, and he had become a horrible man, but here was someone who made an effort to read his mind, to 'connect', to sense his desperation and despair – someone whose promise was tangible and appeared sincere. Kevin, furthermore, had scoured Frank for an agenda, a motive for personal gain, but had failed to find one.

And so, he agreed to readmission, and he did this with a dogged determination to succeed. The result was that psychologists were able to build on gains made by Frank's pills, to offer him insight and hope; physiotherapists, occupational therapists, and podiatrists were able to splint his contractures, design soles for his foot drop, use hoists to have him standing, and then, incredibly, were able to have him upright and walking (sort of), with the aid of parallel bars; while a speech therapist with the patience of a Tamil fisherman was able to help him converse, effectively, using cards, pointer boards, hand signals and 'technology'.

It was a battle, as it always is, and progress was apparent only in retrospect, but Kevin showed a resilience that Carol had hoped alien to him, and persevered. He emerged, just a month before the house extensions were completed, with the ability to make himself understood to all but the most disinterested; with a determination to inch his way to the dining room unaided by all but a walking frame; and to eagerly accompany Evan to his first Agricultural Field Days event in years, where he purchased, without any attempt at bargaining, a brand new mobility scooter, complete with a flapping flag.

Each step in his progression – for instance his mastery of the buzzer that summoned help when he had soiled – was applauded by Carol with an "Aren't you clever, my dear?" and, because irony passed him by, Kevin absorbed these utterances as utterances of praise and thanksgiving – as evidence of how well he had trained her.

The partitioning of their Hillcrest house offered Kevin and Carol independent living in a two-bedroomed home, with, at Carol's insistence, two toilets – each en suite. Kevin's room was equipped with an adjustable orthopedic bed, a walk-in cupboard, and a small but smart television. The expectation was that Kevin would spend most of his life in that room. Their lounge-cum-dining room/kitchen led out and onto a long and covered veranda that faced west, towards Mt Pirongia. Carol's conservatory, part of the original design, was retained at one end. The laundry was accessible to both Angela and Carol through their respective back doors.

Kevin, for the first time, began to show an interest in the project, and Evan (sweet-natured as always) enthusiastically arranged for last-minute adjustments of design to remove the impediments to his father's access that these inspections exposed. The one that galled Carol the most was the smoothing of the lip entering her conservatory. It had been three centimetres in height – just enough to block his swinging leg! 'Why', Carol pondered, 'would anyone not want Kevin to trip? His foot is so ugly!'

Since his stroke Kevin had lacked the dexterity to dry between his toes, and the retained moisture, sweetened by diabetes, had served as superphosphate for his fungi; but her pedal revulsion predated colonisation. It was the size – the grossness of bone, vein, and corn. His feet were like those of a Brobdingnagian! His toes, and particularly those bent and euphemistically termed 'small', were grotesque. There were times in the past, years before he became sick, when she was tempted to incinerate his slippers.

And his lips! Those thin, bloodless strips of fish flesh overhung by coarse hair, were repulsive too. But what part of him was not? How could she have touched him before it was compulsory? Allowed him to fumble her? Perhaps it was the embroidered sheets that her mother had secreted away in her bottom drawer? Perhaps it was the news reels, Debbie Reynolds, or Deborah Kerr?

Bitter spit began to gather at the corners of her mouth as she remembered. 'Contact' had endured, as least until he became disabled, as obligatory and prudent, but now, now that he had no power, she wanted no part of him – no sight of his fat feet and fish lips, no smell of his leakage, and certainly no role in making his wretched life more bearable.

It was this that niggled her about Evan and his niceness.

Joey was born just two weeks before Kevin moved back. Angela's approach to her pregnancy had, from the very beginning, surprised Carol. It was so different from her own austere and isolating ordeals. First news of the pregnancy was communicated to her in the most unorthodox way, while she was watering the garden. Both prospective parents emerged from their car grinning like happy dogs, and walked towards her smiling, but in tears. Her first thought was that they had over-imbibed, but it soon became apparent that this was excitement, joy – fear – their foremost wish granted – and that their lives would never be the same again. But what surprised her more, as the months went by, was that the ebullience refused to subside, and that she was made part of it. Angela's family was large and boisterous, and her mother was a mother hen, but they lived up north, and Carol found herself included in the antenatal and investigative procedures that marked the pregnancy's progress. The most memorable of these remained her participation in Angela's first ultrasound, when viability was confirmed by a pulsating blotch of white. The three of them, Evan, Angela and Carol, stopped in Grey Street on the way home, she remembered, for a coffee to celebrate, and Evan's excitement was comically irrepressible. His effervescence reminded her of 'Soliloquy' from the Rodgers and Hammerstein musical *Carousel*, which Gordon MacRae sang in anticipation of the birth of his child, offering her the earth. It had been one of her mother's favourites.

But being present at the birth of Joey was the most inclusive thrill of all. Carol was apprehensive prior to the event because Angela's mother, Joyce, was coming down with the intention of being at the delivery, and of staying on for a few days after, but she needn't have worried. Joyce took control of the kitchen and of the dishing out of wine and wisecracks, leaving a trail of flour, mud (tramped in from the herb garden), and used utensils; and, in effect, raised all of their spirits, preparing them for their summons, so that the labour, with all four as participants, was a happy event. And Joey, with her squeezed face and pink feet! Joey was a joy to behold. Photos taken by the midwife, a nursing friend of Angela's, captured the chaos, and were shown to Kevin the next day, with others taken of him being helped holding the child. What she found extraordinary was that this encounter marked his first, witnessed, submission to affection. She called it the 'Joey effect', an unforeseen underbelly, and she added the observation to a growing list of hurts available for exploitation.

Thus began a new phase: Joyce returned to Northland, Kevin took up residence, Joey grew exponentially, and Carol, spending most of her time in her garden, got a dog. It was quite by chance that Evan took her with him to the SPCA pound, where he occasionally worked voluntarily over weekends, to check on a newly rescued pup. That pup wasn't there, but another one was – an abandoned white mongrel with a brown patch over its right eye, and dispro-portionately large paws. It looked like a cartoon character skip-ping on paddles: simultaneously tripping, squealing, peeing, jumping and licking – losing its footing on the wet concrete floor – demonstrating a desperation for affection.

"What will happen to her, Evan?"

"What do you mean?"

"If we don't take her? If nobody takes her?"

"They're lovely here, Mum. She won't suffer."

"I know, but …"

Evan looked at her and smiled. "Do you want her, as a pet?"

"Well, no … I haven't had a dog since I left my parents' home."

"But do you want her?"

"Well, no, but … you know? Besides," she continued, "there's Dad … and Joey?"

"Don't worry about Dad, and Joey? … All kids need a dog."

Carol felt a momentary pang. Pets, she remembered, had been forbidden in the home that her children had grown up in.

"You're right, Evan," she said quietly, trying to suppress a smile. "What breed is she?"

"Several, I would think."

And so Alice was added to the household, bringing with her the softest and most compelling eyes imaginable, eyes that were nuanced purveyors of Carol's every mood. An initial flailing objection on the part of Kevin to the dog's acquisition was summarily ignored, as was his insistence that it remain outside. Carol was quick to realise, in fact, that Alice offered potential as a 'hope hazard' – as an animal that could trip – and she made no effort to keep her from her husband's sleeping quarters.

The puppy phase was adorably chaotic, exasperating and expensive, but, coupled with the passage of Joey's early milestones, added an unfamiliar dimension of joy to Carol's life. Some of her best times were outings to offer an exhausted Angela an hour or two of peace. Joey would first be fastened into the back of her yellow Nissan, then the pushchair would be placed in the boot, and, finally, Alice, barking at a frequency above high C, would be allowed to leap into the passenger seat and dribble – content that she was not being left behind. An old curtain served, inadequately, as an upholstery protector. Spotify would be cranked up, and then the three of them would proceed to the river. (Yes, Carol returned to the river.)

Alice was as docile as a dolphin – indiscriminately friendly to other walkers, joggers, cats – even cyclists – and fellow members of the canine species needed look no further than her energetic tail to satisfy themselves that she posed no threat.

One morning, however, things went awry. Alice had a habit of running ahead of Carol when not restrained by a leash – her tongue dripping and her nose twitching, calling on a bladder of seemingly unlimited capacity to mark every leaf, stump or blade of grass identified as having been marked by other dogs in the recent past – but her primary intent was to befriend. One morning, while running free, she was the first to notice the approach of a pram propelled by a lady of considerable age. Carol, aware of Alice's tendency towards over-exuberance, would normally not have allowed her to approach such a vehicle without the owner's express permission, but she was too late. The dog bounded up to the perambulator with even more than her usual spring, leant over, and stuck her nose into its open side. Expecting a doll-like infant cry, Carol was startled by something quite different – a discordant combination of yelp and squeal, and, before she could process what was happening, Alice was beating an undignified retreat with a punctured nose – quivering and pushing against Joey's pushchair.

It took a full two minutes for a semblance of tranquillity to be restored. Suffice to say that Joey was left least perturbed, while the occupant of the old lady's pram was in no mood to be pacified! He revealed himself in all his fury as something resembling a marmoset with mange – yapping so frantically that his few remaining fangs risked auto-extraction.

Eventually, and most fortunately, fatigue came to his aid, and Andy – the name that he answered to before going deaf – began to wilt, with fewer and weaker expressions of outrage. He was, it turned out, a very old and irritable poodle, of the miniature variety.

"I'm so sorry," Carol offered, "the dog's still young and doesn't listen. I …"

"No need, no need, I haven't seen Andy that feisty in years. How is your poor puppy, my dear? Will she survive the shame?" Laughing again.

Carol laughed herself. "Not sure about that. She certainly won't be poking her nose into the next pram that passes by."

"No, not by half – and how's the poor little one? What a tumble that was!"

"She … Joey … no, she seems fine, thank you. I got the bigger fright", and then Carol added, laughing, "Your Andy is quite something!"

"Was. He's almost sixteen now. Arthritis, pins, pills – only one or two teeth. Much like me," she added chuckling, tickling him through his tunic. "I also have 'Arthur'" (her term for osteoarthritis), "and I too am supported by very expensive scaffolding. Eighty-nine is a ripe old age, but I have to outlive Andy."

"You do indeed. I'm Carol," she added, "and this is Joey, my grandchild. Alice, you have met."

"I'm May."

They finished the walk together, Alice weary and subdued, and Joey waking when they reached the car. It transpired that May had also been raised in Taranaki, and that she too had walked the mountain contours with a father.

***

Kevin had never allowed Carol to spend more than was necessary on the garden. "Keep it tidy" was his simple command; but now she could indulge her passion. In April she had planted bulbs –

mainly freesias and Sparaxis; in winter, poppies, pansies and a scented damask, as well as azaleas and rhododendrons for old time's sake; and now, in the early spring of September, her garden was ablaze. Twice a week she had driven over to her favourite nursery to purchase more: polyanthus, violas, sweet peas and more pansies, as well as an irresistible white clematis that she wanted for the side fence. The front, though, she decided, as she walked out on her way to the doctor, the wicker, was going to have sunflowers towering above it.

It was a clear day with the remnant of a winter-blue sky forming a backdrop to buds and clenched leaves as she walked down to the medical centre. Edith, her usual GP, was away, but she was not unhappy to be seen again by Eleanor Hutton, a younger doctor who had helped her through a flat patch two months prior.

"You're looking half your age, Carol, and happy too. What is it that's changed? Do you think the medication's made a difference?"

"Well, I … maybe."

"You have a grandchild too now, don't you? She was going to be living with you, as I recall."

How did this woman remember these details? Carol wondered, with some irritation. "Not with me, exactly, but on the same property."

"That's lovely."

"It is," she conceded, "to some extent, and I also have a dog."

"A puppy."

"Yes."

"Happy chaos, I suppose?"

"Yes, she does … she is …"

"And your husband? He was going to be moving in, and that was worrying you. Has he settled in?"

The questions were beginning to grate, and her affirmative reply was curt.

There was a pause before Eleanor continued. "Is there a

problem … with your husband? He had a stroke last year, didn't he? That must be very difficult for you?"

"Difficult?" Carol replied, smiling bitterly. "He's more than difficult. Always has been. He's a pig," she added.

"The stroke …"

"The stroke should have killed him."

"You don't mean that?"

"I do."

"Does he know how you feel?" Eleanor asked quietly.

"No."

"Have you thought of a solution? Him moving back into a facility?"

"Won't happen."

"Or you moving to a place of your own?"

"No, no, it's okay. Quite good really." Carol reassembled her face before continuing. "I have my garden – Joey – the puppy. I can do what I like now. He's pretty much paralysed."

Eleanor then said something that rattled Carol. "But you must want more, Carol. You're not trapped, remember. There's always another way, but it's up to you. It really is up to you."

And that, plausibly, led to her seeking her first job since leaving Taranaki. While waiting in the pharmacy for her medication to be dispensed she noticed a sign on the counter advertising a position in the cosmetics department, and she surreptitiously folded up an application form and placed it in her bag.

FRANK

It is fair to say that broccoli soup sparked an existential crisis –
another one – and that cream, butter, cheese and, of all things,
onions, prolonged it. One day Frank was purring along, content
that he had negotiated his stroke scare unscathed, and the next he
was as inflated as John Bull. He determined, after promptings from
his belt and grumblings in his belly, that he finally needed to
follow the advice that he had so frequently pressed upon his
patients: "You need to lower risk …" (of clogged arteries, cancer,
diabetes, dementia, depression, etc.), "… by getting off your easy
chair; by reducing your intake of alcohol, red meat, pastry, bacon
and 'anything sweet'; by eating copious amounts of oily fish,
coloured vegetables, fruit (especially pip fruit, citrus and berries),
nuts (especially brain-like walnuts), legumes, garlic and onions –
whatever is in season." Broccoli was in season, and so broccoli
it was.

His lunch in the next week, he decided, would comprise a pear,
a handful of tree nuts, and a generous container of the said soup.
Milly sniffed but demurred when Frank approached her with his
request. What Frank was fortunately unaware of, however, was

that Milly's cruciferous soup came from a recipe that was designed by wives-past, primarily for its taste and not for its links to longevity; and into the pot went a quarter of a cup of butter, one white onion, a quarter of a cup of white flour, two cups of cream, two cups of chicken broth, one large carrot, a cup of Cheddar cheese, salt, cayenne pepper and, finally, a half-kilogram of chopped broccoli florets and stems.

On the Monday afternoon and night of that week Frank's stomach churned more than it had in the months prior, and by the Thursday it had become a washing machine, a gas bag of borborygmi. He had to leave his room between patients to save them from suffocation, and he took virtual ownership of the staff toilet. Frank's stools took on the form and trajectory of molten pumice, and by week's end he had convinced himself that the end was nigh. There was no blood, no melena – mere splatter – but the change was dramatic enough to engender first fear, and then fatalistic resignation.

As with his carotid crisis he attempted to soldier on so as not to worry anyone, but, as before, the women in his life saw through his deception as if he were a child. "What is it, Frank, are you unwell – unhappy?" was Milly's question when he nibbled at his dinner.

"No, no, I'm fine."

"Nonsense."

"No, really, it's nothing."

Milly put down her fork. "What is it, Frank? Are you in pain? Is it your stomach? You were up and down all night. Come to think of it, you haven't been right for months."

"It is a bit upset."

"Upset? What do you mean, upset? Diarrhoea? Cramps?"

"Yes, well, both … and gas."

"Gas? What does that mean? Do you need a check-up?"

"No, not yet. We'll see. I had that colonoscopy a few years ago."

"Maybe you need another?"

"Maybe. We'll see."

"Stop saying 'We'll see', Frank. It means nothing."

"Well, I …"

"It's not my soup?"

"Of course not."

"Speak to someone at work."

"I will."

Frank had no intention of speaking to anyone at work, but Eleanor came in carrying a cup of tea, sat down in his room, and then asked him outright, "What's wrong, Frank?"

He was somewhat startled, even annoyed, and his eyebrows assumed their most belligerent formation. "Not you too?"

"If you're not hiding in here, you're hiding in the toilet. Do you have gastro?"

He looked at her directly, wanting to transmit pique, seniority, but he of all people should have known that Eleanor was immune to intimidation – it amused her too much. He realised that his petulance would get him nowhere.

"I have, actually," he answered finally. "Possibly something worse than that", and then went on to explain, with some level of gravity, his sorry story.

"Just this week?" Eleanor queried.

"Yes, well, sort of. There's been a bit of discomfort and irregularity for a while, but yes, this week it's been much worse. Why do you ask?"

"Your soup, what's in your soup?"

"Broccoli."

"Anything else?"

"I don't know, Milly made it. Water, I suppose, and a bit of salt."

"Have you thought of FODMAP?"

"FODMAP?" He hadn't thought of FODMAP.

"FODMAP, the short-chain carbohydrates that are poorly absorbed in the small intestine in susceptible people."

"I know what FODMAP is."

"Eating them can exacerbate the symptoms you describe."

"I know. I know about FODMAP, Eleanor, but are you saying that even *broccoli* is bad for you?" He'd become frustrated and, to be frank, extremely irritated by some people's (and usually well-heeled people's) food faddisms. They complicated their lives, let alone those of their doctors', by taking on a spiritual and smug interest in conspiracy theories, by gullibly and uncritically absorbing the musings of 'wellness' gurus, and by wilfully ignoring the pleadings of one of the more subtle of their five senses – taste! Their 'diets', always over-priced, ranged between dinners of bird seed, coconut and kale at one extreme, to that of lard, locusts and raw-red venison at the other. Surely Eleanor wasn't into this nonsense!

"No, no," laughed Eleanor, "but you can develop an intolerance for broccoli, as well as several other foods like garlic, and onions, and pears …"

"*Those* are bad for you too?" Frank was incredulous now.

His reaction, and especially that of his eyebrows, was too much for Eleanor, and her mirth got the better of her, causing near collapse. Frank loved to see Eleanor in this state – it was one of her most endearing qualities – but he was afraid that people might rush in. "Shush, Eleanor. Shush. What will the patients think?" he added as he jumped up to close his door.

That simply exacerbated her mirth, but she was finally able to collect herself and say, "S…sorry, Frank, but you're so lovely!"

Lovely? 'Lovely' was hardly the word that he would have used to describe the whoopee cushion that he had become!

"But, seriously," she struggled to continue, "I would suggest a stool test – just in case."

"In case of what?"

"In case you have an infection. This sort of intolerance doesn't come out of the blue, Frank. Are you sure the bloating didn't start before the soup?"

"Well, yes, it might have. Come to think of it I've been gripey since getting back from the States."

At his first opportunity Frank googled FODMAP and realised that Eleanor was probably right. In predisposed individuals, incompletely digested food components pass through the small bowel and enter the large, offering *E. coli* and their companions a banquet. The article used the apt analogy of the feeding frenzy that results from white bread being flung into a fishpond, and it described the end-result as a production line for malodorous gas. Cruciferous vegetables, onions, cream, even pears, were implicated, and, after checking, Frank realised that his soup provided the perfect substrate for the gastronomical eruption that had occurred. What's more, he learned that in individuals who had not suffered from irritable bowel syndrome as a chronic condition, an upsurge in FODMAP intolerance should prompt a hunt for an infective trigger. Eleanor was spot on, and, lo and behold, his stool test confirmed a giardia infection – something that had probably been lurking since his visit to New Orleans!

Eleanor provided him with a script for a five-day course of metronidazole, and his gas factory imploded like a punctured meringue; but the experience persuaded Frank, finally, that he needed a doctor of his own, and Eleanor was asked to assume that role.

The experience, and his ignominious enlightenment, had him thinking again. Was it time to retire? Was he slipping? Why was he not as au fait with the nature and implications of FODMAP as he should have been? Would he have reached the diagnosis as effortlessly as Eleanor if a patient of similar age had presented with a similar problem to him? Put bluntly, was it still safe for him to continue to practise?

Self-criticism and self-doubt had served him as both curse and saviour throughout his career. He had been confident, of course he had been confident, but he had never been cocky. Many a night he had wrestled with his sheet, often disturbing Milly, wondering whether he should have withheld a medication or prescribed it in higher dose; whether he should have admitted an asthmatic, or whether he had been foolish to do so; whether the shortness of breath that he had treated as an infection could have been the result of a clot. And sick small children in particular were beginning to spook him. People had such faith that he would fix them. It was unnerving. After his forty years in the same practice their confidence was understandable, but it also served as a burden.

If he were to stop, what would he do? Play golf? Never. Garden? Cook? Join a boring book club? Attend university lectures? Travel? Yes, maybe travel. The holiday that he and Milly had had in America – ostensibly for her birthday – swelled his heart with sweet memory. The Americans had been unfailingly courteous and helpful – so different from what he imagined they would be. Even the immigration official at Houston Airport was not officious. And what about the bus driver who had offered them water?

They were in Washington DC on a very hot day, and they had walked back over the Potomac and into the Mall after spending several hours of reverential peace at Arlington. They were close to the Lincoln Memorial and Milly was bent over a water fountain trying to fill her bottle when a bus driver, a tall, elderly African American man waiting for his run to begin, suddenly leapt out of his throbbing vehicle and strode towards them holding out two large, ice-cold bottles of water. "Here," he said, "that water ain't no good on a blazin' hot day." And then he was off again, walking faster than was wise, back towards his bus. They were surprised – startled even – both Frank and Milly, and barely had time to wave as his bus burst into life. How kind, they thought, how lovely! Frank had read somewhere that for an act of kindness, of generosity, to be recognised as truly meritorious, it had to be both unheralded and unsolicited. The act of this man fitted that category, and Washington, for all its colossal symmetry, its sirens, its brutal politics – its magnificent and imposing resurrection of imperial Rome – took on a soft hue.

And in New Orleans, that sad, doomed and abused city, with its menacing Mississippi, its Cajun fish, and its uncouth, pissing visitors out for a good time, it was in New Orleans that Frank witnessed another act of kindness, and one of the same order. They were sitting in the French Quarter in a small courtyard on a hot day having a beer under a blood-red bougainvillea when Frank noticed an old, wire-thin man on the busy pavement beyond. Milly had her back to the street and didn't see, as he, not begging, began rummaging in a garbage bin; didn't see as he pulled out discarded greaseproof paper and began licking the tomato sauce off it; didn't see as the driver of a cab pulled up and held out what looked like a hamburger, and then pulled away. It was carried out like a drug drop, with sleight of hand, an act of unsolicited, singular, and spontaneous kindness in an atmosphere of grotesque over-indulgence and contrived gaiety. The intention was not to have the act observed, not even to linger long enough for thanks, enough to witness the meal torn at and swallowed without mastication. (The starving man had no teeth after all.) No, the intention was to respond, without deliberation, to the most noble of all human impulses – to someone in need. Frank, momentarily frozen by the incident, wondered how many lunches the cab driver gave away – how often he had had to clean vomit off his back seat!

Their tour of the greater city gave them further insight into its suffering and celebration. They were hosted by a young, humorous, intelligent, and knowledgeable African American man whose ancestors had been herded, traded, and hidden in the mosquito swamps north of Lake Pontchartrain by the indigenous population in the eighteenth century. He took them to raised graves, showed them mangroves and 'moss trees'; was mainly silent while driving around the derelict districts devastated and abandoned during that disaster of biblical proportions, Katrina; parked outside the house of his recently deceased hero, Fats Domino, and played *Blueberry Hill* and *I'm Walkin'* while telling us of the singer's great faithfulness to the city – of his humility and generosity; he talked with pride about many of the city's other famous sons and daughters – people like William Faulkner, Tennessee Williams, Edgar Elgar, Mahalia Jackson, and, of course, Louis Armstrong. Fats, though, was number one!

They arrived back at their small French colonial hotel enlightened, humbled, happy that they had visited, but never wanting to return.

And, finally, there was that city of cities, the city that had embedded itself in image and sound in all who had lived through the better part of the American century – New York! Expecting to be overwhelmed, intimidated – exploited for their naivety – both Frank and Milly felt quite the opposite. New York had an energy, a vitality, a confidence and a determination that was exhilarating. It made the most of life.

Their one-week stay was well-planned, with pre-booked alternate-day excursions, and rest days in between. They stayed in a quiet hotel in north Brooklyn, just one stop from Grand Central, and the walk from their hotel to the subway had views over the busy East River and beyond – to mid-town Manhattan, with the United Nations block, the Chrysler (Milly's favourite), and the Empire State itself! They felt at home in Brooklyn, but they felt at home in Manhattan too. Their first day, walking over the Brooklyn Bridge, knowing the history of its construction and of the Swedish divers who developed and first described the bends, looking out to Staten Island and the famous, melancholy island to its right – Lower Manhattan drawing closer as they walked – was magical!

There was not a hint of arrogance in the people that they briefly conversed with, with the individuals that they followed with their eyes – the people were simply too busy. Jay walking, for example, was a given. Even the NYPD cops, guns slung low, turned a blind eye to such trivial misdemeanours. Provided people were scurrying along, going about their business, any business, it was okay with them. Frank found it hard to imagine anyone being depressed in Chelsea, the Meatpacking District – the Upper East Side adjacent to Central Park. One of their days was spent in that area: absorbed by Giacometti's skinny sculptures in the Guggenheim; sobered by the crowd still gathered next to the Dakota Building on the other side of the park and paying homage to the man who preached love; and rejuvenated, in a time of reflection, by a Fifth Avenue French prawn and tomato broth.

And on their last day, the heart-breaking highlight that had choked them into prolonged silence, a pilgrimage through the mausoleum of 9/11 – a vast cavern of dignified and reverent remembrance for the day that changed the world.

Looking back on his career, looking back at his considerable time in Hamilton, there were many memories to savour, and so few to regret. Was there any job that offered broader or better insight into the permutations of human behaviour – to people stripped of façade? Despite the prestige and superior income of specialist colleagues, was there any more challenging job in medicine? Because of the 'income gap' there were fewer and fewer full-time colleagues entering general practice – certainly far fewer males –

yet it was still drawing people of the calibre of Eleanor, who was as committed a doctor as anyone that Frank had ever known. She would never own a manicured mansion in Matangi that was shaped like an aeroplane, one wing never used; she would never own a stone and steel beach-front bungalow at Pauanui; she could, but never would, accompany a cravat in an old convertible; and she would never, ever, withhold service from someone who could not pay. Yet, with her focus on patients rather than possessions, she would always be plentifully compensated and would never have to shiver with fright when the fridge broke down. Her special gift was to make people feel safe and listened to, and she, like Frank himself, would be showered with gifts.

> *Gifts grown, picked, caught, or even*
> *slaughtered on a farm – gifts wrapped*
> *roughly – offered awkwardly – with fat,*
> *cracked hands; bread, knuckle-kneaded,*
> *seeded, and smelling of mother; cherry*
> *plums; leek roots flush with sheep*
> *manure; plucked duck stuffed*
> *with sage; and annuals unarranged.*

Frank needed time to think this through. He needed to make his own decision, before speaking with Milly, and before informing Edith and Eleanor. Maybe he would write in his retirement? Somerset Maugham claimed, he remembered reading, that family practice provided the best substrate for writers. Frank had substrate all right, but 'writing' might be a step too far! Besides, he had to be sensible.

With Milly being five years younger than him, and likely to live for at least ten years after he had died, Frank had to be sure that she was well provided for. Neither of them was interested in cars beyond their colour, comfort and reliability, neither needed a home bigger than one that their books could fill, but they hadn't exactly been skinflint either, and it would be difficult after all those easy years to cut back on what they called their 'happy spending' – on holidays, on accessing Jane, on their home and beloved garden. They had also been, in hindsight, inattentive to investment advice. It was something that did not interest them as much as it should have, and their slowly accumulated 'nest egg' had substantially more white than yellow. But was it enough? Surely it was enough?

"Of course, it's enough," was Milly's response when he tentatively broached the subject with her. "I'm not helpless, you know."

"I know, Mil, it's just that I don't …"

"I know what it is, it's paternalism."

Frank laughed. "Paternalism?"

"Yes."

"Must say I never thought about it that way."

"Well, it's time you did, Frank. We're in this together – always have been. There's no way I'm sitting home knitting. My four-day week is busy and suits me fine for the foreseeable future. Besides, it brings in more than enough for groceries."

"It does indeed, but is it enough for Bluff oysters?"

"Don't patronise me, Frank," she said quietly, and then, turning her burning eyes towards him, continued: "No, we've never made an issue out of money, and we won't start now. It's a difficult time for you, I know that, but it's up to you. Do you have the capacity and desire to carry on? I don't know. Life makes a mockery of long-term planning. You know that – especially when it comes to money. People worry that they don't have enough, won't have enough, even when they have billions – and then they go and squeeze yet more out of others. We despise them for it, for their greed. We have enough, Frank – I will have enough. You worry about how I would manage financially if I were left alone, you worry about how everyone will manage, but what would leave me depleted would be the absence of you – not the absence of your income. A luxurious suite in a retirement home would be the last thing on my mind."

Frank was taken aback, and tears streamed down his face. Milly began sobbing too. "We are comfortably well off, Frank, but not intentionally. Thank God we're not rich. We can be proud of that."

He drew her to him, this miracle, this half, this extension of everything that he held dear. "I'm sorry," he murmured, and then, as he drew her closer, he whispered, "I'll pull myself together."

"Don't joke, Frank. Not now."

And then, for some reason, perhaps because his encounter with the elderly patient that he had seen the day before had never really left him, his thoughts turned, even while he held Milly, to his consulting room, and to Ellen:

'My one son, the one down in Levin, has got cancer, in his prostate, and they are just going to watch it. The other one, who lives here, he fell the other day.'

'A bad fall?'

'He broke his leg – it was all twisted – and now he can't work, doctor. Can't do nothing.'

'I'm so sorry, Ellen.'

'Caught his leg in a ladder. Got twisted. We can't go down to Levin now.' She looked at and beyond him with bright, dry eyes, before adding, 'The world's going bad, doctor. The whole world.'

'Are you taking your worry pills, Ellen?' he asked gently.

'The half ones?'

'Yes.'

'No – not for a month or two.'

'Are they difficult to break? Did they disagree with you?'

'No.'

'Do you think they helped?'

'I think they did, doctor,' she answered quickly, searching his eyes. 'I breathed better.' There was a pause, before she added, 'A friend told me – told me to stop. She said I didn't need them. Said they was a crotch.'

'Maybe you shouldn't have told her that you were taking them, Ellen.'

'You're right, doctor. Maybe I shouldn't of. Maybe I should try them some more.'

'Maybe you should, Ellen. See if they help. Things are difficult for you now.'

'They are doctor.'

He wondered whether those pills really were going to help – whether he should simply have allowed her to talk for longer.

QUINCE

Quince fantasised about cancelling. Headache, head injury – family crisis – another more pressing engagement that had slipped his mind? But how would he word his lie? What intonation should he use? He could talk through a tissue and hold his nose! He'd done that before. Another engagement? No, that wasn't plausible. He retained the hope that a message of cancellation and apology would meet him on his return from his walk with Pound: "So, so sorry to cancel at this late hour, Quince, but our visitors have had a divorce." Or "Ever so sorry, Quince, but our electricity has been cut off." Even, "We just don't like you as a person anymore, Quince." But there was no flicking light on his mobile.

If he was serious about cancelling, he knew that he had to act quickly – before Mary started her preparations. It wouldn't be fair otherwise. He glanced at his father's clock – ten-thirty. Too early to put on a roast, braise a fillet, toss a salad – but not too early to marinate duck! Joe liked duck. And pudding? A summer dessert should be whipped at the last minute – a berry and sherry bowl perhaps! With vanilla bean ice cream! But then again Mary couldn't be trusted to make things simple, and a pecan pie was not out of the question.

But Quince was determined. He deserved his peace. Reaching for his iPhone 6 he scrolled down contacts until he found the Rowlands, poked at the telephone icon, and sucked in air. Their ring tone responded and rang until it stopped with a click: "Hello, hello, Mary, Joe? Sorry to …"

"You've reached the phone of the two and only, the other, non-New Testament, Joseph and Mary. We are so, so sorry that we missed your call. Please, please leave us a message after the beep, and we'll call you just as soon as we can, BUT, if we've won the lotto, call Joe on 027 674 7582, or Mary on 027 541 7486. Ciao!"

"Um … Mary, Joe. I … it's me, Quince. Just wanted to know what to bring. Pansy has early plums … okay, bye."

He sighed, swore, and sat back. If it hadn't been for her 'happy' voice, he wouldn't have been so irritated. She was a good person, he knew that, but sometimes, he suspected, the goodness went too far – beyond authenticity – compensating for something undisclosed. And there were times, like today, when he simply did not want to be cheered up – especially at a gathering with people he didn't know. Besides, he had so much on his mind after Frank's talk. It had shaken him to be honest, the accusation that he was idle rather than ill – that his head was empty – unused. He needed time to think.

Just then, Baker, his cat, came in with a sparrow between its teeth. The bird was alive and terrified – leaving a trail of blood, feathers, and black excrement. If Quince had remembered his early and abbreviated reading of the birth of existentialism he would have recognised this moment for what it was, a point of 'apricot cocktail' ignition, because everything other than the bird disappeared

– his self-pity, his indecision, the kettle to his left. The creature and its terror were his only coordinates, the substrate for a thousand books, and sparked a detonation. What Quince did not realise as he lunged at Baker was that the dining room tablecloth was wrapped around his left leg. His only heirloom (apart from his father's clock), a large, crystal vase, was whipped up into the air, and then down, smacking onto unforgiving hardboard. There was an explosion of glass and water, and Baker, just momentarily, lost his poise – but the moment was enough for his prey to flap free.

Quince, meanwhile, did not at first realise that his foot's entrapment had caused a cascade of bodily misfortune to match that of heirloom loss. He had sustained lacerations to both forehead and foot, with the added possibility of mild concussion resulting from his head's brief encounter with table wood as it plummeted, accounting, at least in part, for his initial bewilderment as he tried to take stock from his perspective on the floor. Human and bird blood intermingled, and it was impossible to distinguish one from the other. "Isn't bird blood cold?" he mused. "Aren't birds evolved from reptiles? Does hot blood not look different from cold – more indigo than red?" He felt embarrassed that he did not know for sure. It was something that he should know – that everyone should know. "No," he decided, as befuddlement started to clear, "bird blood is hot. Of course, it's hot."

It was then that the phenomenon of the sunflower momentarily supplanted that of the sparrow. The giant bloom, which had been the solitary occupant of his crystal vase, now hung precariously over the table edge, staring at him like a compound eye, and it was the seeds, or the arrangement of the seeds, that mesmerised him. They were packed tight, like chocolates, into whorls emanating out from the centre. Every space was occupied and orderly – mimicking the sort of mandala that a mathematician would construct. He remembered reading that the arrangement optimised space to a degree that surpassed any conceivable, geometric alternative. "How clever is that?" he murmured.

The paradox of peace precipitating from chaos was not lost on Quince. He became conscious of the stinging pain in his foot and forehead – of the water that continued to fall in drops from the table – but his being was centred on the sunflower, and what it symbolised. It was a gift of light, of hope, of exposure and wild energy that a stranger had offered without hesitation – it was a connection, a conduit, to something noble. The woman had appeared from behind her fence like a genie and gifted him an emblem of vitality that he had the freedom to either seize or ignore.

A sensation unlike any other that he could recall welled up in his chest. It incorporated tenderness, wonder and yearning; it tasted, curiously, of pomegranate; and it summoned, for the first time since puberty, a longing to commit. Dr Edge was right: he would never be more than a pretty fool until someone was found.

His reverie was broken, however, by a disquieting, throaty growl. It emanated, he quickly realised, from Baker. The cat was attempting to reach behind the bookcase with his paws to retrieve his prey. Quince hobbled over to Baker and grabbed him. This was not an action that the cat endorsed though, and he demonstrated his disapproval by using his claws to delay ejection through the dining room window. Once the cat had been successfully ejected, however, Quince was able to gingerly extend one of his mauled arms behind the bookcase to feel for and grasp the sparrow. It was beyond terror, the bird, but not beyond inflicting yet more pain on Quince by puncturing his thumb skin with its beak.

It took until lunch time for Quince to re-establish his equilibrium. In the normal course of events he would have called on Pansy for help, but he felt, in the circumstances, that this would have been a call that lacked prudence. After staring once more at the bloom, Quince got up and limped off to the bathroom to swab his foot, face, and arm in Dettol while gingerly probing for crystal fragments in his flesh. Then, meticulously, he applied Betadine solution to the wounds – Betadine was something that his mother swore by – before going back into the dining room to save his sunflower, and to tackle the mess.

After completing the vacuuming of glass and feathers, and just before cold-sponging the bloodstained mat covering part of the tiles, he heard his favourite sound – Bonny banging her way in. She was accompanied by a gleeful Pound, and by her own Bottom (a name that they had come up with together when he gave her the Boston terrier for her birthday). Bottom was a female, and her mother argued, rather weakly, that 'Bottom' was a boy's name, but Bonny countered by pointing out that girls had the same number of bottoms that boys did, so the name stuck.

"Hiya, gorgeous. Hi, Bottom. Whoa, Pound, don't be jealous. Maybe we should let these two out. What do you think?"

"Sure, Uncle J." (Because her mother called him 'Q', Quince insisted that Bonny call him any letter of the alphabet that came into her head, except 'Q'.)

"Back from swimming already?"

"Yeah, Dad fetched me," and then, after looking more closely at her uncle and his dining room, she added, "What happened? Are you okay?"

"Yes, yes, I'm all in one piece, thanks, Bon. It was Baker. He brought in a bird, and I saved it, but my little world fell apart in the process. You really need to help me with parenting duties. Baker has me beat. He needs a firm hand and I just don't have one."

"Okay," she giggled.

"You hungry?"

"You bet." (Another of their games.)

"French toast and wild honey?" She nodded furiously. "Right, go and see if you can rustle up four or five eggs from under Esmeralda and her brood. They haven't stopped cackling all day, so there should be plenty."

"'Kay", and she was out in a flash.

Quince found himself humming like Frank as he hobbled over to the fridge to take out milk, and then to the pantry for Tabasco, honey, chilli flakes and salt. He would have savoury, and Bonny sweet, but he always added a smidgen of chilli flakes to hers. It was another of their private jokes. She would pretend that she didn't know that he'd added them, and he would pretend that he didn't know that she was pretending. They combined operations like chefs in a tapas bar. Each had his and her own specialist job: Bonny beat the eggs and milk into a froth before dividing the mix into two bowls for the soaking of their slightly stale bread; while Quince was in charge of readying hot chocolate and coffee, before donning his apron to fry.

They always made a ceremony, weather permitting, of taking their respective trays out onto the veranda. This was carried out in solemn and stately procession: Bonny's with her bread smothered in honey and cinnamon, and Quince with his in Tabasco, salt and chilli. The animals gathered around expectantly, while a light afternoon breeze carried his gaze down over the family farm and towards the lake. Bonny chatted about school, about a new friend that she'd made, about a weekend coming up when she hoped to water-ski; and then added quietly and after a pause, "I'm going to be a vegetarian, Uncle P."

"Are you, Bon?" he asked somewhat surprised. "When?"

"After Christmas."

"Do you have a friend who's vegetarian? The parents of a friend?"

"Nope."

"Will you still eat my French toast?"

"Yip, but only if the eggs come from happy hens like Esmeralda."

They sipped their chocolate and coffee watching hawks until their cups were dry.

"You love animals, don't you, Bon?"

"Yip."

"Good on you."

"Thanks, Uncle Z. Want some plasters on your cuts?"

"Yes, please, Florence. You know where they are?"

"'Course."

The paradox was that although Quince now had an excuse to absent himself, he didn't think to use it, and as he drove down his driveway through fields of maturing maize, passed bucking geldings, and into the suburb of Leamington, his mind was more on tomorrow than today. Tomorrow he would pull himself together – start working for a living.

Leamington, with its streets presumptuously named after English poets, is the newer and less affluent west wing of Cambridge, and it is separated from the older, east wing (established as an army outpost in the New Zealand Wars) by the Waikato River. The river courses under a high-level bridge that arches like a gymnast over steep banks of fern. Bends north and south of the bridge make the water on the outer curves rush, as eddies on the inside brake. Although it was never the intention of the bridge to do more than span a stretch of swiftly running water, it had evolved, at least in people's minds, into a metaphorical drawbridge – a marker of division. The east side, with its mature trees and quaint cottages, is seen by the east-siders as 'settled' and 'authentic'; while the west side is seen by the west-siders as more 'Kiwi' and community-spirited.

Quince did not need to cross the river because he lived well beyond the western boundary of Cambridge, on 'the other side', where the evening sun was touching up Mt Maungatautari. The mountain – hill, really – had been enclosed as a world first in a specially designed predator-proof fence, tracking over many kilometres and costing millions of dollars. Once complete, peanut butter was used to trap and eliminate stoats, ferrets, cats, rats, mice and possums – leaving the glorious natural fauna and flora to flourish. The only loser was the native owl, the 'morepork', or ruru, which had developed a palate for rodents; but other birds spilled out of the nursery, and into the wider district. Quince once counted fourteen tui in his kowhai tree during flowering – something his parents would never have seen.

With Maungatautari, tui and Baker on his mind, Quince drove into the Rowlands' driveway before realising that his way was blocked by a vehicle belligerent enough to lead a Washington motorcade. He backed out and parked on the kerb, reached behind him to retrieve his packet of plums, his Côte d'Or chocolate selection, and his bottle of wine, eased himself out of the car – and then swung around, almost colliding with a fast-approaching woman. It is a wonder that he didn't hear her as her heels clicked loudly.

"Whoops! Sorry."

"No, not at all. My fault really, I was focused on the house." She too had her hands full, with a bottle of wine in one and a bunch of mixed annuals in the other.

"You're not going in here, are you? To Mary and Joe's?"

"I am, actually."

"Me, too. I'm Quince," before adding, "It is my real name," and holding out the hand that held the wine.

"Eleanor," she responded by doing the same. Their bottles collided, causing them to smile. "Should we go in?"

"Sure."

Eleanor placed her bottle of wine on the doorstep so that she could knock, softly at first, and then more loudly. The wait was awkward, but Mary finally appeared. "El – Quince," Mary exclaimed with the delight of a *This is Your Life* subject! "You came together!"

"No, no, just at the same time, Mary."

"And you want me to believe that?"

"We …"

"Only teasing, Quince. Good to see you. Have you met?"

"A minute ago."

"What happened to your forehead?"

"A sunflower …"

"Sunflower?"

"Well, sort of." He really did not want to start explaining: "Should we go in, Mary? I can't talk with my hands full."

"Of course. Of course, come on, El, Quince. Lovely to see you both. Harry not coming?"

"No, he's looking after Mum."

Mary was younger than Quince, about forty, and dressed in a smart black and white outfit, but it was Eleanor who distracted him. She looked – well – gorgeous, and the self-conscious brushing of wind-blown hair off her forehead as introductions were made unsettled his poise and produced an urge to impress, but with no idea how. He felt adolescent, awkward, and found himself handing the chocolates to Joe while hanging on to the wine.

"Aren't you going to let go, Quince?" Mary laughed. "That must be some vintage!"

He apologised quickly, and they all laughed. Joe's university friend and his wife were visiting from Wellington, and the friend, Derek, relieved him of the burden. "Thank you. Derek, is it?" And the next ten minutes were mercifully consumed by the selection and pouring of drinks, as well as by the customary placement of each by occupation. Quince learned not only that Eleanor was a doctor, but also that she was, curiously and disconcertingly, in practice with his own doctor, Frank Edge, in Hamilton. Mary had mentioned 'Harry'. A husband? Partner? Child? Joe, he knew, was a mechanical engineer with his own business in Cambridge. Mary, he knew even better, knew everyone's business, but only with their best interests at heart. She was also an art teacher at the local high school. Derek, he discovered through Mary's reverent announcement, was a criminal lawyer in Wellington. And Jo? (Not to be confused with Joe!) Well, Jo was Derek's wife – his second by all accounts. 'Wife' was a role that she in the main accepted, relished even, but not one that she took as seriously as her husband would prefer. Derek came to discover that although she was someone who would help him spend his money, she refused to be obsequious. Playing host to the right people? Yes. Absorbing innuendo while serving stuffed olives? Of course. Standing one step back when it mattered? Absolutely. But she also on occasions, and especially when prompted by carbonated wine, allowed spontaneity to overstep status, and at these times she spoke what was on her mind, whether this irritated Derek or not.

Something that was on her mind now was a nagging curiosity, and so she turned to Quince with her query: "Quince? *Quince?* Never heard of anyone with that name before. Is it American? A nickname?"

"No, I was named after the fruit," he responded, causing all to smile. Quince would normally have proceeded with the tree-and-mother story, but something, someone, made him stop. Mary, having been a recipient of the tale more than a few times, sensed his reticence and deflected conversation away from his name and back to his bandage. "So what happened to your head, Quince?"

"Baker, my cat ..."

"Scratched you?"

"Yes, but no, not on my head."

"You're scratched elsewhere?"

"My arm, but it's nothing, really. No," he continued after sucking at his glass, "he caught a bird."

"The bird scratched you?" she countered, chuckling.

"No, no, it was just a sparrow. It's a long story. I'm sure that you don't want to hear it." This was turning into an uncomfortable inquisition.

"Of course, we do," Mary replied quickly. The opening repartee, she knew, could well determine the evening's outcome, and Quince had a way about him.

"Sit down, sit down," Joe prompted, shooing Skunk, their fat Staffordshire bull terrier, off one of the chairs. "Everyone have a drink?"

Once seated the pressure was on Quince to deliver. There was no escape. "Well, as I said," he started off tentatively, "Baker, my cat, surprised me by bursting into my dining room with a bird."

"Cats!" exclaimed Jo.

"Yes, well, Baker is definitely a cat – but it was the bird, the terrified bird that led to the accident."

"So, now the *bird* is to blame?"

"Shush, Jo, let the man get on with it." (Her husband.)

And Quince did, despite his reticence, proceeding to lay the foundation for their evening as Mary had hoped by describing the course of events. The incident was inherently comic, misfortune usually is, and, equipped as he was with his props of Elastoplast and limp, Quince was able to spin the tale in a way that drew them in.

"Did it get away, the bird?" Jo asked.

"I managed to grab it, yes, Jo, but only after our blood was splattered all over the room." He paused, before continuing with a serious look on his face, "It looked like a medieval battlefield." They all chuckled.

"That's terrible," Jo intervened, "but what about the sunflower? You said that the sunflower cut your head."

"No, no," he paused, "but it had the greatest impact."

"Why?"

"Well, it wasn't just any sort of sunflower," and he went on to explain briefly how he had been given the stem by a lady he didn't know in Hillcrest. "I'd placed it in the crystal vase," he said, "but it tipped out when the vase went flying."

"So?"

"When I looked up from the floor, rather dazed, and with the wounds of a harpooned whale …", suppressed chuckling, "there was the eye of the sunflower, bent over the edge of the table, looking right at me."

"The eye?"

"The arrangement of seeds – much like an insect's eye." He was quiet a moment, and, when he continued, they couldn't decide whether Quince was joking or serious. "Have you ever looked – really looked – at the arrangement of a sunflower's seeds?" His eyes were on Eleanor, and her nod was almost imperceptible. "They're tightly packed – you just can't fit any more in!" Jo had her glass, lipstick-smudged, poised for a sip, but held it there, waiting for him to continue. But how could he go on? He sensed that Eleanor might understand – but the others? How could he possibly convey to them in words the rare moment of peace and enlightenment that the gift from an unknown gardener had provided in that emblem of rational energy and challenge? How important it was to him.

Finally, an impatient Jo blurted out, "But how did it *cut* you?"

"Metaphorically, dear, metaphorically," Derek explained. "Stop interrogating the man. He's not in court." And then, because Derek liked to hold court, he diverted conversation into a domain where his command was unchallenged – wine. "Any chance of a top-up, Joe? That Cabernet/Merlot blend is smooth, don't you think? A drop that our Judges Wine Club singled out on its last excursion. Did you taste the blackcurrant? The pepper? We're not quite up there with our reds – not yet – but give us five years, give us three – even our Syrahs – and we'll knock the baggy caps off the Aussies."

Having captured their attention and created an air of expectancy, Derek raised his replenished glass to the light and studied its contents with the intensity of an alchemist as he swirled them in a mesmerising ellipse. He then levered the glass to the level of his long, thin nose, before sipping slowly, like a snake – catching overflow in lip hair – before completing the ceremony with a right-sided facial tic that could have been mistaken for a sniff. "Mm," he murmured. "We brought three bottles, didn't we, dear?"

"No, two, dear."

"But I asked you to pack three. I bought a case, remember?"

"I do."

"Oh, well, that's that then. Can't be helped now. Should have packed them myself." He fired off a tic, and then another, momentarily exposing his right upper canine. "Might have to dust off a bottle or two of yours, Joe, if the evening plays out. You don't have a Kiwi Cabernet/Merlot lying around, do you?"

"Not sure. Probably not, but we'll find something."

"Not South Australian plonk, I hope."

"Well …"

"Only joking, Joe, only joking," he sniggered, and twitched.

"Of course. How's your glass?"

"Thirsty."

But Jo was not going to be marginalised, certainly not while sipping her third standard drink, and so she pivoted back towards Quince to resume her interrupted interrogation: "Well, you obviously survived the seed, bird and cat attack, Quintin?"

"For God's sake, dear, it's *Quince*."

"Any name's fine," Quince shot back, and then proceeded, "I did indeed, Jo, thanks to Bonny, my ten-year-old niece. She doctored me with Dettol, vinegar and brown paper."

"That's impressive – pretty good for a ten-year-old. I would have run a mile at that age – at any age, actually," she added after a further sip.

"Yes, Bonny is both pretty and good. I couldn't cope without her."

"And," Jo added with emphasis, "you have a doctor all to your-self tonight," placing her arm on Eleanor's. "You wouldn't mind staunching the flow if his plaster fails now, would you?" Eleanor was about to mouth a reply when Jo swung back towards Quince. "And what do you do, Quince? You must be a rower, or a horse breeder, or something?"

"No, nothing," he answered quickly, "I don't really do anything."

"Oh, Quince, you're so funny," she laughed. "I bet I'll guess before the night's out."

Mary jumped up. "What about music? Any requests? We have Spotify – that Bluetooth thing."

"Talking of Bluetooth, why do you have such a ridiculous Wi-Fi password, Mary?" Tic, tic.

"They gave it to us."

"Who?"

"The Wi-Fi people – I don't know."

"But, dear Mary, you can change it. No one needs a more effec-tive firewall than we do, at the firm, yet we get by with the names of one or other dog – birth year – that sort of thing." Tic, tic.

"But then I wouldn't have the pleasure of causing you difficulty, now, would I, Derek?"

"You could at least have printed it out. Your handwriting is very much open to interpretation – like so-called modern art," he added pointedly. "I managed to get past the 'o'/ '0' quandary by trying both, but an 's' is an 's' and cannot be a '5'."

"Boo-hoo, Derek. You got there in the end."

Pique is not comfortable at a party. It puts participants on edge – raises expectation that 'things' might come out. Quince, sensing that this might spoil Mary's night, might even imperil a marriage, jumped in. "What about classical guitar, Mary? Any Julian Bream? Lovely with dinner."

"Possibly. Do we have him recorded, Joe?"

"Not sure. Not my thing really," Joe replied, laughing, "but I'll check. Could always use Spotify. It's Spanish acoustic that he plays, isn't it?" he added.

"Mostly, Joe. Bream's great, but don't, whatever you do, watch him."

"Why ever not? Is he ugly?"

"No, Jo, but he screws up his eyes all the time. You end up looking rather than listening if you know what I mean."

"But what do his eyes actually do?" Jo persisted.

"They squeeze tight with every high note, then open," (demonstrated) "as though the peaks cause unbearable pleasure – as though he's been tickled down below. It really is quite disconcerting," he added thoughtfully.

There was a moment of silence as this was processed. No word – not even from Derek – while Skunk, back on the couch, stopped slopping his … whatever it was he slopped. Eleanor, he noticed, sat with head bowed, but with her hair bouncing.

Finally, Mary blurted out, "My God, we need to see this. Derek, where's your phone, and don't come up with that bullshit about not being logged on."

Derek had no difficulty finding Bream on YouTube, while Joe found the same on Spotify; but every time his guitar reached the exquisite pitch of a high note, they burst out laughing. The effect was to substantially lighten the mood, and Mary beamed; but Quince did notice just a hint of anxiety in her eyes as she rose to fetch the main course. Eleanor, laughing, rose after Mary, to join her.

Quince was tempted to join them himself, to offer help, but instead he followed them with his eyes as they entered a kitchen illuminated by late afternoon yellow. He was aware that hosts generally preferred not to be distracted, particularly when preparation reached the point of plating, but he could see that Mary was comforted and calmed by her friend's easy presence – that their whispers were in sync. They would be focused on the food, he was sure, on the early success of the home-made bread, feta and black olives – on the main being served – but he allowed himself a hope that they would flick their eyes his way – mouth a consonant followed by a 'u'; but his conceit was doused by Derek and degustation.

"The best of evenings those, with the club, on the foreshore, for a five-course marriage of morsel and grape. Have you tried it, Joe?"

"Yes, we did actually, just the once, with friends."

"Nothing like it. What about you, Quince? Are you into wine?"

"Yes, usually, but I'm no expert. Can't have much tonight though – not with the recent clampdown."

"Easily solved. Get an Uber."

"If there is one, dear. We're not in Wellington, you know?" Jo had subsided somewhat since Mary and Eleanor had gone through to the kitchen, but now she raised her voice. "Should we sit, Mary?"

"Yes, yes, wherever you feel comfortable," came Mary's reply. "Light the candles, would you, Joe, and top everyone up," then in she swept with her accomplishment.

It was a beef sirloin salad, placed on a large white platter, topped with tomato salsa, sprinkled with chopped parsley, and eaten cold. The beef had been sliced, nervously, into pink medallions with her Swedish knife while the pair were in the kitchen. Every 800-gram sirloin selected from The Hoof & Trotter butchery posed its own challenge, as each had to be rolled in the right combination of crushed peppercorns, salt, cumin and coriander before being baked, then seared, at the right temperature for the right period of time – hence the tension around the ceremony of slicing. But perfection had been achieved!

Six is a good number for a dinner party as it lessens the importance of seating. It also opens the table to conversation without cliché or exclusion. For Mary, it meant that her signature dish could be placed within reach of all, in the middle of her oval table. Her steaming potatoes and beans found space between candles muted by Indonesian shades, shining wine glasses, and two, simple, bowls of nasturtiums. Quince noted with pleasure the surprise in Derek's eyes and the in-drawing of breath from Jo; but, most of all, he noted that Eleanor, although she kept quiet, was basking in her friend's triumph.

A toast proposed by Joe preceded their first forkful – a forkful followed by another, followed by a sip, followed by Quince turning to Mary and asking, "What on earth is in this salsa, Mary? It's delicious!"

Mary beamed. "Oh, Quince, it's nothing really. Just chopped tomatoes, spring onions, fresh coriander, lime juice, salt, and pepper. That sort of thing."

"But it's subtle too. Doesn't diminish the beef."

"Is the beef okay? Not underdone?"

"Perfect, Mary. Perfect," interjected Derek. "Lovely and moist. Must find the right drop to go with it though. What have you there, Joe?"

"A 2014 Koonunga Hill Shiraz – Penfolds. Will that do? It is South Australian," he added with a smile.

"I'll risk it if I must. Get me a fresh glass, will you?"

They resumed eating, oohing and aahing, but were stopped mid-mouthful by Jo. (No one was counting, but the number of her standard drinks was clicking over.) "I once heard a fellow say the funniest thing," she mumbled, appearing to have some difficulty in saying the funny thing herself. She was peering into memory as she continued. "The fellow fancied himself as someone who knew his barbecue." Pause. "He asked each of us how each of us preferred his … or her … meat." Pause to underscore grammatical exactitude. "Most said, because it is what most say, 'medium rare'." Pause. "One woman said, 'burn it, then burn it some more'." Pause. "But I wanted to know how the fellow himself liked his meat."

"Oh, get on with it, Joanne. We've all heard it before."

"No." Pause. "Your friends haven't." Pause. "Anyway, before I was rudely interrupted, I said to the fellow, I said, 'How do you like *your* meat?' And *he* said, holding his tongs like a cow prodder, 'Put it this way, lady, *cut off its horns and wipe its arse*.'" Derek ticked, Skunk scratched, and the rest of them watched intently as Jo triumphantly took another sip, her lips grappling for her glass.

Finally, Eleanor, her mouth split by a broad smile, broke the silence. "That really is one of the funniest stories that I've ever heard, Jo. It would have made his day."

"I think it did." Pause. "Made mine too."

All except Derek laughed and general chatter resumed, reverting to non-contentious issues like royalty, ocean plastics, global economics, and the end of truth; but later, after candlelight and wine had time to mingle, their conversation, as so often is the case at this time of the evening, defaulted to occupational anecdote. 'Medicine' is normally up there in terms of interest, but it was no match for criminal law, and they were treated to titbit after titbit from Derek. He appropriately assumed a more authoritative demeanour as he offered personal and collegial insights into cases that were in 'the public domain'. Nothing that was sub judice, mind you, but prison encounters, court protocol – even organised crime – were elucidated. Finally, and inevitably however, the question came up, posed by Mary (possibly because she was still niggled by his Wi-Fi tantrum):

"But how can you defend monsters? How can you grill the aggrieved?"

Derek smiled patronisingly before answering, "Quite simply, Mary, by fulfilling the duties of a civilised state. Every man, or woman for that matter, is, by statute, entitled to the best legal defence, and ..."

"Yes, we all know that, but how do you *feel*?"

"Feelings don't come into it. I'm simply doing my job – giving it my best shot."

"And if you get the guy off, you feel good?"

"As I said, feelings don't come into it, but if your question is 'do I see a win as a job well done?' then, yes, of course I do."

"Mm."

"I'll tell you something else though, for what it's worth," he added, "if I were guilty and could choose, I'd choose a jury trial, but if I were innocent, I would settle for a judge ... or three. A panel of three would be my preference."

"That's scary!"

"That's the law."

As a teacher Mary often railed on about 'obscene income', and she suspected from the size and unsuitability of Derek's vehicle that his was hard to spend, but Joe anticipated where this was heading, and he cut her short before she could ask Derek directly for his hourly rate. "Top-ups, folks? Eleanor and Quince, you're not both driving, are you? How about you, Jo, do you want to switch to red?"

"Wash your mouth out, Joseph," she snapped, and then added wittily, "Like Coco Chanel, 'I only drink Champagne on two occasions: when I'm in love, and when I'm not.'"

"We won't ask you which state you're in now, Jo," he laughed, "but I take that as a yes for a top-up?"

"Actually no, thank you. A water would be nice though."

Joe, Quince realised, was an ideal foil to Mary – her safety valve. His light engineering business, which served the farming community around Cambridge, was dismissed as too technical and too boring to discuss at dinner parties, but Quince determined that he was comfortable with that. He surmised, and might well have surmised correctly, that Joe was the happiest of them all to wake up and dress for work. Overalls, in Quince's albeit selective work experience, brought out the boy in men, and workshops, so often dismissed by professionals as dirty and undesirable, for him, of all workplaces, struck the right balance of skill and teasing cheerfulness. He had always thought of Joe as Mary's husband – the pale version – but now he felt a pang of envy. She leant on him. He could see that.

But his reverie could not be sustained, not while a water-fortified Jo remained curious: "Right, Quince, let's guess! You've played things close to your chest tonight – summing us all up. You're not a bloody psychologist, are you? Or a boring rowing coach, God forbid! What is it that you do? What have you been doing?"

Mary had intended waiting another ten minutes before bringing through dessert – pears soaked overnight in red wine, cinnamon, star anise, orange peel and sugar – but she half-stood now ... to divert attention. There was no need, however, because Quince's response was swift and unexpected, although it was preceded by an ever-so-brief glance at Eleanor. "I generally don't do anything, Jo, but I had a colonoscopy last week."

"Oh! How lovely for you!"

"It was okay. The procedure was okay ... interesting even ... an out-of-body experience after being shot up with opiates and who-knows-what ... watching an exploration of my innards on a big-screen TV."

"But was it normal? No diverticula? My mother has them apparently. She has to eat cardboard pellets every day to stop them becoming infected – to keep things moving." (Those at the table blessed with good hearing could be forgiven for having detected just a suggestion of an 'h' added to her 'was', to her first and second 'has', and to her 'stop' … as if she herself had pellets tucked under her tongue.)

"No, that wasn't mentioned. They said that it was normal, although it didn't look normal to me."

"What were you expecting?" asked Joe.

"Probably not the right time to say, Joe, but ripe, white tripe, I suppose; but it turned out to be pink and squirming." He was silent a moment, faced by ten expectant eyes, before continuing, "The preparation, though, is something else – the worst ordeal imaginable."

"Oh, come on, it can't be *that* bad … and Joe, I might just have a little glass of something after all. This could be good." Those additional 'h's again?

Mary, still standing, reached behind her. "Will a Sav do, Jo? We're out of cold bubbles, I'm afraid." She then sat down, smiling. "Carry on, Quince, we're all in suspense."

"It starts with starvation," he began. "Two days prior to procedure no bread, no rack of lamb, no wilted spinach, no cling peach, no almond, sesame or artichoke – no baked tomato topped with Maldon salt and chilli!"

"How ghas(h)tly!" interjected Jo in mock-horror.

"That's not the half of it. It's what you *can* eat that's worse. Steamed white fish, boiled chicken, low-fat plain yoghurt, white bread, peeled pumpkin, clear jelly, and gallons of clear (i.e. tasteless) liquids!" Even Derek was staring to chuckle now. "But if you think that day two was bad, consider day one." He paused for effect: "A paltry breakfast of boiled egg and dry white bread, followed by …?"

"Approved fluids," Eleanor answered with a broad smile.

"Absolutely, you would know. Water, apple juice, black tea,

bouillon – approved ice blocks. It's worse than water-boarding." Pause. "And then …"

"More horror?"

"The worst, Jo, the worst. And then," assuming a tragic pose, "Prepkit-C." Joe and Mary smiled broadly; Derek (who had presented in a panic to his doctor just the previous week after bleeding from an anal fissure), laughed nervously; Jo struggled to concentrate; and Eleanor started shaking.

"What is(h) …?"

"Prepkit-C is a package of poison, Jo, and it comprises two packets of PicoPrep – one taken at five on the night before, and the other at four-thirty on the morning of the procedure; with Glyco-prep-C, dissolved in a litre of water to make its consumption interminable, taken in between at eight o'clock."

"And what … what's(h)o difficult about that?" Jo was genuinely puzzled.

"The taste, Jo. Have you ever tried to swallow fridge-fuls of supersaturated urine?"

"Can't s(h)ay I have," she answered truthfully.

"Well, it tastes worse than that."

"My goodness(h)!"

"It's a toxic brew, but it's the aspartame that triggers the gag reflex."

"As(h)p … what?"

"I looked up the ingredients. Aspartame is a non-saccharide sweetener added for flavour, for flavour! Can you believe it? A possible carcinogen. It can even cause Gulf War syndrome … maybe Parkinson's." Eleanor was struggling for control, with cosmetic lahars tracking down her cheeks.

"Did it work?" Derek was curious.

Quince turned to him. "It did, Derek. Within minutes, and for endless hours, I was converted into a stormwater drain. The evacuations torrential – torrential – booshh, booshh, booshh. Not sure how my septic tank coped." Eleanor stood up. "Pound, my dog (and I don't blame him for this), abandoned me in disgust." Eleanor spluttered an apology and headed down the passage. "By morning there was nothing left."

He was quiet then, as they all were, because they could hear a crescendo/decrescendo of muffled cries and sniffs. 'Was it mirth or misery?' they wondered as they looked towards Mary for explanation. Quince was concerned that he might have gone too far, but Mary placed her hand on his shoulder, beamed, and said, "Would you give me a hand with the dessert, Quince? She hasn't laughed like that in years."

Mary's marinated pears complemented the steak perfectly, and no one demurred when a scoop of coconut ice cream was offered as an accessory.

It was close to midnight when they took their leave, and what should have been awkward was not. Mary's considerable culinary effort, along with laughter and the lubricant of wine, had broken their carapaces and bound them in goodwill. Quince, responding to Mary's request, dropped Eleanor off at her home in Hall Street before driving back over the high-level bridge to his side of town.

She had touched his right forearm on reflex as she had exited his car (as she did her patients as they left her room), and he was left with the warmth of acknowledgement. There was no suggestion of eroticism, and none taken, but the pleasure carried him home. Neuroscientists now label this the pleasure of 'social touch', a pre-lingual sensation of belonging triggered by touch afferents located in the skin of forearms, backs, shoulders, trunks, and faces.

ELEANOR

Harry and Eleanor followed a routine on Sunday mornings, and it was no different on the morning after Mary's party. On weekdays her alarm had her up and on the road to Hamilton by seven. Any later and the road was too busy, any earlier and she would miss her hug from Harry. He started school after eight and she would leave him to sleep for as long as possible but wanted him woken and washed by the time her mother came over to start preparing his breakfast. Saturdays they would be off early to soccer, sometimes swimming, but on Sundays there was no imperative, and she was awake and waiting when she heard him stir, pee, and then slip into her bed. Whitey slept on his mat in Harry's room, but on Sundays he was 'allowed' to leap onto the bed to join them. Eleanor pretended that she couldn't see him as she rose to fetch their tea and rusks.

A rusk is a form of hard buttermilk bread that was originally baked by Boers for ease of preservation and portage, and Eleanor got the recipe from Leah when she was staying with her in Bwazi. The first time that she had tried them was with Aaron, Harry's father. They had travelled to a river in the bush where he had made tea over an open fire. There was a kingfisher, quite close, with eyes piercing the drift of water, while cowbells, she remembered vividly, sounded melancholy on the other side. "You must try one of Leah's rusks. The bought ones don't compare."

"How do you eat them though? They're as hard as rock."

"Like this," he said, smiling, before dipping one into his mug of steaming tea. "But don't dip it for too long, or a chunk will break off and splatter your blouse."

That first taste, she remembered, seasoned by the wood ash in their water, was divine; and now, as she watched Harry dip with the fingers of his father, as she watched him in his tousled pyjamas pick out and nibble burnt raisins, she experienced again that first taste of contentment. Harry was careful in selection – he knew that the fatter chunks were more likely to break off and fall – and Eleanor smiled as he chose those that were longer. When he was smaller, she would purposefully prolong her dunks to the point of collapse, and the ensuing plop would splash them both. He was too smart for that now!

Chatter came easily after their tea. This Sunday, as on every other, he lay sideways with his head cushioned on her tummy, Whitey pressed up against his thigh and his right arm flailing, as he debriefed. Eleanor was privy to the goings on of everyone from Miss Bartlett to the groundsman, to Tommy Walters, to the goal he let through, to fractions and division, to picking up Whitey's poo, to preparations for 'Green Day'. Eleanor mostly kept quiet, but she couldn't resist stroking his cheek with her thumb.

This morning offered a slight variant, however, and one that caused disquiet. Her focus was on Harry as it always had been, of course, but she found her mind drifting off occasionally and focusing on the enjoyment of the previous night. Despite her misapprehension, it had been fun. For years she had seen no point in gatherings for enjoyment – the planning and preparation, the pointless repartee, the reciprocal effort – but Mary had pulled it off! The food? Of course, it was delicious. But there was something else, something that allowed a mellowing of the eclectic mix, and stamped the evening with authenticity. Each in his or her way had had a good time, and each had been an indispensable contributor to the enjoyment of the other. Jo, Eleanor mused, may not be convinced of that this morning, but her barbecue cameo had set the tone. Quince, though (what a name!), lingered in her mind. It was he, with his Elastoplast, compound eye and catastrophising, who had helped them all reveal themselves.

The evening had momentarily deflected her focus form Harry's sweet face, she realised, and she felt a twinge of guilt.

"How about brunch out at Karapiro, mister?"

"At Podium?"

"Absolutely! You can order whatever you like."

"Even Black Forest cake and ice cream?"

"Of course, a double helping … and you can play on the ropes … go down the slide."

"Will you go down the slide too?"

"Of course."

"And Nana?"

"Nana might stick to the ropes."

They would sometimes gather in their lunchroom after work for a wine, a room that no one could say was tidy. Medical magazines, notices and open packets of biscuits occupied most of the table space and a photograph would not have served it well, but for the staff it was their common and comfortable place – their dining room of old. Edith and Rae (a practice nurse) were the ones alert to opportunity, and when they realised that Eleanor had completed her first year at the practice, they decided to mark the milestone with a gathering. Rae, Frank and Eleanor enjoyed Sauvignon

Blanc, Edith preferred Pinot Gris, while Geraldine, the reception-ist, and Corrie, the younger nurse, drank Diet Coke. All were partial to savoury biscuits and Camembert, but on this occasion additional items were purchased – chips, cashew nuts and jelly-beans. The reason was their surprise: Rae had secretly slipped out earlier in the afternoon to collect Marion and Harry from Cambridge. Milly had been tipped off too, and she called in briefly with a potted gerbera.

Eleanor, meanwhile, had been buried in paperwork and was unsuspecting as she walked in. Her mind was still on an abnormal blood test result when she came face to face with Harry. "What on earth are you doing here, young man? And Mum too!" she added with delight, seeing her mother crouched in a corner. "How did you two get here?"

With chuckles the plot and its implementation were revealed. Harry had proved that he could keep a secret. After the initial laughter, tease and toast they settled into their easy pattern of inclusive chatter. The initial hesitancy of both Marion and Harry, Eleanor noted, were swiftly dispensed with. Edith, remembering her own (now adult) son's preference, opened and poured a glass of Royal Crown Cola with ice (stirred with a miniature umbrella) for Harry, while Rae piled Marion's plate. Frank was chatting to Geraldine about his fig tree. "It's gone mad – completely cuckoo – branched out every which way! I went overboard last winter, paring it down to a stalk. Milly said it looked like a plucked leghorn and I suspected that it would refuse to fruit, but no, a glut is imminent. Figs are sprouting every which way."

"When do they ripen?"

"In March, just two months. I'll be hauling in basketfuls. Time to get your jars out, Gerry."

"Do you cover them with netting? Hang shiny CDs in their branches?"

"No, there's enough for everyone: the waxeyes, fruit flies, bats, neighbours – enough for everyone in the known world!"

"You should dry them."

"I do dry them, but there're only so many that a man can dry."

"Stew?"

"Milly stews them, but there're only so many that a woman can stew!"

"True."

He turned to Harry, cupped his hand over his mouth, and whispered loudly, "Do you climb trees, Harry?"

"A bit."

"Will you climb my fig tree for me?" Harry glanced at his mother, who raised her eyebrows in mock shock. "I won't tell your mum." Harry nodded his head hesitantly. "Good man. We'll make a plan closer to the time, okay?" Harry nodded again.

It would not be long before the figs ripened, Eleanor realised, and soon after that she would, at Frank's insistence, 'take off and take stock'. Watching him with Harry, she recalled more of the conversation that followed her confession of disinterest: *"You're stale, El, and one-dimensional – all output – going through the motions."*

"But my life is fine. Our house, Cambridge, this practice – I couldn't have hoped for a better move. Mum's settled – Harry's made friends."

"So, are you enjoying coming to work?"

"Who enjoys *coming to work, Frank?"*

"I do – Edith does. Rae definitely does."

"Always?"

"No, not always, there've been periods when I've loathed work – long periods."

"I don't loathe work," she'd laughed.

"You will though, if you don't wake up."

"Come on, Frank, that's a bit melodramatic."

"Is it? When was the last time that you really looked forward to something? Got excited? Felt nervous? Tossed and turned?"

"Well, I was very nervous for Harry when he started at his new school."

"For Harry, for your mother – for your patients. You have more compassion, empathy and kindness than you know what to do with, but they're qualities that need context."

"How?"

"I don't know, but as I said before, a complete break away might help. A social life would be a good start," he had added mischievously.

"I do have a social life."

"Really? Apart from playgroups, philately clubs and school fundraisers?"

She had laughed again. *"Actually I had a lovely evening at a friend's house a few weeks ago."*

"Tupperware?"

"Much more interesting than Tupperware, Frank."

"A loose male?"

She remembered grinning. *"Several males, actually."*

"But any of them loose?"

"Loose? That's old-fashioned, Frank, but yes, one of them was unattached."

"Excellent!"

She'd laughed again. *"We have dating sites now. Match-making, if it's desired, is carried out online."*

"Well, get online."

"A male is what I'm lacking?"

"Maybe, maybe not, but you need someone or something to cause a disturbance."

"He happens to be a patient of yours," she'd remarked quietly, surprising herself.

"Mine? Really? Who, for goodness' sake?"

"Quince – his name is Quince."

Frank, she recalled, had looked quite taken aback, and then murmured, *"How interesting! How very interesting!"*

"I just met the bloke at a dinner party, Frank ... as part of a group ... highly unlikely that I'll bump into him again." Frank's continued silence had prompted her to add, *"Don't read anything into it,"* and, *"Why, is there something that I should know? Is he dodgy?"*

"No, no, quite the opposite. He has something – something very special."

Corrie couldn't stay, and left reluctantly, but the rest of them lingered and were happy in their chatter, and Eleanor, with her busy day, her surprise party, and her single glass of wine blending, looked on with sweet affection. 'How can I be "stale" and "spent" when I have these people in my life?' she wondered. 'What right have I to feel the way I do? With all I have?' She looked across at Frank, still speaking with Harry, and knew that he was right in his prescription – she did need a jolt – an almighty jolt to shock her out of apathy – but was escape the answer? Did she deserve a holiday? No, she knew that that was not what Frank was meaning – he was after risk – provocation; and another older man, she remembered, her dying patient Ted, had forced her into risk for the same reason, posthumously sending her off to a godforsaken country to fall pregnant! 'You wouldn't want *that* now, would you, Frank?' she murmured, smiling. 'That would be more than stupid!'

But then she looked across at Harry and burned with love. Without Ted's jolt there would be no Harry, and that was inconceivable. He wanted, he needed, to see his father's country. But was that too big of a risk?

At the very least she would want to spend some days in Bulungani, show him the jacaranda-lined streets that were broad enough for ox wagons to turn around in; drive him out to Aaron's country school among the msasa trees; spend at least two days, at least two, in the granite magnificence of the nearby Mpopo National Park where she and Aaron had climbed giant boulders, seen the black mamba and Leah's lizards, and where they were caught in a fierce storm; and Portland, the village of Alec and Leah, Aaron's home, would that be possible? A walk through mopani scrub? Would that require a permit? M'zunga, the area in the Limpopo Valley where Aaron was captured and killed? M'zunga was out of the question.

She would have to research current conditions, restrictions and access to ensure that it was safe. Harry was her greatest concern. If the authorities realised that he was the son of Aaron? If Aaron's sister, an apologist for the ruling regime, found out that he was visiting? Would the child be removed from her and forced to stay? A shudder went down her spine. 'Maybe we should wait,' she thought, 'delay or postpone? But then again, what if I am catastrophising – paralysed by mother-fear?'

Eleanor decided to reach out to Alec and Leah in England. They would still have contacts on the ground – help her to assess risk. They would know if Noah, the hotelier whom she had befriended, was still in Bulungani. She had not been explicit with Harry after all. 'I'll take you there someday,' she had promised, and nothing more.

"You're awfully quiet, El! It must have been a long year?" Edith's question prompted a return from reverie.

"Sorry, Edith. No, I was a million miles away. It's been a hugely significant year for all three of us, with no small thanks to you lovely people. Thank you for the surprise, for spoiling me – us," she added, placing one arm on Harry and another on her mother. "I'm a lucky girl."

"Yes, thank you," beamed Marion, as she rose to leave.

***

Eleanor had not intentionally tried to make herself look pretty for years. She had no nominated hairdresser, her clothes were replaced when worn, her shoes were 'summer' and 'winter', her nails were never polished, and her face, her eyes and lips were accentuated only occasionally and with little effort. Yet her beauty remained undeniable, and this, together with her misinterpreted warmth, had attracted the odd approach. These approaches had been quickly and gracefully rebuffed, as if they had not been noticed. She had neither room nor desire for 'complication'; but, over the latter part of summer, a subtle transformation became noticeable, fermented perhaps by Frank's awakening, but triggered by a chance meeting.

Eleanor was leaving work to go home one afternoon when she decided to stop off at the medical centre's pharmacy to buy sunscreen. Walking to her right on entering, she approached a counter where there was a woman standing on tiptoe and with her back to her. There was a familiarity to the woman, but it was only when she turned and affected a smile fixed by foundation that Eleanor recognised her.

"Carol! Hello, good to see you," she exclaimed in surprise. "Looks like you could do with a step ladder?"

The foundation held its tensile strength as she answered, "Hello, doctor. I have one somewhere."

"Please call me by my first name, Carol. Everyone else does. Are you enjoying your job?" she added.

"Gets me out the house. I'm doing three days now, and the occasional Saturday morning."

Eleanor sensed a weariness. "You okay?" she asked before she had time to check herself.

"Yes, I'm okay? What about you? Busy?"

"No, not too busy. It's summer."

"Of course. What can I do for you?"

"Oh, thank you, Carol. I was looking for sunscreen."

"It's over there," she pointed with a hand that held a pretty-looking bottle. "I'll show you."

"What's that that you're holding?" Eleanor asked as Carol started to step out from behind her counter.

"Opium," she answered and stopped.

"Opium!" Eleanor laughed. "Now that sounds naughty. Is it the brand that you wear?"

"No, I prefer a floral perfume, like Black Orchid – when I can afford it."

"Oh, that's right, I remember the lovely scent of chrysanthemums when you last came in. What's Opium then?

"It's more musk and spice. You want to try it?"

"I don't normally wear perfume, but why not?" she laughed.

"Try both." Carol then proceeded to apply a drop of Opium on Eleanor's left wrist, followed by a drop of Black Orchid on her right. "There're several others."

"No, no, these are both enchanting, thank you." She was genuinely intrigued but found herself sniffing her left wrist more than she did her right. "I really like the Opium … for myself, but do you think that an older lady would prefer the floral one?" Eleanor was thinking of her mother, but quickly realised that this could have been misconstrued. "Sorry, Carol, I didn't mean you."

"You could have, I am getting on," she replied, smiling, "but no, it's horses for courses really."

"Well," said Eleanor decisively and reaching for her purse, "I'll have a bet each way."

"A bottle of both the Opium and the Black Orchid?"

"Yes, please."

"Do you want them wrapped?"

"Just the black one, please. It's for my mother."

Eleanor walked out having forgotten the sunscreen but feeling a lot lighter on her feet. She didn't rush off and make an appointment at a hair stylist or cash in a token for a pedicure, and her lipstick remained the colour of flesh, but … but … there was a bounce in her step.

The upshot (although it could have been coincidence) was an invitation that doubled as a date. It emanated from the staid setting of one of the GP CME (Continuous Medical Education) meetings that Eleanor attended at Waikato Hospital. These meetings were held regularly, every alternate week, in the evenings, and they were preceded by a light informal dinner which encouraged 'cross-pollination' with colleagues from around the Waikato. The dinners catered for both vegetarians and carnivores, with a third dish for the gluten-free. Some stood as they ate, while others found a seat at a side table. It was inevitable that cliques formed over the years, and Eleanor, to appear inconspicuous, gravitated into corners to read and reread the evening's programme, holding the sheet with her one hand while forking food with the other. Polite and well-meaning introductions inevitably came her way, however, and the questions were stereotypical, "Where is it that you work? With Frank Edge? Has he not retired?" and "Is your portal consultation service up and running? We find that ours saves time … keeps the worried well at home. Not sure how we managed before."

Eleanor was pleasantly surprised at her most recent meeting therefore when she recognised someone of old approaching. He had been two years ahead of her at medical school but had dated and subsequently married a friend, and they socialised as a group. His glasses were different, he wore groomed stubble rather than student beard, but his grin was unmistakable. She was genuinely pleased to see him: "Henry, where have you sprung from? Haven't seen you for years. Thought you were doing paediatrics?"

"Eleanor Hutton! Well, I never. Paeds? No, not for long."

"It's one of the toughest."

"Not really, it's a mug's game – too much work for too little money. But what about you?"

"I was in Taupo, general practice, but moved to Hamilton about a year ago – Frank Edge's practice. And you?"

"I run my own joint … would never work for a boss. You should come across."

Eleanor laughed and was about to reply when the bell sounded for the start of the meeting. "Got to run," he said pointing to the toilet, "but give me your number. We'll catch up."

And he did, the following week, by text: *stop off at matador after work tomorrow bout 5.30 few mates Henry.* Eleanor wasn't quite sure what to make of it. Mates? Beth? Eleanor had lost touch with Beth and had had no time to ask after her at the meeting. She replied: *Thank you, Henry. Look forward to catching up but can't stay long.*

Matador is a tapas bar with a pleasant setting above the river. Entry is via a descending staircase offering a view of noise and crowded tables – tables that spill out onto a leafy patio. Squinting from one to the next, Eleanor initially missed Henry. Rather than sitting in one of the groups, he sat alone at the bar. His right foot, housed in a pointed tan-polished shoe, was hooked behind the lower rung of his stool, while his left was tapping a rhythm on the floor. She walked up, smiling: "Hi, Henry, have you booked a table? Are the others here?"

He partially extricated himself from his seat to give her cheek a peck. "This is our table – it's where you get the quickest service. A drink?"

"Sure, um … just a soda, thanks."

"They're half price till six. Happy hour." He added, "Cash in, girl."

"No, just a soda to start, thanks."

"Where's Beth?" she added.

"Beth?"

"Yes, sorry, Henry, I wanted to ask after her when we caught up last week."

"She's long gone … living in Oz, as far as I know."

"Oh … I had no idea. I'm sorry."

"No need to be sorry, I'm not. And you? Are you hooked up?"

Eleanor smiled and was about to relate what had happened with Aaron, then checked herself. "No, no husband or partner … but I do have a beautiful son."

"Son?"

"Yes."

"How old?"

"Eight – going on eight."

"And the father?"

"It's a long story."

"Octopus?"

"Sorry?"

"Do you like octopus – baby octopus?"

"Yes, I …"

"Let's order then. I normally get two tapas per person. You okay with that?"

"Yes, but where're the others?"

"Couldn't make it. Fried haloumi? Chicken wings?"

"Yes, okay."

"Here's the menu. We need a fourth."

"Um … I don't know. Asparagus?"

"Out of season. Pork belly, we'll have pork belly – it's glazed with bourbon."

"I can't stay long, Henry."

"But you can have a wine. Only six minutes to go."

"Okay, just a house white, thank you."

"We could share a bottle of good stuff?"

She smiled. "A glass would be fine."

Sitting up on a stool made Eleanor feel conspicuous, as if the restaurant patrons could smell her Opium – could sense her legs' uncertainty – and the tapas dishes could not arrive quickly enough. Over the course of her one drink and his three, Henry swivelled on his stool, offering various preconceived inclinations of his profile, his bare forearms – his shoes – all the while pontificating through his teeth as he sucked and chewed at his pork, chicken wings and tentacles of octopus, succeeding only momentarily to suspend his self-aggrandisement when he slipped away for a quick 'slash'. The fried haloumi, he found, was not to his liking, and he pushed it Eleanor's way.

In the ninety minutes that followed she was treated to a precis of his accomplishments:

1. Professional – Senior Fellow of the Royal New Zealand College of General Practitioners with a Diploma in Sports Medicine; sitting Waikato Branch member and lobbyist for higher patient co-payment contributions. Rumoured to have received nomination for GP of the Year.

2. Financial – not fully disclosed, but listed ownership of a two-storeyed home on Raines Road; a retreat 'on the water' at Papamoa Beach; as well as a recently purchased BMW 3 Series with a retractable roof.

3. Romantic – again alluded to obliquely, through mention of his overworked Tinder account which he subscribed to under the pseudonym (disclosed in confidence) of 'Panther Grey'.

4. Sporting – winner of the 2018 River Course, Bogey Stableford Competition. Life member but non-participant in the Hamilton Martial Arts club. Advertised sponsor of Let's Get Going and Jump for Your Life (offering celebrity access to mayoral banquets). GP to the Waikato Chiefs rugby team's masseur.

. . .

Eleanor was standing to leave, when Henry added, "I've been offered two corporate tickets for the Chiefs' next big one, against the Sharks – the South African outfit – you game?"

"No, thank you, Henry. Another time. Can we pay here?"

"Sure. Fifty-fifty okay with you?"

"Of course."

His parting kiss lingered longer and landed closer to her lips than the greeting had, and it imparted a smudge of chicken fat on her cheek.

Every Saturday morning and throughout the year, regardless of wind or wild rain, mobile stalls are corralled into laager formation on the Cambridge village green. Arranged within the ring are plastic chairs and tables where patrons (after replenishing their weekly stocks of cured meats, smoked fish, fruit, preserves, and fresh seasonal vegetables) can sit sipping coffee, sample home-made pasties and pies, look skywards at the nibs of redwoods drawing clouds, or toss their coins into caps as buskers sing and strum. In winter offerings are meagre, but in late summer the barrows brim with sun-peaked produce at reasonable prices; and it was at this time, late in February, that Eleanor, her mother and Harry walked down from Hall Street to see what was to be had at the Cambridge Farmers' Market.

Marion, being the age she was, knew to make sauce when the sun shone, and, armed with a handful of five-dollar notes, wondered from stall to stall picking out overripe heritage, beef-steak and cherry tomatoes, multi-coloured capsicums, bird's eye and habanero chillies, as well as aubergine and fresh garlic. Eleanor trailed after her with a large cloth bag and more cash, while Harry, licking at an ice cream, was left listening to a blues duet. But on the greater green and beyond the rim of stalls something caught his eye – cricketers were gathering to inspect their pitch. Harry had the habit of playing with anything that bounced (at home he used the back of the garage wall as his playmate if his mother was away or busy), and he always had a selection of balls at the ready.

He had one now, an imitation cricket ball, in his hand, as he walked past the stalls to the white rope boundary to watch. His mother's radar, meanwhile, normally locked onto his coordinates, had been momentarily deflected. In sandals, hat, and jean shorts, lost in thought and happy, she was about to scan back to the blues players when she noticed a man with a young girl. He seemed taller and slimmer than she remembered from six weeks prior – he had no Elastoplast on his forehead – but he was, unmistakably, Quince. Her first response was to retreat beneath the canopy of a stall and shade her eyes with her hat. Eleanor noticed that he was trailing after a young girl and tickling her neck with a carrot tip but pretending that he wasn't, and, when the girl turned, laughing, and wagged her finger at him, he feigned outrage and surprise. They were having fun, and it was fun to watch. As she smiled, a thought flashed through Eleanor's mind: 'It would be nice to have him as a friend, someone kind – an open book!' but she checked herself, surprised, and recoiled further into the stall, aware that an approach could be misconstrued.

Her mother's voice brought her back. "This is the last bunch, dear. Can you manage?" And then she added, "Where's Harry?"

"Harry? He's over there." But he was not over there, and a knife iced through her chest. "Harry, *Harry*!" she called, as bad people trampled through her brain. "I told him not to move," she added sharply. "Wait here, Mum. See if you can spot him." She dropped her sack of vegetables and then took off, striding nowhere quickly, her long thin feet pointing the way, pouring fear-sweat, and almost knocking over Quince.

"Eleanor!" he exclaimed, surprised. "What is it? Are you all right?"

"Harry – my son. He's disappeared."

"A little boy?"

"Yes."

"About eight or nine?"

"Yes," she said more slowly.

"Isn't that him watching cricket?"

She followed the line of Quince's finger as it bisected two stalls, and there, beyond a busy generator and only ten metres from where they stood, sat Harry in his floppy, blue hat, his chin cupped in both hands as he gazed ahead at the game.

Eleanor flushed as she smiled and dabbed her eyes. "I'm sorry, that was ridiculous. Mum," she called, "he's fine. He's over here."

As they walked across to Harry, introductions were made. "My mother, Marion."

"Hi, Marion, good to meet you. This is my boss, Bonny. I'm your beast of burden, aren't I, Bon?"

"Uncle F! They'll think you're serious," she laughed.

"They *know* I'm serious, Bon. They can see what you're making me lug around." And then he added, "Bonny and I are making dinner for her mum and dad tonight, fresh salad and salmon pie. What are you doing with yours, Marion? You have some serious bounty in your bag."

"Roasting, for winter sauce and soup."

Quince stopped. "Winter soup? How?"

Marion smiled happily as she explained: "I roast a variety of ripe tomatoes" (opening her bag to show him), "capsicums, eggplant, garlic, salt – sometimes chillies – in plenty of olive oil, and then liquidise them into a rich sauce for freezing. Delicious for soups and pastas in winter," she added.

He turned sharply to address Bonny. "Did you take that down, boss?"

"Yip, Uncle P."

"Bon is a wild-fish and free-range eggs vegetarian," he announced proudly.

Harry was absorbed in the cricket ritual and didn't notice them when they first joined him. Eleanor bent down and tugged at his hat. "Thought you were listening to music, mister. Couldn't find you." Harry started to point and talk, but went quiet when he noticed Quince and Bonnie – quiet until Quince started asking him who the two sides were, which had won the toss, and the name of the lanky fast bowler who was striding towards them to mark his run up. He wasn't able to answer but wanted to know, and so the two of them walked round to the players' pavilion to find out, while Bonnie stayed with the ladies.

They were chatting away like old men when they returned, and Quince made a suggestion: "What about a coffee, or tea? Harry and I want to see if this Morrinsville bowler has a bouncer in him."

"Thank you, Quince … I'm not sure … Mum, are you hot?"

"A little, Ellie, but it's cool here under the elm. Martin loved his cricket," she added quietly. "Went to every test match he could."

"Settled then," Quince declared. "Who's for tea? Who's for coffee? Who's for passionfruit juice with crushed ice and a liquorice straw? I have a couple of fold-up chairs in the car too."

"I'll get the drinks, Quince," Eleanor insisted – remembering the treats that she and Peter had enjoyed with their father at local cricket matches – "while you fetch the chairs. Anything to eat?"

Quince picked up a fallen stick on his way back from the car, and, after they had had their treats, he arranged a game with Harry's ball. Rules were formulated and sides selected (adults versus children), with Marion nominated as umpire. The game was disrupted at one point when a straight drive from one of the cricketers caused a ball to come scooting through their playing space, but the result was a foregone conclusion: a win by some considerable margin for the younger participants. It also resulted in an insistence on the part of Quince to be provided, at some time in the future (and preferably with a proper bat), the opportunity to secure revenge. Telephone numbers were exchanged to facilitate this.

Eleanor was rocked by her reaction to Harry's 'disappearance'. It was wild, irrational, and stupid – embarrassing – pathetic. The Cambridge green on that summer Saturday epitomised safety. It was the very caricature of safety! A demarcated grassed area cradled by towering trees set beside a town clock with pointless hands chiming above a rose-enclosed epitaph where Prince William had placed a wreath. Her son had walked a mere ten metres past infants, grannies and shallots to watch cricket, for goodness' sake. Cricket! What was the source of her paralysing fear? Was it her indecision about taking Harry to Bwazi? Was it her chilling realisation that people saw him as 'different' – as 'other'? As someone who could be stereotyped as a threat to the way things were! But this terrible thought was intolerable and quickly quashed – dismissed as solo parent paranoia. New Zealand, she was confident, was entering an era that was post-racial, post-sexist, post-anti-Semitic, post-Islamophobic … post every whiff of myth-based hatred.

And then, in Christchurch on 15 March everything changed, or nothing changed, and her lurking fear materialised. The distortion of reality in the pursuit of power; the contemptuous dismissal of fact as the founder of truth; the Machiavellian manipulation of fear to formulate fantasy through distorted historical emphasis and innuendo; the repetition of wish list Santa Claus slogans on Twitter, on red caps, and in Nuremberg rallies; the fanatical right to sever heads – to slaughter and destroy on command from on high. The barbarity of righteousness had revealed itself in amplified fashion, at home! The Muslims were targeted in this atrocity, but it could have been the Christians, the Jews, the Hindus, the gays or the browns, like Harry.

But the bewildered response that she witnessed offered hope: school children in their thousands, gang members, priests, librarians, politicians, the idle and the old, all glassy-eyed with revulsion. Eleanor watched the film of flowers trembling and grief embraced, of numb love and leadership, of healing and repair coupled with the covenant of commitment and purpose in the aftermath, and she was comforted, and could send Harry off to school.

PART III

CAROL

As a young girl Carol would stand at the shoulder of her mother as she consulted her mirror. The mirror was long and could pivot, catching light from the overhead lamp. The child's role, like that of a theatre nurse, was to adjust and direct the beam towards its subject (in this case a face), fetch tissue and cotton wool, but mainly to anticipate and hand to her, her instruments of application. Bearing in mind procedural risk, words were necessarily few, and they were seldom assembled into more than half-sentences.

As the wife of the club chairman her mother was frequently called upon at prize-giving to smile and finger-squeeze triumphant sporting competitors. Sunburnt and desiccated victors would feign humility as they threaded their way between chairs, good-natured jeers and applause, exchange mumbles with Her Majesty, and then hoist their trophies high. Carol's mother wanted to do her husband proud, to show 'the other half' of their esteemed duality; and to achieve this it was essential to follow Doris Day's Hollywood lead by presenting herself well.

First, and usually on the day prior to the great event, she would perm her hair, an enterprise that demanded a substantial degree of olfactory fortitude, and one which absorbed most of the said day. Next, and on the afternoon of the event, she (in a spiky rubber cap that looked like a rock-pool crustacean) would take a bath – a bath infused with rendered-down rose water. Finally, and late in the afternoon, she and her assistant would repair to the bedroom vanity where the ceremony of facial transformation would take effect. Foundation (or concealer) was a prerequisite for success. Often underrated or ignored by the lazy or ill-informed, it was as necessary in preparation as the work of a plasterer upon his wall. Rouge, or blush, was the next to be applied, and Carol would be ready with pot in hand for the pigment to be accessed by her mother's right thumb. Too little and nuance was lost, too much and she would be the laughing stock, but, once a natural rose had been achieved, she would ascend to the area of her visage that posed the greatest challenge – her eyes and their surrounds. Deftness and dexterity were the order of the day, and neither participant exhaled as horsehair enhanced lid, brow, and lashes. Carol, armed with tweezers, came into her own at this point, as she was responsible (due to the reflective limitations of the mirror) for the plucking off and out of unwanted hairs or 'shadow specks'. Next, and with mounting tension, her mother would approach closer to her mirror and blink, and blink again, before artfully smearing her lips with an angulated oily red applicant that she screwed out of a shiny metal stick. This was a silent prompt for Carol to pass her mother a tissue to blot and smack – to form her full lips into the shape of a letter 'M'. The penultimate act was powdering, not only of her shiny nose, but also of her potentially obnoxious intertriginous zones, each of which received a generous puff. Finally, and almost as an afterthought, her wrists and ear lobes would accept their dabs of eau de Cologne.

The finished product never failed to impress Carol, to fill her with a curious combination of envy and pride.

Her father, having played some game or other all day, would come to fetch them in the late afternoon in his badge-laden blazer and member's tie, and then hold open the passenger door of his automobile. Her mother, dressed in shawl and long-sleeved Crimplene, would step out on her precarious heels, calling back to Carol, "Have you locked, dear?"

"My word!" her father would say, "My word," as he took his wife's hand. He knew better than to smudge her lips with a kiss; but Carol he would hug and peck, happy that his girls were sent from heaven. From the back seat of their old but excited Buick she would bask in their collective glory, praying that she herself could one day wear fake mother-of-pearl.

How this contrasted with her own married life!

Carol herself had only recently acquired a vanity drawer with a pivoting mirror that mimicked that of her mother's (she had purchased it on impulse from an antique shop in Te Aroha), and Kevin, irony of ironies, was on hand to register its delivery with a tremulous squiggle. His habit after lunch, now that it was getting warmer, was to position his mobile scooter at their gate so that he could stare at cars and passers-by, and he probably had no clear idea what the furniture was for. In his day he had tolerated a bathroom mirror, quite a long one in fact, but a second sheet of reflective glass, and in particular one that was attached to a bedroom vanity ('the name said it all'), he would have viewed as an absurd indulgence. She, Carol recalled, had not been permitted to purchase cosmetics of any kind – even sweet-smelling soap – and jewellery had been out of the question. She had been encouraged to shop at second-hand outlets using her audited allowance, and cobblers resoled her shoes. Any purchase that could be perceived as an attempt to make her look 'pretty' had been ridiculed by

Kevin as 'cheap', 'trashy', and provocative. His third beer, we have already learned, sharpened his derision and belligerence: "Where'd you get that flimsy top from? The emporium in Hood Street?"

"No, Kevin, I told you ..."

"If you want to show your tits, show your tits."

"The boys, Kevin. Please ..."

"Don't 'boys' me. What *boys* are you talking about anyway? The pimps at the emporium?"

"I'll take it off, Kevin. Sorry, I thought ..."

"Don't think. You're too stupid to think." Pause. "You think you're lamb?"

"Lamb?"

"Yes, lamb, but you're not lamb, you're goat – and you got goat tits."

Defiance took the form of window shopping. After dropping Evan and Stewart off at school, and on days when Kevin was away on business, Carol would walk into town and 'shop'. Victoria, Alexander and their side streets were her favourites, as in those days they accommodated the main multi-level departmental stores. She would ride up and down the escalators peering out and over *Men's Wear*, *Women's Wear*, *Kitchenware*, and *Whiteware*. Occasionally she would indulge herself by stepping off at the *Tea Room* to savour a hot chocolate and a fresh scone – straining to catch the gossip of nearby ladies with rinsed blue hair. Most had store bags at their sides, some wrapped in beautiful paper, and Carol would imagine that she herself had made purchases of English sweets at Farmers – ordered Irish linen to be delivered.

<hr>

The day of one's emergence is the end of a hazardous journey marked by pain, anxiety, and relief for others. Because we have no memory of the initial drama, its significance is built around cumulative celebration of self as special through the loving actions of those who wake us with gifts, bake gingerbread cakes, build Wendy houses, and sing 'Happy Birthday'. Carol could look through snaps and cine-clips to recall her parents' efforts; the hired magicians, the decorations, the invited friends, the sleep-overs, her first watch – even their tentative embrace of rock'n'roll themes in her teenage years – but she chose not to. It was too painful. Photographs, she found, juxtaposed celebration with sadness, and she avoided taking them out. She lived for the tenth of April as a child because she was elevated on that day to the prominence of a princess, and she looked forward to the next, and the one after that, because each promised to deliver her onto an ever-higher plane of happiness.

But after she married and moved, the tenth of April became a day that came and went much as others did – a takeaway pizza and a bought pudding, a practical gift partially wrapped, a "we should think of going out for your thirtieth", or fortieth, or fiftieth – a second glass of sweet sherry. Kevin expected nothing more for his own birthdays, even those that marked the decades, and he preferred to select his own gifts. It was prescribed that the children's parties take place midweek (when he was at work), and remain low key, but this provided Carol with the opportunity to indulge them with games, surprises and secret treats from the two-dollar shop.

Their family's failure to celebrate birthdays was brought into focus for Carol by Angela's effort for Evan while Kevin was still in the rest home. It wasn't a special birthday for Evan as she recalled – probable his twenty-eighth or twenty-ninth – and she was initially perplexed when Angela stealthily approached, cupped her hand close to Carol's ear, and whispered, "It's on."

"What's on, Angela?"

"The party. The surprise party for Evan."

"Oh, were you serious about that?"

"Absolutely. Can't wait to see his face, Carol. He has no idea that we're doing more than blowing out a few candles."

"What exactly are you planning?"

"I'll get him out of the house for half an hour or so – I'll think of something – while you slip in with the others."

"Others?"

"Yes, Jeff and Hazel have a van and they'll drop off eats, drinks and balloons. If you could wait around the corner until I send a text – I'll send them one too – so that you can open the door to let them in. Would you mind helping set things up?"

"Yes, yes, of course."

"The rest will be there to help too."

"The rest?"

"A few from Evan's work – a couple from mine. And you know Barry and Brenda? Barry was at school with Evan."

"Yes, yes, I do." She was relieved to learn that someone she knew was coming. There seemed to be so many.

"What about Kevin, Carol?"

"Kevin?"

"I thought of trying to sneak him down for the party. That really would surprise Evan."

"It would, yes, Angela, but I don't know. He's not really a party type. The noise, the strangers – just getting him here without Evan's help could be difficult."

"Suppose you're right."

"Another time. A lunch perhaps."

"You're right, but it's a shame."

"It is. It is."

"Don't forget to turn the lights out," Angela added conspiratorially.

"The lights?"

"Can't have Evan getting suspicious."

"Of course not."

"And tell everyone to park around the block."

It was Angela's enthusiasm and determination to spoil Evan, to make him feel special, that most surprised and impressed Carol. She and Kevin had had no friends as such, and they had never hosted anyone other than 'business associates' for a barbecue. Making a fuss of someone for its own sake was something that she associated with her childhood, for children, and she was apprehensive about the role that she was expected to play. What was it? Was she to offer drinks like her father did? Or snacks like her mother? What attire would be most appropriate? Was it her role to 'mingle'? And if it was, what was she expected to say? Evan, of course, she could talk about – his boyhood and occasional prank – but what else? There was really nothing that she could think of.

But the night was a great success. Jeff and Hazel arrived within minutes of Angela and Evan leaving the house, and their boxes of eats, drinks, paper plates and loose cutlery, as well as bunches of pre-inflated balloons, were ushered in smartly. The other guests began appearing too, greeting one another in hushed giggles, and they quickly assembled in the lounge to await further instructions. Hazel took charge: sparse lounge furniture was moved out to the periphery of the room; an outdoor trestle table was opened and clothed in bright-blue crinkle paper for food, drinks, plates and cutlery to be spaced along it; balloons were tied to an overhead fan in bunches; and gifts were stacked under a standing lamp. It was time to lock the door and turn off the lights.

Surprise was accomplished, and three sunflower heads, the last of the season, were in the best position to frame Evan's face as the lights came on. Carol had placed them in a vase on the mantelpiece earlier in the day, and they, better than any camera, were able to record the startle reflex and momentary bewilderment that a delay between perception and comprehension provokes. 'Happy Birth-day' followed, however, allowing time for the gap to be breached and a grin to be formed – a grin that remained a fixture on Evan's face for the rest of the evening. Carol could see that he was deeply moved by the effort, and it caused her both shame and anger. Angela, if she wasn't holding food, was hanging off his arm – it was obvious that she adored him – while his friends mingled easily with one another. They even made an effort to chat with Carol herself – to top up her glass. The puzzling thing was that they all seemed to *like* one another – wanted one another to have fun! 'Is this all it takes?' she mused. 'Could happiness be this simple?'

If both of their bedroom doors were closed, and provided there was no leak in his mask, Kevin's CPAP machine did not bother Carol unduly, but not infrequently one of them was left ajar. Carol convinced herself that the lapse was intentional, and it made her seethe. It also added to her resentment of his doctor, Frank Edge. It was Edge, after all, who had turned Kevin around – had had him crawl out of his hole of self-pity. Without the doctor's pep talk Kevin would never have put in the rehabilitative effort that 'restored sufficient function to elevate the patient above hospital level care', thereby enabling his return home. Home! What home? Prior to his return, and for the first time in her adult life, Carol had been able to enjoy the sanctuary of a space where she could drop her guard; where she could eat in her underwear if she chose to; stir two, or even three, teaspoonfuls of sugar into her mug of morning tea; have long baths and soak until her soles crinkled; record *The Great British Bake Off* while she watched *Downton Abbey* – *please herself*. But the good doctor had resurrected the curse of Kevin and soiled that space. He had also, through the acquisition for his patient of a stupid breathing machine, ensured that the curse would continue into perpetuity. Without its assistance, Carol fumed, Kevin's sleep apnoea would likely have taken him away long ago; but now, despite having closed both doors before going to bed, she had been woken by the repetitious farts of escaping wet air. 'Should I smother him?' she asked herself, 'or should I simply flick the switch? Which would be less likely to lead to detection?'

Carol had discovered at their last visit to the hospital's Sleep Clinic that a complete record of Kevin's CPAP machine's performance and utilisation was automatically captured and stored remotely. This record, she realised, could prove damning if he died in the night! She wondered what effect a soft pillow would have on the tracing. It was, after all, a weapon that had featured frequently in *C.I.*! Oxygen saturation levels would drop of course, but that could be ascribed to a sudden and unfortunate breach in the mask's integrity – to a catastrophic leak. But the machine, and this was critical, the machine would keep puffing away. There would be no record of an interruption to power supply.

A struggle, though, could offer clues through blood, bites and bruising, but Kevin, if approached from the side of his paralysis after his good arm had been restrained, would offer no more resistance than a flailing turned-up tortoise. And saliva on the slip? That would prove nothing – he always slobbered. No, it was feasible. She could do it … or could she?

Alice was scratching next to her bed as she rose and padded noiselessly through to her husband's bedroom. Both of their doors were open, and his night light (fitted for safety!) illuminated her path. The mask appeared to be well-positioned, but the noise of the escaping air was a give-away. They had been advised by the technician to shave off Kevin's facial hair – even his moustache – as it was likely to interfere with the seal; but keeping his face fur-free required effort on her part. It required, at the very least, that she remember to charge the battery of his electric razor, that she find the time, daily, to be meticulous when mowing along the ridges of his cheeks and jaw (the points of mask contact), and, finally, that she maintain the sharpness of the razor's blades through oiling and emptying, so as not to cause discomfort. Unfortunately, if one were to try to quantify Carol's level of effort (effort directed towards the ongoing comfort and survival of her husband), one would have to place it at the margins of 'perfunctory'. Consequently, one could argue, Kevin's blood oxygen was never destined to reach the saturation percentage that his machine was capable of delivering, and, as she looked down, absorbed by the ongoing struggle of bellow, beard and fat, hope rose. 'Stubble would be less problematic than pillow', she decided, 'but it might take too long!'

The idea of a holiday arose out of another visit to her doctor, Eleanor, the month before her April birthday and soon after they had met briefly at the pharmacy. She had considered a change of doctor – even a change of practice – after having been told, in effect, that her happiness was up to her; but the pharmacy encounter, she felt, had gone well, and she was tired – dead tired.

"You did look tired last week, Carol. Is work too much for you?"

"No, work's good."

"Are you still walking with your dog?"

"Yes, when I can, and we often take Joey too – my grandchild."

"Of course. That must be lovely?"

"It is," she replied, and then added, "she keeps me going, really, she and Alice."

"And living with your son? Is that working out?"

"With Evan, yes, and Angela. She's good to me."

"But?"

"What you mean?"

"You don't look happy."

Carol laughed, but with an edge of bitterness. "Happy! Who's happy?" Eleanor remained quiet as she continued. "I look at Evan and Angela – they're happy, I suppose – especially now that they have Joey. But they seem to want to make each another happy," she added, looking directly at Eleanor. "I never hear them fighting – not really. They remind me of my mum and dad."

"They were happy, do you think? Happy together?"

"I think so."

"But you haven't had that?"

"No," she replied sharply.

"It must be difficult living with an invalid?"

"No, it's much easier actually."

"You don't want me to try to arrange for more help – his washing, toileting – that sort of thing?"

"Can you put him back in the rest home?" Carol shot back.

"Only if he agrees, Carol. You know that. Or if he deteriorates and needs hospital care."

"I know," she laughed, her face resuming its default expression, "I'm only joking."

"I could have a word with his doctor, Dr Edge, to see if there's anything ..."

"No."

There was a short but awkward pause before Eleanor changed tack. "Let's get you up on the bed, Carol. We need to check a few things – get bloods, urine, and possibly follow up on the results next week, if you don't mind?"

"I don't mind."

"How's your son in Australia?" she asked, while Carol was taking off her shoes. "He lives near my brother, on the Sunshine Coast, doesn't he?"

"He does, but he's busy. Don't see much of him. Doesn't come home much."

"Why don't you surprise him?"

"What you mean?"

"Go over. Have a break – a holiday. He'd love that."

"Not sure."

"Of course he will."

"Not sure … and I've never been on a holiday, not a real holiday … not since I was a child."

"Time to start, Carol. You've been to Australia though, haven't you?"

"I've never been anywhere – not even the South Island."

The blood tests revealed that Carol was hypothyroid and on her return visit Eleanor was delighted to be able to tell her that thyroxin replenishment would quickly correct the imbalance and make her feel like a new woman. "You'll have more energy, not feel the cold as keenly, and you'll find it much easier to lose weight."

"Really?"

"Really," Eleanor beamed. "Just give it a month or so – time to arrange your holiday," she teased.

"No, I have, Eleanor."

"You're going?"

"I am, or at least I hope so," she added.

"What do you mean, you hope so?"

"I don't have a passport … never have, but Angela helped me fill out an application online."

"Good for her. That won't take long. And where will you stay? With your son? Have you told him yet?"

"Yes, I have told him, but no, no, I won't stay with him and his girlfriend. They're busy and don't have a big place."

"You'll have to stay somewhere posh then, but close by."

"I am, I think. Stewart, the son who lives here, has booked me into a one-roomed apartment overlooking the sea."

"Really? That's wonderful, Carol. Fantastic! You'll have to send me a picture of you in your bikini."

Carol flushed. "I'm nervous though. Never been through customs and stuff. Not sure how I'll cope over there either."

"Just ask, Carol. Tell them it's your first time."

"I will."

"And your son will meet you at the airport in Brisbane?"

"Hope so."

"Of course, he will."

"Hope so, but he's very busy."

Because Taranaki is out on a limb, access to destinations other than those cradled within the shadow of its mountain necessitates long-distance travel, and, as a consequence, the greater portion of Carol's childhood holidays were spent, as she recalled, in the back seat of her father's car. Her maternal grandparents lived in the Auckland suburb of Mount Roskill, and they would make the pilgrimage every Christmas to stay with them. There would be the visits with her cousins to the zoo, the climbing of the pohutukawa trees that overhung small beaches, the occasional film – usually a musical – and bus rides into the city to eat ice cream and toffee apples, or just to walk along the street taking in the busyness of it all; but the enduring memory was of the back seat. There were no restraints in those days and Carol was free to lie flat, to sit side-ways on the hump of the drive shaft as it passed through to the back wheels, or simply to sit on one or other side staring out at the passing farms. Her father seldom spoke, but her mother would play 'I spy' and '20 questions' when Carol became too restless. Packed breakfasts comprised boiled eggs, fresh brown bread spread with farm butter, and tea sweetened with tinned condensed milk. They would stop in small towns like Te Awamutu for pies and walnut slices while her father filled up the car with petrol, and then the journey would resume with the monotonous drone of tyre on tar.

But this holiday promised to be different. Evan drove Carol up to Auckland from Hamilton and helped her to check in. The process, using an automatic machine, Carol found bewildering. Being a Saturday, it was loud and crowded with queues at every luggage kiosk, but they had arrived with plenty of time to spare.

"Let's have a quick cup of tea upstairs before you go through Departure, Mum."

"Have you time, dear? Won't Angela be worried?"

"Not at all. I'll text her. In fact, I'll send her a photo of you chilling out in the lounge."

"No, not now. I look a mess."

"A very excited mess!"

"It's scary, Evan. I'll tell you that."

"It is scary, but you can't deny being excited."

After their tea Evan directed his mother to the departure gates, ensuring that she had hold of her passport and boarding card. "Now, remember to ask for help when you get to the e-Gates for immigration clearance. And don't forget to breathe."

"Okay."

"And have something to eat once you're through."

"Yes, yes, you're making me even more nervous."

He laughed and gave her a hug. "You'll be fine, Mum. I'll be here to fetch you next week."

"You sure? It's so far to travel."

He laughed again. "Give my little brother a pinch and a punch from me."

Evan and Angela had primed Carol for her immigration and security processing through verbal explanation and YouTube illustration in the previous week. They had even shown her a clip of a first-time traveller placing himself instead of his hand luggage on the X-ray processor's conveyer belt. The expressions of incredulity on the faces of the security officers were very funny, but it was the passenger's eagerness to please, to do the right thing, that struck Carol. He had acted out of innocence, not stupidity, she argued. His intentions had been honourable.

"I could also make a fool of myself, you know! End up on YouTube like this poor man, despite being told what to expect."

"Nonsense, Mum," Evan laughed. "You'll be fine. Just hold your passport out to anyone who comes near, and they'll wave you by."

And they did. Within twenty minutes she was through, clutching onto her passport and boarding pass with clammy hands, and heading for Gate 9. There were only ninety minutes till departure, but the Gate 9 lounge was still accommodating passengers for an earlier flight – one destined for Hong Kong, she noted. Carol decided to venture back to the closest shops within hovering distance. Perhaps there was time to have a snack at one of the food outlets, as Evan had advised? She had measured the time/distance from the cafes to her gate (walking quickly and avoiding the horizontal escalators) at six minutes. There were several food stalls, but the Vietnamese one chose her as it had the shortest queue. Photographs of meals were displayed above the prim lady serving. Being conscious of time, she pointed at a soup near the top, and asked for green tea. The soup was called a beef pho, and, apart from gasping on a slither of chilli that had surreptitiously floated into her third spoonful (chopsticks had been set aside), it was delicious – savoury and subtle with a hint of ginger. As a parting gift Angela had handed her a small exercise pad and pencil. "Jot down anything you want to remember," she had suggested. After a sip of scalding tea, Carol opened the exercise book, licked the tip of her pencil (a habit dating back to the time of indelible 'ink'), looked back up at the board to confirm the unusual spelling, and made her first entry.

She also, because she had promised, sent Evan a text to let him know she was through. He and Angela were so good to her, so kind, but she knew not to expect the same from Stewart.

***

Her one mistake was to buy a dark blue suitcase. "Stewart will be there to meet you when you emerge, Mum," Evan had reassured her. "Just follow the signs for 'Luggage Collection' after you've gone through the Australian e-Gates. You aren't carrying anything that you need to declare, and you'll be directed down the 'green' corridor and out before you know it." What Carol did not know was that most travellers, certainly those navigating Australasia, favoured the self-same pigment that she had selected, and she watched with growing apprehension as replica after replica tumbled down onto her flight's rotunda. She snatched at one, and then another and another, unaware that the chugging belt was on a rotisserie that offered more than a singular and fleeting opportunity for capture. Still clutching her passport and customs form with the white knuckles of her right hand, it was left to her left to lunge at each of the appendages of blue luggage that passed her by, even those adorned with pompoms, but the number of suitcases and surrounding passengers gradually thinned out, and hers finally materialised.

Carol, dishevelled and suffering from a headache that had her afferents on edge, emerged into a blast of indecipherable noise. Distorted faces, hugging, squawking, and milling chaos merged into nightmare. She hesitated at the exit, obstructing those behind, then shuffled forward, her eyes scanning the crowd like a lizard – hoping that Stewart would appear. Children, mothers, and men with bare burnt legs bumped into her, and their possessions formed a barrier to escape; but she finally pushed past the horde. 'What if he isn't here? Couldn't come? What then?' She gripped her passport and boarding card even tighter. 'A taxi? A bus?' Evan had advised her not to exchange money at the airport. "It's too crowded, Mum. Stewart will take you to an ATM when you get to Mooloolaba." "What a name!" she had laughed. But now! How would she pay?

She was frightened, breathing fast and feeling dizzy – not sure whether to step outside onto the concourse. She felt her fingers going numb, her toes too, and wondered if she was going to pass out; but finally, and mercifully, her son was at her side, grabbing at her case and leading her into the heat before she could touch his cheek.

"Stewart! Oh Stewart, it's so good to see you."

"Yeah, good to see you too," he offered, turning briefly to catch her eye as he exited the doors. "We need to hurry. I'm in a drop-off zone." And hurry she did, until they reached the safety of his car, a low, black, two-seater something with little space for her suitcase.

"How are you, Stew?" she was finally able to ask once they were buckled up and ready to go. "Thank you for picking me up. Don't know what I would have done otherwise."

"It's only Brisbane, Ma. You haven't landed in bloody Mumbai."

She sensed that it would be better if she kept quiet until they reached the open road, and Stewart's thudding, brain-jarring bass sound ensured that she kept her word. Smells emanating from his dangling potpourri made her feel nauseous too. She couldn't pinpoint the offending ingredient – it could have been musk, or even marzipan – but its effect was that of ipecac.

"Could you stop, dear, just for a moment?" she whispered.

"What?"

"Stop ... *could you stop, please?*"

"*Why? We're on the M1.*"

"*Sick. Might be sick,*" she shouted.

Stewart swore, swerved, and stopped abruptly, then swore again because his mother could not get her passenger door open. It had no handle, no lever – only a number of dimly-lit buttons. With one hand cupped over her mouth, she was using the index finger of her other to strike at the buttons with ever-increasing desperation. Her window darkened, paled, slid down, then up, then down again, but her door held fast. Fortunately, Stewart's response time was rapid enough for him to lunge across and effect Carol's release before her bile-soured airline meal of smoked fish, coconut slice, stale roll and sweet, cold coffee could be ejected over his mock-fur upholstery. Instead she watched in misery, through heaves and long nasal drips, as the roadside of the M1 became its recipient, her every effort accompanied by a passing car's shudder. 'Perhaps I should have selected the blander, braised beef option' she pondered.

Poor Carol was not a sight to gladden the heart of her son as she slowly placed her legs back into the car. "Please could we turn the radio down a little, dear? I have … I have a bit of a headache." Angela had helped her to choose her travel top. It was white with a lace frill, and it had looked so smart in the shop mirror. "Wear that with these navy pants," Angela had advised, "and you'll get an instant upgrade to Business Class." Carol looked down at the fresh stains and knew that she would have to toss the top away.

They passed names like Burpengary, Caboolture and Beerburrum, drove through eucalypt forests, rocky outcrops, and endless suburban developments. Carol had anticipated the two of them chatting excitedly during the trip from the airport to her apartment, having him tell her about his new life and land – perhaps point out a koala or a kangaroo – but instead, just as she did as a child, Carol stared out of the window, longing that the journey would end. She had also anticipated a night of celebration on the Saturday of her arrival, but all she wanted was a hot shower, a cup of black tea, and bed. Stewart appeared happy to acquiesce.

Carol woke twice in the night and sobbed the second time, trapped in disappointment. Stewart had never been affectionate, and she could understand why his response to her initial greeting was perfunctory; but there was something else. He appeared to be jittery, on edge, and his eyes were dark and darting. The dirty hair she could understand, but his teeth! Carol had never subscribed to the conspiracy theories around fluoride, and she had been meticulous about her boys' dental hygiene. Their teeth had always been immaculate! Why then were Stewart's stained and beginning to stump?

She sat up and looked at her watch, still set on New Zealand time. Eight fourteen! How could that be? And then she remembered, of course, Queensland was two hours behind – or was it in front? Hard to think of Australia being behind NZ! And then there was daylight saving to consider. That confused her, even at home. "We don't do daylight saving in Queensland, Ma," Stewart had informed her sharply after she had once mistimed a call. "There's a *three*-hour difference in summer. Remember that." Was April considered summer in Australia? Anyway, there was definitely a difference … one way or the other … but whatever it was there was enough faint and curious light filtering through a crack in her curtains to orientate Carol to the layout of her studio apartment. She had been too exhausted the night before to notice how comfortable and cosy it was. Her queen bed occupied one corner, her kitchenette another, but it was the gangly pot plant on the coffee table of her two-chair lounge that her eyes rested on and recognised as an orange kangaroo paw. She rose, padded over, and fingered the plant, expecting it to be artificial, but tubes of the 'paw' came off in her hand. 'Water', she decided, 'it needs water.' Her kettle had been pre-filled, and she poured a little around the plant's base before flicking on the switch for coffee. There were options for instant or filter, and two two-biscuit packets had been set out on a tray for 'complimentary' use. With coffee cupped and steaming, she drew open her curtains and sliding doors, shivering slightly as she stepped out onto the flat's small balcony, set thirteen storeys up. She was met by a warm salt breeze accompanied by the hush of her childhood's sea, and beyond, way beyond the shoreline below, was the pinkish hint of dawn.

The balcony rail obscured her view if she sat, and so Carol stood, sipping, watching as the transforming light woke waves – discernible first as distant ripples that marshalled themselves into lines like infantrymen. She picked out one, and then another, following the advance of each as it gathered pace – swelling, curling, and striking, before collapsing into froth on the hushing sand. She remembered doing the same when tramping as a child with her father on a western contour of Mt Taranaki, high above the Tasman Sea. "Waves don't live long, do they, Daddy?" she had asked. "Ah, but they do, sweetie, these have travelled all the way from Australia, and it takes a long time to get here from there." She wondered whether the waves that she was watching had come all the way from New Zealand, and how they had managed to intersect.

<hr>

The sweet biscuits and coffee had started to make Carol feel lightheaded and affect her vision. She realised that she should eat. Not sure what to wear, or whether to apply her make-up, her stomach determined that a skirt and blouse would do. Out of habit, and just before closing the door, Carol grabbed her waterproof jacket too.

Her intention was to stock up at the Coles supermarket advertised in her guest manual, but first she had to find an ATM. Her lift door opened into an arcade and there was one just opposite. Within minutes, and much to her relief, her card had been recovered and she was walking out with a pack of fifty-dollar bills.

Coles was situated behind the building, but delicious smells directed her onto the street. Being early there were few people around – mainly delivery personnel, joggers and garbage collectors, but the enticing smell was coming from a campervan kiosk parked above the beach. Inside was a bronze and scrawny man of indeterminate age with blond leg hairs. He was wearing a faded bandana, baggies, and a cane toad T-shirt, and he was bent over a hot plate, singing.

"Gidday, love, what can I do ya for?"

"Have you opened yet?" she asked hesitantly.

"If you're buyin', I'm open, love. What takes ya fancy?"

"Um!"

"What about eggs any way but fertilised?"

"That would be nice."

"An' a mussel fritter?"

"You have those?" Her mother made them in Taranaki when whitebait wasn't in season.

"Fetched the little beauties meself this mornin'. Fried tomato? Banana? Spuds?"

"Just tomato, please," she laughed. "And a coffee – a flat white."

"Only serve perc, love, with as many top-ups as you like."

"That's fine. Lovely, thank you."

"Comin' up."

"Do you always open this early?"

"Only when the tide's out, darlin'. You out from Kiwi?"

"Yes, Hamilton – in the North Island."

"First trip to Queensland?"

"Yes, first to Australia actually."

"No kiddin'?"

"My son lives in Mooloolaba. He's doing very well," she added.

"Good on him. Got a mate who's a Kiwi. He's not short of a crust neither. Bit o' sweat is all it takes. Bit o' sweat."

And the man was sweating, even though the sun was still low – angling in over the sea and casting shadows back off the rocky outcrops that buttressed both ends of the beach. Surfers, some without wetsuits, were clumped like baby seals beyond the breakers, and swimming groups were starting to gather on the sand in front of her. The closest comprised elderly males – big-bellied men in bright speedos that barely concealed their unmentionables. Their leader, handing out red life-saving caps, had to be a relative of the golfer Greg Norman. To their left was a smaller group of women, fit, desiccated and formidable, not bothering to towel themselves, who had already completed their swim. Carol watched as the men took to the sea, three abreast, to traverse the bay; and she watched the women, cackling like crows, walk up to the hose next to her, to wash their feet. Two, she noted, had bunions like her own.

Angela had insisted that Carol buy and bring togs, but she wasn't sure that she would swim ... not with all that she'd read about great whites, bluebottles and jellyfish ... not with her fat, white legs. The fine, warm spray was enticing though!

"Here's ya tucker, love. Help yaself to coffee," the man called out. Had she ever, ever been this hungry?

Both the breakfast and coffee were served in biodegradable containers, and she carried them to a nearby bench to eat. The mussel fritter fried in batter, the poached eggs, the tomato, the raw coffee – even the banana that he had forgotten not to give her – were as good as anything she had ever eaten. Having a meal, a delicious meal, cooked by a man singing, was unfamiliar to Carol, but it added a complementing condiment that she could not, and did not want to, articulate. She remembered, while seeking dietary advice about her weight a few months prior, that Eleanor had recommended that she focus on 'taste before content' and enjoy her food before all else. It had seemed unprofessional at the time, but now it made sense. "I won't give you a calorie counter with reams of dietary dos and don'ts, Carol, I just won't. You know what's bad for you. You'll end up using the information to punish yourself ... six hundred calories over the limit on one day, eight hundred the next! Eat when you're hungry and savour the experience with all your senses – enjoy your food, and it will know where to go." And now, satiated but not overfull, with every sense satisfied, she managed a smile.

People carrying bright umbrellas, towels and togs were gathering on the beach – couples, families, sparring adolescents, fitness groups – and balls of every size and shape began to fly. Carol closed her eyes and breathed in evenly, carrying the scent of the sea deep into her memory. She wanted to capture and consolidate this moment as one of her happiest.

The plan was for Stewart to come for lunch, and it was hoped that he would bring his girlfriend, Heather. Carol felt that it would be easier to eat and talk in the apartment, and so she selected items from the supermarket delicatessen that she thought they might enjoy – cold meats, pickles, olives, fresh rolls, mixed salad and a ripe pawpaw. She even threw in a few exotic treats like artichokes, dried tomato, and smoked peppers with paprika. Chocolate, of course, too. Carol was not sure what drinks they would like, and so she selected a variety – freshly squeezed guava, ginger beer, sparkling grape juice, and milk for tea and coffee. At the checkout there were tubs holding bunches of flowers. They were expensive, and she hesitated, but three long, scraggly sunflower stalks with heads the size of side plates caught her eye. Ever since her own imperfect blooms had stopped a stranger's car, had linked the better selves of him and her, Carol had determined that she would never pass them by. Her unexpressed hope was that these would work their magic on her son.

But it was not to be.

Stewart arrived later than he had promised, and he was alone. "She works nights, and was too tired," he said of Heather.

"Oh, what a pity, Stew. Maybe we can catch up this evening, or tomorrow. What work does she do?" Carol added.

"This and that."

"What do you mean?"

"What I said," he flashed. "She works in hospitality." He grabbed the TV remote and started flicking through channels. "You got Netflix?" he queried.

"I don't know, Stew. Haven't tried it yet. Let's sit outside, dear. I thought that we could have lunch on the balcony. Would you like a drink?"

"Sure. What beer you got?"

"Beer? No, sorry, I just have soft drinks – or hot chocolate? You've always liked your hot chocolate."

"I'm not bloody two, mate," he flashed suddenly, fixing his eyes on his mother's until they began to tear – and then he softened and smiled. "Just messing with you, Ma. Just messing with you. I'll zip down for a half pack. Looks like you need a stubby yourself," he added, laughing. "You're on holiday, Ma. Time to party."

She did have one beer, at Stewart's insistence, and they did sit out on the balcony as she had envisaged, but Carol did not taste her lunch. She heard again how well he was doing, how often he was going over to Bali – how easy it was to 'make it' in Queensland. What exactly he did 'do' escaped her, but the bullying swagger, the bragging, the way he slurped his beer while his mouth was full – the dead eyes – did not. There was little mention of Heather, and no interest in his nephew, Joey. Stewart had become Kevin with a Queensland accent, but there was also something else, something that stabbed at her heart with an ice pick.

By the time he left late in the afternoon Stewart was approaching pleasant, and he promised to pop in often over the week. "We'll go out. I'll take you to a steakhouse. You'll have to try crocodile, or wallaby," he laughed. But, as it transpired, Stewart was too busy that week, and they met only once, with Heather, at an Outback bar two streets up from the beach. It was fortunately too loud to talk, but Heather seemed genial enough once she had consumed a few dark ales. Her teeth though, Carol noted, were pegged, and stained, just like Stewart's, and she cowered when he spoke.

Returning that Tuesday evening to her apartment, to her kangaroo paw and wilting sunflowers, Carol poured herself a glass of Tasmanian cider and stepped outside. There was a warm, stiff breeze blowing off the water and a half-moon racing cloud – their interplay painting streaks of fleeting dark and silver on the sea. Stewart had ordered fried barramundi, chips, and salad for her dinner, and she was left with an aftertaste of batter, which the cider soured. Carol poured a second glass, and then a third, licking viciously at the bitter tears that reached her mouth; and the following morning, after a fitful, thirsty sleep, she fashioned a solemn covenant, self-to-self, set out as a legal document on apartment paper, and signed, using her maiden name, and her original, sixteen-year-old signature:

I, Carol Elizabeth Cummings, do hereby and forthwith vow to make myself number 1 in all future considerations and deliberations. These will include decisions around meals, matters concerning dress, matters to do with finance, garden, house, holidays, family – and any other matters outstanding.

Signed ...

Her first post-covenant action was to temporarily sever contact with Stewart by turning off her phone. The second was to book a bus tour to the Australia Zoo at Beerwah, which advertised an all-inclusive:

1. *Koala cuddle*
2. *Crocodile feeding demonstration*

3. *Morning tea*
4. *Photograph with python*
5. *Prawn lunch*
6. *Interactive walk in primate enclosure*
7. *Movie tribute to the late Steve Irwin.*

The highlight of her day, however, was catching sight of a blue-tongue lizard swallowing, very slowly, a child's fallen chip.

Her second tour, taken on the day before leaving, was to the Mary Cairncross Scenic Reserve, a subtropical rainforest that was so different from, yet reminded her so much of, the Mt Taranaki forests of her childhood. A young, female PhD student from the University of Queensland led them on hushed walks under the canopy of towering red cedar, black bean, white beech and strangling fig. Birds were easier to hear than see, but Carol did catch sight of a pair of fluttering rufous fantails – relatives of New Zealand's own piwakawaka – in an overhanging branch. It was the calm though, the damp of the moss and fern, the exposed roots that searched out and steamed in the developing day, that, at least temporarily, helped her to suppress her grievance.

By the afternoon, however, her resolve was back. After a first ocean swim, Carol sent a farewell message to Stewart, informing him that she would be out that evening, and that she was taking the shuttle to the airport the next day. He was in trouble, she knew that, but it was his father's doing, and they could both go to hell.

FRANK

Frank's knees were perished: 'sore' was too weak a word, 'agony' too strong – perhaps 'ache' would do – but, regardless of nociceptive nomenclatural niceties, they forced him, against his better judgement (with Milly on one side and Henry, their opinionated cat, on the other), to embark upon a series of twists, flops, stretches and turns to try to alleviate its effect. When tugs at the top sheet coming from his left flank turned violent, however, and a slapping tail signalled imminent attack from his right, Frank decided that it might be opportune to extricate himself from the bed completely, and to search for pharmacological relief; but to achieve this without further provocation proved far from easy. He had to draw himself up towards his pillow like a caterpillar, consecutively shifting bum and feet until he was in a position to haul himself out of the bedclothes, pivot on one elbow, raise his left leg up and over Henry (while maintaining a safe margin), and, finally, plant first one foot then the other on the carpet.

Frank was fortunate in that he took no regular medication, but he kept a small supply of paracetamol and ibuprofen – even some codeine that the dentist had prescribed for him – for nights such as these. They shared a plastic bag with batteries, paper clips, antacids, and ear buds. He padded through to the kitchen, poured himself a glass of water and swallowed two of each. Wide awake now, and with an ageing Emma joining him, Frank decided to make himself a cup of black tea.

It was cool, but not cold, and the two of them sat out on the edge of the wooden deck under the walnut, watching the ascent of a quarter-moon that offered just enough light. A faded white rope hung off a bough above them, attached to a bird feeder – a rope that Frank had originally slung to support Jane's swing. It was useful now, for sparrows, mainly sparrows, those tiny but ubiquitous creatures that appeared from nowhere and within seconds when food was put out for them. Cooked rice was their favourite, but bread and barley too, and, although he was careful to place most in the middle of the feeder to keep it above Henry, some bits fell, and the little chirpers would fly down to fight over scraps – often roughed up by nasty mynahs. To protect the sparrows, and when he was able to find him, he would lock Henry in their bedroom until the food, and birds, were gone. It never took long.

He noted that the tree was more elbow than arm, offering angular frames for blanched stars. Some nuts had fallen but many remained poised, ready for a nudge from the wind. A walnut, Frank mused, would not be everyone's pick as a house overhang! With the possible exception of chestnuts, it was the messiest tree by far! Clean-up started in March when black tannin-staining pods began dropping. Next came the nuts, in their tens of thousands, which had to be gathered, shelled, dried and frozen; and following them leaves – clogging, toxic leaves, falling till late June. Not to mention rats! Cats and Coumadin, Frank found, were no match for walnut-hungry rats.

But, what a tree! What would they have been without it? It was the walnut after all, which had prompted Frank and Milly to raise their bid. Had he even looked inside? he wondered. How long ago was that? Over forty years? When the tree itself was well past half a century and far too large to climb. Like everything familiar it seemed not to have changed, but photographs begged to differ. One large bough overhanging the roof (which Milly subsequently cured and fashioned into a bent man with a bullet in its head), had had to be sacrificed, but the rest was left to the elements. In summer it offered filtered shade and an avian perch – in winter, a lattice for the moon, but mostly its offering was its faithfulness and mystery. At Jane's wedding it came into its own.

As someone who had transcended the confines of nationhood, she had talked of marrying in Baja, Mexico, in America, in Istanbul – even Guatemala, but Milly and Frank received an overseas call one weekend with a decision that settled the issue and seemed so obvious: "Would it be okay if Phil and I married under the walnut tree?" And, on a brilliant afternoon in late December, fifty guests drawn from almost every continent on Earth assembled in front of where Frank and Emma were sitting. Frank recalled the summons of the theremin that linked parents and daughter and led them through a garden in its prime to this very spot, where the ceremony took place. It was the walnut that bore witness, though, not only of the ceremony, but also of the celebration that continued deep into the night. Their hired Macedonian band, which had travelled down from Auckland, refused to lay down their guitars, and a paternal aunt broke her arm while dancing.

The trunk had been adorned in an apron of laced light for the night of the wedding, and its might concealed, but now the girth was unashamedly exposed – monumental and unmoving – an ageless sentry. To Frank this strength was most apparent when it was naked, in winter, when he and Milly would sit around a brazier sipping wine – watching white smoke ascending.

> *Like ice against enamel*
> *the wood coal squeaks*

as xylem splits and phloem
spits out fat-hot sap.
And smoke – the alluring
fume – curls unmolested
into spirits, not all solemn,
but no one speaks.

Up then, up the lichen-
smothered trunk it creeps,
smudging one by one
the witch-long walnut
digits, and licks them dry,
dry as tongue, eburnean
sculptures, not all solemn,
but no one speaks.

And further still, through
halted winter night, it seeks
to filter constellations
that I know but cannot
name, primal/parent smoke,
the burning eyes of children's
hope, not all solemn,
but no one speaks.

Conscious of the deepening cold for the first time, Frank turned to get up. Emma had moved and was lying with just her nose protruding from the door. "Come on, old girl. Time for bed."

Prior to calling Evan in, Frank made a quick scan of clinical notes dating back to before Kevin's stroke. The brief on his appointment palette read, 'Requesting a consultation about his father'. In Frank's experience these encounters were usually cordial and complementary to patient care – a concern around a deterioration in driving skill or a worrying symptom not divulged – but occasionally they provided a platform for inquisition or unreasonable demand. He liked to be prepared.

Frank recognised Evan when he called him from the waiting room, and it was immediately apparent from his awkwardness that he posed no threat. "Would you mind if my wife came in with me?" he asked quietly.

"Of course not. Evan is it?" holding out a hand.

"Yes, thank you."

The wife appeared more confident than the husband, and she introduced herself with a smile: "Angela."

"Hi, Angela … and the little lady?"

"Joey."

"Hi, Joey. Come on in."

Frank ushered them onto two seats, before sitting himself. The infant arched and began to cry. Evan glanced across anxiously. "I'm sorry."

"Don't be silly. Babies don't bother me a bit."

Angela was trying to stifle Joey's cry with a dummy. "Maybe you should take her out," Evan murmured tensely.

Frank put out a hand and touched his arm. "Joey's fine, Evan … honestly," then added after a pause, "You're worried about your dad? What is it? Is he in pain … getting worse?"

Evan shook his head. He was finding it difficult to speak. Angela intervened. "Would you like me to explain, Evan?"

He shook his head but didn't look up. "It's my mum." The noise of a squeaking dummy filled a pause.

"Your mum? Is she finding it difficult to cope? Is it your mum that you're worried about?"

Evan shook his head again, then glanced despairing at Angela.

Holding the infant with one arm, she reached over to squeeze her husband's hand, and then turned to Frank. "We weren't sure whether to come … whether it was appropriate … but we are worried."

"Worried?"

"There are issues," she added, "things that we've noticed. We're not sure," she continued after a pause, "that Evan's mum is looking after his dad that well."

"I see," Frank replied quietly. "She's under enormous pressure."

"They've never got on – never." Evan had found his voice. "But now it's worse."

"What do you mean, Evan?" Frank asked quietly. "Has she made threats? Has she ever hurt him?"

"No." There was a further pause before Evan continued. "He wasn't the best husband, not when I think about it."

"Was he abusive?"

"Not physically, no … I don't think so. But she was afraid of him."

"And now?"

"Now she can do what she likes."

"And you worry that she might harm him?"

"I don't know. She wouldn't harm him physically by … by hitting him or anything. My mum's not violent," he added quickly, "but … she might not keep him safe." Frank sat quietly, waiting for Evan to continue. "She's away this week, in Australia, and we've noticed things … unwashed clothes in his drawers … dust under the bed … his nails, hair. He was smelling when she left … and his meals."

"Meals?"

"He needs help to eat," Angela said quietly, "because of the weakness – the difficulty that he has swallowing. We're not sure that Carol makes it easy."

"What do you mean?"

Angela looked across at Evan. "They don't eat together generally, and a couple of times when I've gone across at mealtimes Kevin's been struggling."

"Struggling?"

"His tray had been placed out of reach, or his meat hasn't been cut up. And now," she added, "now that he's eating with us, he's seemed quite ravenous."

"Is he losing weight?"

"No, no, I don't think so, but he's given a lot of sugary snacks."

"But Kevin's diabetic?"

"Yes."

"Is he given his regular medication?"

"We think so … we don't know."

"Can you communicate with him?"

"Sort of," Evan interjected. "Ange understands him better than me. She's a nurse."

"Has he raised any concerns?"

"Not really, but he's seemed happier and more settled since Mum's been away."

Frank sat quietly for a moment, and then asked, "I understand that you all live together?"

"Not really, the house is divided. Mum and Dad live independently in one half."

"I see, and your father couldn't move in with you?"

"No, not with Joey. There isn't space."

"And you work, Angela?"

"Not yet, not with Joey, but I'm starting part-time work at the hospital in June."

"Do you think it would help if your Carol employed someone to assist her with his personal cares? I don't think that the state would pay, unfortunately, because of his assets, but it might take the pressure off."

"Possibly, although we've suggested that ourselves in the past, and it hasn't gone down well." Angela paused, before continuing, "I can do more … oversee his medication and meals too if Carol will let me, but … it's her manner, doctor … the cruelty that really worries us, and we can't be watching things 24/7."

"No."

Evan's head was still bowed, and his eyes were focused on a pattern in Frank's carpet when he resumed speaking. "It's not her fault, doctor. My mother's a good person. She adores Joey. She's good to us, to everyone really, except my dad." The infant was asleep now, and the only sound was that of her even breathing. "Mum's life had been hard with him, and in some ways it's even harder now. She came alive when he was in the rest home. I worry about her as much as I do him." He looked up and directly at Frank: "I just don't know what to do."

There was nothing in the demeanour of the pair facing him that raised suspicions of inauthenticity or self-interest. Quite the opposite, in fact! Their anguish was obvious, and Evan's eyes said it all; but Frank had been put on notice. It was likely that his patient was being neglected – possibly harmed – but what was to be done? He had often been confronted by the 'soft cruelty' of resentment arising out of an end-of-life mismatch, and physical separation (not always possible) had offered the only solution. Before suggesting that, however, he responded, intuitively, to Evan's appeal: "You're doing all you can, Evan. Both of you are. Most children would simply walk away, make a life somewhere else, send flowers on Mother's Day, and no one could question their right to do that; but you are burdened with the gift of kind-ness – the greatest gift of all – and your parents are very fortunate indeed." He paused. There were three patients waiting to see him.

"Your brother, Evan, the one who lives in Australia?"

"Stewart?"

"Would your mother consider living with him? … at least for a while? … until something can be put in place?"

Evan gave a short laugh, before answering "No".

"And you wouldn't want your father moved back to the rest home?"

"No, we've thought of that, but no, not now – not unless he gets worse – has another stroke or something. He really would hate that, and it would be very expensive. It might mean us having to sell the house."

"Would you like me to speak with your mother?" Frank thought that it might be useful to gauge for himself the level of animosity and the threat that it imposed, to mediate a de-escalation. "Or ask her own doctor to see her? There might be an element of depression, or ..." But this suggestion was promptly rejected.

It was finally decided that Frank would make a prearranged house call on the pretext that it was an annual service that was routine for patients, post-stroke. He would ask Rae, his practice nurse, to accompany him. He wasn't sure what the visit would achieve, but the hope was it would put Carol on notice that there was going to be a higher level of professional scrutiny with respect to her husband's care.

Frank leaned back in his chair after the pair had left with their child. He glanced over to his shuttered window. It was small and hadn't been opened for years – perhaps it couldn't be – but ... but his scooter was parked on the other side! They could take off, the TGB and he, with a book and a packet of almonds. They could find an unoccupied bench at the river end of Hamilton Gardens, and read ... sketch comments in the margins ... stretch the day!

But his bladder brought him back to earth. Three patients were waiting to be seen, and one, a ninety-four-year old, had been sent down by rest-home transport with shortness of breath, leg ulcers and fatigue. The option for the receptionists had been either to wedge her in between two octogenarians as a double booking as they had done, or have Frank see her at the rest home after work.

Frank and Milly had settled friendships dating back, on both sides, to school days, to their university years in Dunedin, and to their over forty years of living in Hamilton. Some friendships waned due to geographical separation (a relative concept in New Zealand), some due to a breakdown in the collective through marriage, divergence or divorce – even the occasional premature death – but most endured and offered them an under-appreciated asset, a familiarity and comfort generated by decades of inter-secting experience. They had family within reach too – siblings, cousins, Milly's elderly aunt in Tauranga, nephews, and nieces – Jane down in Wellington – and each added cushion to what was to come.

Conversation had necessarily metamorphosed over time, but in the past several years preoccupations had naturally shifted from jobs, pairings, offspring and pets, to grandchildren, travel, ailments and infirmity. Everyone had an ache! Whether or not to downsize was the current obsession – whether to move to 'single level' with a lawn that others could mow; but most were stridently opposed, 'over my dead body', to a shift into a retirement village. Their opposition was understandable because the temptation was so great. Advertisements were offering everlasting purpose, peace and security, and enticements in the form of glossy brochures were slipping past the 'NO JUNK MAIL' stickers on their letter boxes, in pop-ups online, in posters, television clips and lavish on-site open homes. All featured a caricature of geriatric serenity – a silver-haired couple with perfect teeth sporting the smug smiles of post-coital bliss.

Apart from the submerged automatic sprinklers, the fellowship hall, the lap pool and gymnasium, the visiting Pilates teacher, the men's shed and mobile hairdresser, small print promised security cameras, electric fences and frail care. (Assurances were added in whispers to the less decrepit spouse that the essential emergency services of ambulance, doctor and funeral director had twenty-four-hour access to confidential entry codes.) What was in the smallest print of all, however, print that only a developer or real estate agent was young enough to read, was the cost; and what became apparent as their evenings with friends progressed was that many had made enquiries – tentative and only out of interest, of course – about this very consideration.

In the past there had been no need to shepherd the elderly into comfort camps. They had remained tethered to the family, however tenuously, and they had continued to contribute through nuisance or knowhow until their demise. But demographic imperatives, occupational and geographical mobility, family contraction, and the expectation of disengagement from life's tribulations that had been driven by the baby-boomers' accumulation of easy wealth, drove the transformation. Developers, financiers and famous sportspeople saw the opportunity for 'substantial returns' – how can you lose when your dividend is dependent upon the death of the dying? – and the transformation became inevitable.

Frank found himself spending more and more time visiting ailing patients in these villages, and while most kept their gates open during weekdays, access codes were necessary at night and over weekends. One fine, windless Sunday while he and Milly were out in the garden, Frank received news that a patient had died at a nearby village. His car was blocked by branch cuttings, and so, to save time, he decided to take his TGB scooter – a black-and-white Taiwanese equivalent of the Italian Vespa. Frank had his code book on hand, and entry was easy, but exit was another story!

After the 'good death' of an elderly patient there was as much relief as sadness, but the round of commiserations, the confirmation of cardio-respiratory cessation, and the formal completion of a death certificate always left Frank with a feeling of displacement when he emerged into the everyday outside. Consequently he was perplexed when the security gate did not open automatically as it usually did when he approached. He waited, wondering whether they had installed a delay. He walked his scooter back, and then approached again. He dismounted, became animated and waved. 'Could there have been a power failure?' he wondered, but lights in the rest home remained burning. He was becoming agitated now … just wanting to get home … back into the garden. 'Should I call for help? But it's Sunday. No one who can help works on Sunday!' He finally realised that it may have been the scooter, that it was too small to trigger a response, and that the only means of escape was to scale the gate, plug in the code on the other side, and then hope that he had enough time to collect his scooter without it, or him, being crushed. Frank briefly toyed with the idea of asking a grieving relative to 'let him out' by triggering the mechanism with their vehicle, but he quickly dismissed the request as insensitive.

It was time to act, and so, bedecked in oversized helmet, black gloves and fluorescent jacket, Frank hauled himself longitudinally over the mercifully spike-free upper bar of the gate and half-landed, half-collapsed onto the other side. He was about to punch in the code when he realised to his annoyance that the code book was not on his person. Agitation removed all semblance of memory and so his only option was to repeat his ascent of the gate and then repeat it again with the code book zipped into his jacket pocket. Finally, and clammy with sweat, he was able to enter the code, pause while the gate slid open, and then hurry his scooter through the gap.

Frank decided to rest for a moment, to collect himself before spluttering home on his 49ccs, but his reverie was disturbed by the sudden squealing of tyres as a police vehicle made a U-turn to pull up alongside him. The officer, a young man with a feeble beard and a flat hat, leapt out of his vehicle and approached Frank menacingly. "What the hell are you up to?" he demanded.

"Sorry?" Frank's voice was muffled by his visor.

"What? Speak up!" he shouted, before demanding, through explicit hand movements, that Frank remove his helmet.

Frank had difficulty taking his helmet off at the best of times. It had a release button which was difficult to locate with gloves. But, after mangling his glasses, he eventually managed to prise it off. "I'm sorry. Hello."

The policeman was clearly surprised by the age of his 'snatch and run' suspect, and there was a pause before he managed to ask, "What were you up to?"

"Up to?"

"Climbing over the gate. Getting out."

"Sorry … no … I'm a doctor. A patient has just died."

A look of incredulity passed over the policeman's face. "A doctor?"

"I'm afraid so, yes."

The policeman stared at Frank for a full minute, then glanced over at a plastic toolbox that was strapped to the back of his scooter. "What's in that box?"

"My instruments … drugs … that sort of thing."

"Open it."

By now traffic was banking up with people peering out of their windows as they passed this curious scene. Frank hoped that none recognised him as he undid the box's support straps and handed it over to the policeman. "Please be careful of the used needles. I store them in a Gaviscon tube before disposal."

The policeman eyed Frank for a moment, and then glanced down. A new battery-enhanced stethoscope lay on top of the box. It straddled an upper tray holding plastic containers, as well as the empty (apart from used needles) tube of Gaviscon. The policeman lifted the tray gingerly, but barely looked underneath. He stood up and faced Frank squarely. 'You seem to be a doctor,' he might have said, 'but not one that I would go within spitting distance of.' He said not another word, however, before shaking his head, getting back into his car, and driving off.

Frank wondered whether he was strong enough to ride home. He felt a great weight pressing down upon his chest and shoulders, as if he were a moon-man landed on Earth, as if he were the age of Methuselah – as if he had been compressed into something amorphous and minute. Was it just the humiliation, he wondered, the mumbling incoherence of his abject capitulation to interrogation by a superior minor? Or was it something more? Did he still have it in him? This doctor thing? He looked back through the gates to the manicured lawns and trimmed hedges, to the alternating postings of standard rose and nondescript shrub; he looked further, to the hospital wing, where a daughter was still folding clothes; and, finally, he looked down at his scooter, to make sure that he had not lost his keys.

When he next met up with his friends, he told his story about the gate, and they all laughed. They laughed too when he said that these prototypes of Elysium gave him the creeps, that they had no soul, that they resembled cemeteries; but he noticed that Milly did not laugh, and that she was quiet when they washed the dishes.

Edith, Eleanor, and Frank gathered early for a clinical meeting every second Thursday, and there was an open invitation extended to Tom Bentley, a colleague who worked nearby and alone, to join them. His attendance, Frank teased, depended upon wind direction: "You only turn up when an easterly's blowing, Tommy, when the aroma of Edith's coffee reaches you."

"True, Frank. Absolutely true."

Edith was serious about her coffee. She used nothing but Colombian Arabica – "Robusta's too bitter" – and had her beans couriered down from Auckland. Each brew was freshly ground and percolated in her battered heirloom on a hot plate. Frank, as he filled his warm roll with salted butter, maintained that he had read somewhere, or that he had been told by someone, that smell trumped taste. "Coffee, apparently," he declared, "is physiologically incapable of tasting as good as it smells. You are a witch, Edith," he added. "You are an aromatic alchemist."

The meetings had been a tradition in the practice for many years, but Frank could not recall a time when he had appreciated them more. Eleanor, arriving only a year prior, had filled a gap that he didn't know was missing. The meetings were ostensibly arranged to fulfil one of their professional body's requirements, the maintenance of competency through peer review, and they provided an opportunity for self-evaluation – an opportunity to compare and refine their approaches to a myriad of clinical permutations. But this group offered so much more: it offered through its diversity, congeniality and absence of ego, a safe zone where doubts, difficulties and dilemmas could be openly expressed, where unease, inadequacy, regret and indecision could be offered context through advice and support. The unspoken objective was for each to walk out and into their consulting rooms unburdened.

There was no formality placed on proceedings, but they seldom meandered because each could 'read' the need of the other, and priority was assigned without prompting. Eleanor, for example, remained silent when she needed to speak, when there was something troubling her, while Tom shuffled and Edith flicked her fringe; but Frank was the most transparent – he pitched in before they had had time to sit down.

"I have a difficult situation. Not sure what to do."

"What is it, Frank?"

"A patient of yours, Edith, or she might be seeing Eleanor now." They waited. "Her husband is a patient of mine. A chap in his seventies who has had a stroke. Sad, really, he's pretty much an invalid." He paused, sipping at his coffee. "Pretty much dependent upon his wife. The problem," he added slowly, "is that she might be abusing him … might be posing a risk."

"Physically?"

"Maybe, Tom, I don't know, but certainly through neglect."

"How do you know? Bruising? Loss of weight?"

"No, he's actually gained weight. A lot of weight, and that might be part of the neglect. He's a diabetic. No, the son came to see me."

Frank went on to explain the consultation with Evan and Angela – how awkward it was for the son. "He found it very difficult … didn't seem the type to cause trouble … to be after anything for himself. My impression was that he was genuinely worried, about both parents. He put me on notice though," he said looking at each in turn, "and I'm not quite sure how best to respond."

"Would the son be happy for you to speak to the mother?" Tom asked.

"Not about his concerns, not directly – definitely not."

"That's difficult. Not fair really. It's usually the overseas relative who passes the buck."

"I didn't get the impression that the son was doing that though, Tom. There was anguish there. Real concern. I felt that he might need help too."

There was a moment of silence as they sipped their coffee, and then Eleanor spoke quietly: "I'm pretty sure I know who you're talking about, Frank." He looked at her and waited. "The problem goes way back, way before the stroke." She turned to Edith: "You dealt with a lot of that, Edith, and I've discussed her with you."

"Oh, yes. The patient who's working at the pharmacy now?"

"Yes."

"Mm. I thought that the stroke, his disempowerment, might have helped."

"I thought so too."

"What's the background?" Frank enquired.

"A life of old-fashioned servitude really," Edith continued. "A life that he controlled from day one. She was effectively his vassal, his thing, but although she was outwardly compliant and submissive, she seethed inside. I often worried about that."

"About what, Edith?"

"Her hatred. Her bitterness. She clung to them. Wouldn't let go. I've never seen anything like it. I advised her many times to leave, to find another life, to get counselling, to take medication; but she wouldn't budge. I gave up in the end. Thank goodness she moved to you, Eleanor," she said, and then added, "Maybe she feels even more trapped now that he's had a stroke – feels morally bound."

The morning light was behind Tom, obscuring his face as he spoke. "Caring can be hell. I've seen Parkinson's, dementia, and, of course, stroke destroy many a love bond in my time."

"That's true," Eleanor interjected, "but I'm afraid that this might be different."

"In what way, El?"

"I saw her soon after her husband had had a stroke, and she was buoyant. He was, it's true, still in a rest home convalescing at that time, but she was excited about new living arrangements, about a first grandchild, a dog, and, as it turned out, a first job. But," she added more thoughtfully, cupping her mug in two hands as if it were winter, "it was her triumphalism that worried me."

"You're suggesting?"

"Not sure."

"An opportunity for revenge?"

"Possibly."

"Then I'd better do something." Frank paused before continuing, "I've made a tentative arrangement to make a home visit with Rae on the pretext that it's routine for stroke patients."

"Has the patient himself raised concerns, Frank? Is he able to?"

"Not directly, Tom. Communication's limited, but the son did say that his father appeared happier when his wife was away on holiday in Australia."

"And the option of permanent placement in a rest home?"

"Not something that the son wanted to consider at this stage. His father's done surprisingly well with rehab and returning home was a major motivation. There could also be a financial impediment."

As a collective they decided that the best way forward was for Frank to undertake the visit, to check on drug dispensing protocols and personal care, to look for signs of physical abuse, to open the door for the wife to discuss difficulties, and to attempt to communicate in confidence with the patient himself.

Arrangements were made for Frank and Rae to make their call early in the afternoon on a day when Carol worked mornings. A white wooden gate had been left open for them revealing the fading remnants of a summer garden as well as a westerly view of Pirongia. Frank stopped to take stock. He had expected a 'tidy' garden with concrete borders and low-maintenance shrubs, but instead it was a jumble of spent annuals, old roses, still-flowering geraniums, unruly nasturtiums, and interesting ground cover intertwined with sage, parsley, and thyme. Up against the fence looking out towards the road, however, were what really caught his eye … drying giant sunflower heads jam-packed with seed.

The front door opened, and a dog ran out to meet them. "Alice!" the lady Frank recognised as Kevin's wife called out. "Alice, come back here. Sorry about that. She's still young." To the side, and next to the conservatory, stood an impressive mobility scooter sporting a New Zealand flag.

"She's adorable," Rae shouted back.

Frank patted the white wagging dog before holding out his

hand with a smile. "Hello, Carol, good to see you again. I'm Frank, and you know Rae."

"Yes," she answered stiffly. "Come in. Kevin's in his bedroom."

Frank glanced back as he advanced towards the door. "What a beautiful garden and home you have, Carol. Those sunflowers must have been something?"

"They've turned a few heads, that's true."

"Do you harvest the seeds?"

"Yes, I do actually. Some of them at least."

Frank stood for a moment longer, looking back, with the dog nuzzling his leg.

"Sorry. She was supposed to be out the back."

"Not at all, Carol. I've got one of my own. She's a real sweetie."

It could have been the garden, or it could have been the dog, it might even have been Edith and Eleanor's account of Carol's diminished life with Kevin, but much to his surprise Frank felt 'connected' to Carol in a not unsympathetic way. 'Could someone who grows giant sunflowers be capable of cruelty?' he wondered.

Kevin was sitting next to his bed in his wheelchair when they walked in. There was enough natural and lamp light to see that he had put on quite a bit of weight, but his face was a healthy bronze. "Do you get out into your lovely garden much, Kevin?" he asked by way of introduction. The response of Kevin's head was a yes/no.

"He spends hours outside at the gate. Watches the world go by."

"Excellent, Kevin," Frank commented, and then asked whether he could briefly check his heart, pulses, chest, blood pressure and abdomen. "Rae will undo your shirt buttons if you don't mind and roll up your sleeves. Your blood sugar's up a bit, I noticed, Kevin." In response Kevin merely stared – his one eye more prominent than the other. "Could I have a look at Kevin's medication packaging, Carol? We might have to tweak things a bit."

Kevin's medication was packaged for ready use in sealed strips by the pharmacist, and clearly labelled with instructions for dispensing. He noticed that some evening doses (and occasionally whole days) had not been taken, but said nothing. The room itself smelled of detergent. There were no signs of bruising, burns or punctures on Kevin's skin, and there was no odour of neglect beyond the faint smell of urine. His hair, though, could have done with a wash and a trim.

"Rae, would you mind going over Kevin's diabetic stuff with Carol? Take the medications with you. See if the two of you can come up with anything in the diet that would help. Insulin is an option, but if we could carry on getting away with tablets it would be easier."

"Sure. You okay with that, Carol?"

"Um, yes, but what have you got left to do with Kevin?"

"Reflexes, muscle weakness … that sort of thing."

"He barely speaks."

"But you can nudge and wink, can't you, Kevin?" Frank joked. "You carry on. I won't be long here."

After Rae and Carol had moved out and into the conservatory, Frank turned to Kevin. "This room is a lot nicer than the rest-home one, Kevin. You seem comfortable here?"

Kevin's head wobbled rather than nodded as he attempted to vocalise a barely decipherable "It's okay" after meeting Frank's eyes with the unfiltered, unabashed stare of the helpless or danger-ously ill – a stare that can be unnerving, but one which Frank took as an invitation to engage.

"Would you like to use the pointer board, Kevin? It might be less tiring than talking." He nodded. "Excellent. Are you comfortable? No pain?" The letters N O were fingered in response with his useful hand. S E P T S K I N. "You have a rash?" He nodded, then gestured towards his opposing armpit. "Can I have a look?" Kevin lifted his good arm, and, after loosening his shirt and vest Frank noted what must have been a very itchy candida rash affecting both sides. This was common in diabetics, especially if they were overweight, and it often involved other intertriginous zones. "What about down below? Mind if I check?" With Kevin sitting in the wheelchair this was more awkward to confirm. Frank thought of calling for Rae to help, but then thought better of it. Carol would be sure to come through too.

"This must be driving you nuts, Kevin." Nod. "Easily fixed though, with cream. We'll also have to make sure that Carol dries you there after showering. She does the showering doesn't she?" S U M T I M E S. Frank waited. S U M T I M E S A N G. "Your daughter-in-law?" Nod. "She must be a big help?" Further nod.

After buttoning up Kevin's clothes Frank was more direct: "Are you happy with this arrangement, with the division of the house … living as you do?" S O K "Better than the rest home, I'm sure?" Nod. And then he became more direct still: "Is Carol managing all right? You don't think she needs help?" N O "She doesn't get impatient sometimes?" M A Y B. And finally, "You don't get frightened at all? Feel unsafe?" Kevin stared at him. "Nothing you want to tell me … something that I can try to help you with?" N O, hesitation … S E P T S P E N D S 2 M U C H, then added, M Y M O N E Y. Frank smiled, but then checked his smile. The asymmetrical eyes had ice in them. "I see."

He rose slowly. "I'll see what we can do about the diabetes, Kevin, and of course the rash. Maybe visit you again in a couple of months, or you could come over to the surgery on your mobility scooter. Anytime though, just get Carol, or your son, Evan, to let us know." Faint nod.

The conservatory had a tiled floor and raw wood walls, and they were stacked and hung with pot plants – mainly bromeliads and ferns. He noticed that there was easy wheelchair access, but little room inside. Carol remained stiff and defensive but appeared amenable to the changes suggested around diabetic medication and diet. She appeared less attentive, though, when he requested that she use a hairdryer on Kevin's fungal-infested nether regions following a shower.

His parting comment as they stepped out of the conservatory was, "It must be tough for you, Carol. Let us know if there's anything that we can do to help."

"It's fine," she replied curtly.

QUINCE

Quince had not read Goethe. The name was familiar – he had heard it connected to a play called *Faust* – but he had not heard of another of the author's creations, that of Werther, the prototype of a young man smitten. It was as well that he hadn't, because there were recognisable parallels in their respective states of mind, and things did not end well for Werther (as the title of the novel in which he features, *The Sorrows of Young Werther*, broadly hinted). But, although the recognised parallels included longing, rapture, preoccupation, and consuming doubt, they diverged when situations were compared. For one thing Quince had age on his side, and age acts as a buffer. For another, Werther made the mistake of falling for someone he couldn't live without despite knowing, before he had fallen, that he would have to, while Quince had fallen for someone who had, at the very least, reciprocated an interest. His instinct was to run – avoidance, deflection and buffoonery had served him well in the past – but, but he couldn't get Eleanor out of his mind.

Like Werther, Quince was at one moment forlorn, the next elated, dissecting every gesture that he could recall, every word, as proof of interest or disdain. Her laugh, especially her laugh, and the flash of tear and tooth that her laugh revealed, made his pulse jump because he, Quince, had provoked it. Their meeting at the market had gone well too, surprisingly so. Perhaps it was the unexpectedness of the encounter and Eleanor's initial vulnerability (the presence of the children and the old lady had certainly helped), but he had managed to be … himself.

But what, really, did he have to offer? She was younger, a doctor, financially secure and lovely. She could choose if she wished a heart specialist, a brain specialist, a famous musician – even a widowed, wealthy businessman who exercised and took his staff to Fiji every year. A lawyer was unlikely, certainly not one like Derek, but a prosecutor in the mould of a middle-aged Robert Swan Mueller? Absolutely! But were they the people she was looking for? Was she looking for anyone? And Eleanor had her son, Harry. What a smart and happy boy he was. How amazing it would be to be a part of his life. But not everyone would see it that way. The brain surgeon might see him as an impediment – the musician too. Hope rose as Quince remembered their game of cricket – how natural it felt.

But then he doubled back again, to himself: a man in his mid-forties without an occupation or an interest – greying, balding, sagging – a waste of a man. It was absurd to even entertain the hope that she would find him attractive. Like? Yes. Most people 'liked' him – there wasn't enough substance to dislike – but he couldn't, he realised, settle for friendship alone. For the first time in his life Quince experienced jealousy: he was jealous of Harry's dead father, jealous of the imagined heart surgeon, and jealous, even, of Frank, his doctor, who worked in the same building as she did. He found himself in puerile contemplation of driving by to see if she was home, to see if fancy cars were parked outside, and he found himself staring more critically at his mirror. What kept playing over and over in his head, however, were Frank's words:

"go and find someone you can't do without, someone who could break your big, beautiful heart." Eleanor had appeared after these words like a glorious apparition, had appeared after he had had time to absorb and reformulate them into a commitment to himself – but what now? Was he up to the challenge and the enormous risks that the challenge posed? He was not sure.

They had exchanged telephone numbers, and hers had been locked into his list of contacts at the first opportunity. All it would take was a contact search followed by the soft press of an index finger, but what would he say? There would have to be a reason for ringing, and how would she respond? "Hello, sorry, who?" It would have to be an invitation, but to what, or where? Dinner might be awkward, just the two of them sharing fish starters – choosing a main that would stick in his teeth. A movie at the Tivoli – taking wine to their seats – might be a better option, but what would they see? 'Films don't hold back these days!' And if they sat in the dark, would he take her hand? Would he take that risk?

Pound, he realised, was restless. Quince had wasted half the morning in silly reverie, and it was time to move. After his talk with Frank, but before the upheaval of Eleanor, he had determined that he would travel for a couple of months, in Australia, to find himself. Plans were somewhat vague but purposefully bold. He would fly to Perth, he thought, and then, because Frank said that he should make himself uncomfortable, he would wend his way to Darwin, where snakes, storms and crocodiles should do the trick. But would that be a bad move now? Would he miss his chance? Did he have the funds? He had never, in the past, had to worry about funds.

Quince's spending could not be called extravagant and his instinct was to abhor waste, but if the deep freeze broke down, if he wanted to upgrade his utility, if an investigation of his entrails was advised … he never thought twice. His accountant, however, was starting to sound a note of caution. "You have more capital than most people, Quince, but interest rates have dropped to almost nothing, and your capital won't last for ever."

"And shares, Ethel, don't I have shares?"

"You do, Quince, in your portfolio, both overseas and local, but they're only worth what you sell them for, and they don't earn much."

"Earn?"

"Income. They don't generate much income, and most of the work that you've done in recent years has been voluntary," she added.

"I can't charge the Maungatautari Trust."

"I know, that's a noble project, Quince. It's good that you contribute. I'm not saying that you're idle, but …"

"But I need to be more productive?"

"Yes, you need a regular income."

He had to find something to do. It was obvious to Quince. The exasperation of his doctor, his accountant, even of his older sister, were nagging at his conscience, but so was an upwelling of disgust. Walking out onto his patio with its sweeping views over the northern slopes of Maungatautari, with a frantic Pound scratching and whining in frustration, he came up with an idea: 'I will grow something, here, in greenhouses if I have to. Flowers? Probably flowers.' The eye of the sunflower was still fresh in his mind. 'Or parsley?' He had heard that parsley was profitable; and it was parsley, as much as Eleanor and Australia, that were on his mind as Pound led him down and across the farm paddocks to Pansy.

But it was mushrooms – *Agaricus bisporus*, to be more specific – that was on his mind when he walked back. Pansy was, and always had been, his confidante, an older sister who had substituted for his mother in many respects, and his intention was to lay out before her the pieces of his puzzled mind – have her identify the corners of the jigsaw and work in from there. But it was Terry, Pansy's husband, whom he encountered after striding in unannounced.

"Oh! Terry! Sorry, I thought you'd be out on the farm."

"Weather's too good to be outside, Quincy." Terry never missed an opportunity to joke. "How're you doing?"

"Good thanks, Terry, good. Is Pansy about?"

"Nope, she up in Auckland. Won't be home till tomorrow. What can I do you for?"

"Nothing really." Quince was only too well aware that Terry could be a difficult man to extricate himself from once he got talking about 'the dollar', the All Blacks, 'suburban creep' and national politics, but he was, after all, family.

"Cuppa tea?"

"Um, yes, thanks, Terry. Just a quick one."

They joined Bill and Pound out on the porch. Pansy's rock and rose gardens, established by their mother, were in autumn fade, but still quite lovely, and it wasn't altogether unpleasant having to have tea with Terry.

"You know anything about parsley, Terry?"

"Parsley?"

"Yes."

"To eat?" Terry was a meat and three veg man.

"No, to grow … commercially. I heard that there was a good return on parsley, especially in winter."

"You talking greenhouses?"

"Yes."

"Set-up can be pricey, Quincy."

The word combination and intonation grated, and the habit that Terry had of 'y' for 'e' substitution was a perpetual irritant. "Well, no, maybe." Quince paused before continuing, "I need to do something, Terry. Parsley seemed sensible but I thought of flowers too … fresh flowers."

"Mug's game, Quincy. Too seasonal, too many bugs. Too dollar-dependent." But then, between sips, he said, "Thought about mushrooms?"

"Mushrooms? No." Terry tantalised him by remaining silent as he sipped. "Why mushrooms?"

"Cos they grow like bloody mushrooms."

Quince forced a half-smile. "I suppose they do."

"Seriously, Quincy my boy, if you're going to have a go at anything on that little mound of yours, it'll have to be all year. Mushies might just do the trick. They don't care a stuff about global warming, and they don't even need the sun." Terry really had captured Quince's attention now. "Thought of doing it myself, but I've got enough on my plate."

"You think it could be viable?"

"Absolutely. Couple of greenhouses out the back and Bob's your aunty. I heard a talk at Rebus last month by a joker from the Commercial Mushroom Growers Federation," he continued. "That's where the idea came up. Got to take some of what those fellas say with a pinch of snot, but this joker did make sense. It's a high yield all year and the greenies eat more of them with their chopsticks than they do peanuts. It'll take a bit of work up front, Quincy," he added, "but once you're smooth and running you'll rake in the coppers. Another cuppa?" he asked after a triumphant pause.

"I might do, yes. Thanks, Terry. Thanks very much." But then he stood, his eyes staring nowhere. "Actually no, thanks, Terry. I might get home and see what I can find."

Terry laughed. "Don't forget the old saying, Quincy: 'Don't sign a bog-roll till you've crossed the t's and dotted the i's.'"

"I'll remember that, Terry."

"Call me any time."

"Will do."

Quince had summoned Pound and was about to step off the porch when Terry asked, "Who're you picking for six?"

"Sorry?"

"Six … now that Squire has pulled out."

"Oh, not sure, Terry. For the World Cup?"

"What else?"

"Um, not sure really. What about Sam Cane?"

"He's a seven."

"Oh!"

"Needs to be a big bastard. Have you seen the South African loosies?"

"No."

"They'd make Samson and his mates look like a midgets."

Quince found this genuinely funny, and he laughed. "Jeez, that's a worry."

"It's a worry all right."

***

It was fortunate that Baker came in with a dead mouse, because Quince had forgotten to feed poor Pound, and he only realised when the rodent was tossed out at ten o'clock that evening. By then he had decided on buttons, *Agaricus bisporus*, both fresh white and Swiss brown, and he had registered for an eight-lesson, hundred-hour course on mushroom production that would teach him the theory of everything that he needed to know to become a grower. The course would include an overview of edible mushroom history and variety, mushroom culture, spawning, beds, growing conditions (dependent upon greenhouse technology), pests and diseases, harvesting and storage, with marketing outlined at the end. Furthermore, he had formulated a list of greenhouse distributors in the greater Waikato region for contact the next day, and he had prepared an Excel spreadsheet in anticipation of cost listings.

Over the next few weeks his mind was preoccupied not only with wheat straw, chicken manure, gypsum, pasteurisation, spawn access, sites for levelling, and estimates of construction times and costs, but also, at Terry's insistence, on consultation with Ethel, his accountant, and Andrew, his lawyer. He made contact too, over this period, with the Commercial Mushroom Growers Federation and sent in an application for membership. The hours and days, which before had stretched out to infinity, now flashed by in an instant, and it became clear through the process that he would not be able to start production until the spring at the earliest.

Meanwhile his preoccupation with Eleanor did not disappear or even diminish during this period of frenetic activity; quite the contrary, she was the very driver of his tumbling mind. While Frank, Ethel and Pansy had pushed him, Eleanor, or the disconcerting feelings that he had for Eleanor, compelled him. He thought again and again of phoning her, but again and again he postponed his impulse. 'I need to complete the course, complete the survey – complete the costings before I contact her,' he decided. 'She needs to see what I am capable of.'

Pansy was amazed by his new-found drive and asked outright, "Have you found a woman?"

"What do you mean, 'found a woman'?" he laughed. "What has a woman to do with mushrooms? No, it was Terry who came up with the idea."

Pansy didn't argue – she simply pursed her lips.

Going away to Australia became a possibility again. By late April, Quince had completed every preparation possible, and a winter hiatus loomed. He had still not contacted Eleanor, nor she him, and he was beginning to look at undeclared infatuation as fantasy – an embarrassing and final farewell to youth – when his phone rang, and his heart flipped. There, staring at him, was a picture of Eleanor and Harry.

"Hello," he ventured tentatively, collecting himself while pretending not to be aware of who the caller was.

"Hello, Quince?"

"Yes, speaking."

"Hi, Quince, it's Eleanor Hutton. We met at the market a couple of months ago, and at Mary's before that."

"Yes, yes, of course, Eleanor. How are you?"

"Fine, we're good thank you, and you?"

"Fine."

"This is probably an imposition, Quince, but Harry is doing a project on trees, indigenous trees, and you'd mentioned your connections with Maungatautari." Quince remained silent. "You're probably too busy …"

"No, no," he interjected quickly, "just getting mushrooms going, but …"

"Mushrooms?"

"No, no, in a few months. Would you like me to take him up Maungatautari? Plenty of trees there."

"That would be absolutely lovely, Quince. He still talks about your cricket game," she added, laughing. "Would Saturday morning suit you? I'm working a shift at Anglesea After-hours Clinic on Sunday."

"No problem at all, Eleanor. Why don't we meet here, at my place? It overlooks the mountain."

"Perfect! But lunch is on us, in Hall Street."

Quince sat back – his brain stinging. 'It was just a call, a friendly call,' he cautioned, 'prompted by Harry.' But this was the contact that he had desired for months – an opportunity to see if she was real – and he had not bungled it.

Bonny was with him when Eleanor and Harry drove up, and both looked pleased to see her. Pound was the first to greet them, and he eased the adult awkwardness.

"Would you like to come in for a minute, for a coffee?" he offered.

"No, thanks, Quince. Thank you. We've just had breakfast."

He was happy to sense a note of nervousness. "Okay then, intrepid adventurers, follow me. We can go in my car."

"You sure?"

"Absolutely."

Although Maungatautari was geographically close, access required a good half-hour drive through quintessential Waikato farmland to its eastern entrance at Pukeatua. Bonny was the converser-in-chief. She'd traversed the route with Quince so many times that she was able to name not only the streams, creeks and hills along the way, but also an Australian harrier, or kahu, caught in a thermal above them and to their right.

Their first stop was at the visitor centre manned by elderly volunteers who Quince knew and chatted with. Bonny and Eleanor helped Harry collect pamphlets and maps that explained the concept and development of the Maungatautari project – the creation of an inland island sanctuary free of predators for the preservation of native animals and plants – and he added brief notes, in pencil, on his clipboard. They were hushed as they passed through the double-gated and electronically controlled entrance to the southern enclosure and remained quiet as they advanced along the tree fern bounded track.

Harry took his mother's hand. "Will we see a kiwi, Mum?" he whispered.

"Not in the day, darling. They only come out at night," she whispered back, "but there are plenty here, aren't there, Quince?"

"More all the time, Harry. They've got a very successful breeding programme going, one of the best in the country, and survival is excellent. There's nothing here that can harm them."

Quince was in his element now, surrounded by serenity, and he stood back as Bonny pointed out the most impressive of the reserve's many trees: totara, kahikatea, tawa, miro, rata, rewarewa, and, Harry's eventual favourite, a towering rimu, centuries old, that dominated the rest. The older pair watched and listened as Bonny and Harry took the lead, and this gave Quince the opportunity to whisper and point Eleanor towards a pair of fantails, or piwakawaka, flirting in a low-growing native fuchsia. Further down the hushed path he stopped briefly so that Eleanor could photograph a rengarenga lily framed in a backdrop of purple groundcover. Nikau palms, supplejack, kiekie, silver fern and orchids in the sub-canopy filled the in-between; but it was the tower that the kids loved most. The wooden structure, sixteen metres in height, shuddered as they climbed. Eleanor was concerned that the height and movement might frighten and deter Harry, but he, following the lead of Bonny, jumped to enhance the effect. From the top they laughed as they looked down on several kaka, North Island parrots, scrapping over reservoirs of ranger-delivered sugar water, and they became statues as a saddleback settled briefly just an arm away; but the highlight was to lie on their backs on the uppermost platform at Quince's insistence, remaining absolutely quiet while watching the interplay of canopy and clouds, and listening, intently, for the only sound in the world – that of bellbirds and breeze-blown leaves.

There was a comfortable silence on the way back, and an easy interchange at Quince's house. Eleanor did go inside, for a glass of water, and Quince did spend ten to fifteen minutes showing her the sites proposed for his two greenhouses, but what gratified him most was that he wasn't having to make an effort to be himself. Bonny needed to be home for lunch, and so he dropped her off before driving over the high-level bridge and into town. En route to Hall Street he called into a florist to buy a potted begonia.

Harry had a ball and bat out ready to play when he arrived, but they only managed a few overs before Whitey got the upper hand. "We can lock him inside later, Harry," his mother offered the exasperated Harry, "but it's time to eat now."

"Muuum!"

"Yes, come on." She laughed. "Your grandmother has made you your favourite. Would you like to wash your hands, Quince?" she added. "Whitey's slobber won't go down well. Show Quince where the bathroom is, please, sweetie, and wash your hands too."

It was a crisp but sunny autumn afternoon, and warm enough to sit outside. The boys had a quick game of cricket while the table was being cleared, and then Harry went inside for 'quiet time' and Marion retired to her flat.

Eleanor, somewhat dishevelled after her walk and the work of the wind, came out carrying a tea tray and sat down. She looked even more lovely than he had imagined over the months, and he was momentarily unsettled. 'Friendship,' he warned himself. 'All she could ever want with me is friendship.' But rusks restored his equilibrium. Instructed to dunk one of the large chunks of hard biscuit that she handed him, the inevitable occurred and a chunk fell from his chin with a splash. "Gotcha!" she exclaimed gleefully as he wiped his mouth, and her delight drew him perilously close to an attempted kiss. Fortunately and instead, he went on to enlarge upon his mushroom plan, but made no mention, initially, of Australia. This contact was what he had dreamed of, and he was in no mood to run away quite yet; but Eleanor, it seemed, had plans of her own.

Harry's father, she explained, had been Bwazian, and she had made a commitment to travel to the country as soon as she was able, as soon as Harry was old enough to remember; and the time was now.

"When are you leaving? And for how long?" he asked anxiously.

"Next month, and for four weeks. We'll be back in the second week of June."

"Is it safe?"

"I think so." Quince was quiet. "I don't want to take any chances. I won't," she added, "take any chances, but I owe it to Harry."

"Does he have relatives in Bwazi?"

"Only an aunt, as far as I know, but we won't be seeing her." Quince looked up and into her eyes. Their focus was miles beyond him, and it stayed there as she began to talk, to talk in a way that she had not to anyone else, not even to her mother, since Aaron's death. She spoke about her initial reluctance to go to Bwazi all those years ago, but of what she had gained through the experience. She spoke about Aaron, about his foster parents, Alec and Leah, about the bush, about Bulungani, about her unexpected pregnancy, and, finally, about Aaron's disappearance and its impact. "His sister may well have played a part in his death," she explained.

"Do you still miss him?" he asked in a whisper.

"Yes and no." Her eyes had shifted to Whitey now, who was begging for more biscuit. "But I barely knew him. Two weeks? How can you miss a man you've known for two weeks? By mythologising him?" She absentmindedly broke off a piece of rusk and held it to Whitey. "I certainly don't hurt any more, and I've forgiven him for dying; but I will never forget." She looked up and into the eyes of Quince before continuing, "I have Harry to remind me that it happened." He expected her eyes to reflect pain, but they were as tranquil as a subterranean pond.

They sat for a few minutes in easy silence, and he held back the hand that longed to hold hers. The sun had dipped, and it was starting to get cold. Eleanor shuddered briefly and smiled. "Would you like another cup of tea?" she asked, but the invitation lacked conviction.

"No, thank you, Eleanor. I must get back to Pound and Baker. They'll be hungry."

"Thank you for the walk, Quince."

"Pleasure."

"I … I'm sorry to have burdened you with all …"

"Don't be silly, Eleanor," he responded quickly, and then added, "You have quite a story there."

She laughed. "I suppose I do."

"Maybe I'll see you before you go."

"I hope so."

"I might be going to Australia."

"Really!" She looked taken aback.

"Just for a holiday … before I grow mushrooms."

"We'll be able to compare notes then, after our breaks."

"Absolutely! Bye."

"Bye, Quince."

Quince was aware that travelling to Perth would not have been foremost in Frank's mind when he had advised risk and provocation. For one thing, with sea on one side and sand on the other, it was a city that was impossible to get lost in. But he had to start somewhere, and, as Rosie had reminded him, Cousin Marcus would see him right. Marcus was a second cousin once removed on his mother's side – a naturalised Australian who had adjusted to the heat. He lived with his partner and two parrots near the airport, an area that was awash with laundromats, juice bars, glaziers, panel beaters, and, curiously, podiatrists. 'There must be a lot of feet in Perth,' was one of his first thoughts after arrival.

It transpired that he had little in common with his cousin, and, after two nights and a gruesome tour of the Fremantle prison, he travelled south in a hired, auburn Toyota Yaris in search of discomfort. Mandurah provided morning tea, Bunbury lunch, but it was Busselton, a seaside resort with the longest pier in the southern hemisphere, that provided his first oddity – an oddity in the form of a couple.

They were the owners of a bed and breakfast establishment who had enticed him into pre-booking by posting a photograph in their advertisement of what he imagined that he was looking for – a classical Australian homestead. It had a pale-green corrugated tin roof that curled over a long, cool veranda partly shaded by bougainvillea. As his GPS guided him closer, however, he found himself in an area of suburbia not dissimilar to that in which Marcus resided. The only difference was that each was enormous, and each sported a pale-green tin-roofed bungalow with a long, cool veranda. The suburb was new, and the tin a little shinier that it should have been.

His next surprise was that the owners were English and not Australian. He should not have been surprised because they had advertised a Devonshire tea on arrival, and, true to their word, they had him slumped in a deep wicker basket nibbling on his allotted blackberry jam and cream scone before he had had time to pee. They were elderly, argumentative, and conversed with a competitive intensity that left him with no opening for reply save the odd obligatory grunt. Adding to his difficulty was their (especially his) diction. It was quite impossible in the main to determine what the man was saying, and his teeth, Quince observed, appeared to be the cause. The kindest comment that one could make was that their assembly was somewhat disordered, but one could go further if one were honest and say that his tusks ignored the very rudiments of symmetrical assembly. And the effect? A disruption in jaw/palate/tongue/lip coordination that was so extreme that words, especially those containing the consonant 'S', had only a passable chance of deliverance in any comprehensible form.

Quince was eventually spared the humiliation of bladder breach, by choking. A scone crumb made the merciful decision to settle on his epiglottis, and this set off a fit of coughing so extreme that it momentarily silenced both woman and man mid-sentence. The woman, who had recently completed a course in first aid, had Heimlich and health and safety flash through her mind, but reached for water, and this worked to the extent that Quince could finally escape. He noticed on the inside of his room door a set of rules, as well as an inventory of contents, down to the last plastic spoon.

The next morning he entered the breakfast room (the couple's kitchen) with justified trepidation, and was met by his decrepit host sporting a Peter Rabbit apron and spraying, by intonation, a question, "Wotshoewantwishawtoasht?"

"Pardon?"

"Toasht."

"Toasht?"

With a hint of irritation, "Yesh, toasht."

"Do you have marmalade?"

"Corsh."

"Thank you."

"Tea or coffee? Can't have bowsh."

"Tea, please." Quince concentrated his efforts at trying to decipher the gentleman's code, but he became distracted by what his visual cortex informed him was a lively rabbit hopping out from under the table. He could have sworn, furthermore, that it was followed by another. "Are those rabbits?" he asked hesitantly.

The wife entered on cue and answered on behalf of the Tooth

Fairy. "Floppy and Bob," she said, "our other guests. Parents are in Bali for two weeks."

"Guests?"

"Yes, we accommodate rabbits, don't we, Victor?" Victor was busy cooking bacon and egg and ignored her. "Do pretty well out of it too."

"I see." Quince then made an error of judgement by glancing over at a cluttered cabinet to his right which housed a menagerie of porcelain figurines, some of which appeared to be rabbits. To his horror his glance was immediately seized upon as an expression of interest.

"Come and look," she exclaimed while striding over to open the cabinet doors.

"But ..."

"Toast isn't ready yet, is it, Victor?"

"Almosht, but wait on," he added, throwing down utensils. "I'll show him. Thoshe are mine."

It transpired that the cabinet housed a complete set of Peter Rabbit effigies, and what followed was an interminable interlude of push and shove as each attempted to outdo the other with detail. First Peter himself was taken out and displayed ("No touching, mind"), then Jemima Puddle-Duck, then Mrs Tiggy-Winkle, Hunca Munca, Benjamin Bunny, Tom Kitten ... and so on. Quince was not spared an argument over the date, price and place of purchase, and every attempt he made to move back to the table and his congealed fried egg was accompanied by a most irritating tug on his sleeve.

Finally, however, he managed to regain his seat, but his ordeal was not over. "Wearsh norsh?"

"Pardon?"

"Norsh. Wearsh norsh?"

"Norsh? I mean north?"

"Yearsh, norsh."

Quince raised his finger slowly, then vaguely pointed it towards Floppy.

"Short you'd shay that," the Tooth Fairy roared triumphantly. "Thatsh easht. Norsh's over there," pointing back towards the cabinet and causing Quince to miss a beat. "Geographe Baysh a funny shape. Dishtortsha coasht."

"I see. Thank you. I must be …"

"Everyone getshed it wrong."

"I really must be going."

"Want direcshins?" the Tooth Fairy asked mischievously.

"No, thank you. I have GPS."

"Thatsh cheating."

Over the next fortnight, and without any definite plan to do so, Quince completed a trek of impressive proportions as he and his Yaris traversed the south-west rectangle of Western Australia – a trek that included stops in Margaret River, Denmark, Albany, Esperance and Kalgoorlie, before returning, just for one night, to Marcus in Perth. His cousin, if he had been less self-absorbed, might have noticed a change in the man who had set off two weeks prior, and this cousin, if he had been more curious, might have wondered why. The change was certainly something that Quince recognised in himself and puzzled over.

Was it the walk along the beach at Prevelly after passing signs warning of dugites in the dunes? Or the nude old lady lying propped up on her sleeping dog, reading? He had waded in beyond her, he remembered, into water, white and indigo because of the kelp, and watched it swirl like distant nebulae; and it was there, after all, after standing on a stingray with furling wings feet wide, that his heart had stopped! That could be it!

Or was it out from Albany in a Southern Ocean storm when he could not decide whether wave or wind was the more terrifying?

Or further east at Cape Le Grand where kangaroos watched as he walked on flour-white sand with frozen feet? Where the water was see-through and sapphire? Where granite heads, burnt orange, cupped the bay?

And his inland arc? Definitely his inland arc! The pink salt lakes on his right driving north? The black crows squawking, flapping, hopping on the hot earth at picnic spots? The endless strip ahead, and the undisturbed deep blue and red that was vast beyond imagination? Of course.

But so much else. The ghost and salmon gums along the water pipeline to Perth; and night? Night most of all. It was as if a barrow of bright gems had been spilled and scattered unevenly across the sky: some clumped, some spread like white metal scrap, and some, as happens with a spill, settling in no-man's-land. Mars was close, the radio said, and he noted that it followed him.

Quince was aware that these encounters, one by one, had lifted his mantle of superficiality, the mantle that Frank, the sunflower, and Eleanor had loosened; and he felt unpeeled. They were encounters which were painfully exquisite, and, in the past, he would have acknowledged them with a mere glance, then turned away; but his exposure had stripped him of protection from the hurt of a beauty aligned with loneliness, and he was compelled to reconsider risk.

Prior to leaving Cambridge he had seen Eleanor twice more – taking her out to dinner on the second occasion – but he still was not sure if she was 'interested'. There had been no signal that invited certainty, but their conversation, even silences, had been unforced. Since leaving he had sent several messages, mainly commentaries on his trip, and he had received two prompt but innocuous replies; but it was time, he realised, to take the next step, and an unexpected email was his cue.

ELEANOR

As the time for their departure approached, Eleanor became more apprehensive. Reports coming in from Bwazi, as well as comments dispersed by the diaspora, described a country at the point of collapse. Utility supplies of power and water were intermittent at best, shelves were bare, fuel queues stretched for kilometres, and the army patrolled the streets. Disturbing images emerged on social media of police brutality against unarmed citizens. Of greatest concern, however, was a coded warning from one of her contacts that Harry's aunt had been promoted and now held high office in the Bwazian intelligence service. There had been speculation at the time of Aaron's disappearance that she, his sister, had betrayed him. Exposing Harry to the infrastructural dangers of a dysfunctional state was one thing, but was abduction a possibility? The implication was chilling, and enough to force reconsideration.

Eleanor questioned her decision to go in the first place. Was it really for Harry, or for her? Was it to reassure herself that what she remembered was real? That Portland, Bulungani – the resurrection bush on a kopje with grey doves calling – were more than romantic reminiscences? Or was it simply to respond to Frank's challenge? He had, she acknowledged, been right in identifying boredom as the cause for her insouciance, but was 'getting away' the answer? "You're stale, El, and one-dimensional," he had said, "all output – going through the motions." And he had left her in no doubt that, in his opinion, her obsessive focus on Harry was unhealthy both for him and for her. Again, that was true, but was a misguided re-enactment of history that placed her child in peril going to reinvigorate her?

It was nonsensical and needed to be called off; but how could she tell Harry? He had been collecting images of Africa for weeks – told school friends where he was going – had smiling pictures of his father on the top of a Mpopo boulder! And what about her? Eleanor? She felt reamed out. How could she survive without a holiday? Without the pause required, as Frank had put it, 'to take stock'?

And then Quince phoned!

Eleanor had thought of him often since he had left, and she'd had to mute her responses to his messages because of the unfamiliar excitement that they'd generated. The excitement had no parallel with the powerful and irresistible thrill provoked by Aaron, but it felt more durable and overdue – like a longing long-unrecognised and neglected. She had felt so comfortable with Quince, so safe – felt that she could have fun again, with him. And it was Quince who had received first notice, in an email that she had sent that night, of her decision to cancel. An alternative to Bwazi had not been considered, nor mentioned, and she was taken completely by surprise when he phoned.

"Hello, Eleanor?"

"Quince?"

"Not too late, is it?"

"No."

"Why don't you come to the Kakadu?"

"The Kakadu?"

"I'm flying to Darwin tomorrow. Then thought of Kakadu, Katherine … maybe even Uluru." Eleanor remained silent, and Quince was more hesitant when he continued: "Just got your email and I'm leaving tomorrow … and I thought … if Harry wants to see some crocs – snakes maybe – Kakadu might be the place." Her silence persisted. "Probably not what you're after. It could be uncomfortable. Nothing is booked … I was thinking of tents – two tents, and …"

"We'll come, Quince. I think we'll come," she said, but could say no more.

<hr>

The race was on! Harry giggled triumphantly as he ran beside and then ahead of Eleanor on the escalator rattling towards Gate 23 at Auckland Airport. They were about to catch an international flight to Brisbane en route to Darwin. Eleanor had considered stopping over for two nights with Peter to break the journey, but this would have meant a further delay for Quince. It would also have subjected her to a brother's teasing interrogation before she herself had had a chance to rationalise her impulse; and, as the plane approached the lights of Darwin, a flutter of doubt threatened to turn her back.

Quince, Eleanor was aware, would be waiting with his own doubts and expectations. Could she meet them without compromising herself? Was she ready for a relationship beyond friendship? Was he the right man? Had Aaron been 'the right man'? These were questions that could only be untangled with time, and at a time when she wasn't exhausted. They'd been up for over eighteen hours and it was one in the morning in New Zealand! Her priority was to have both herself and Harry wash, eat and sleep, and she hoped that Quince was not expecting to talk.

It was apparent, however, from the moment that they emerged into the concourse and saw him standing two-back with his tanned arms folded, smiling, that 'boundaries' would be unnecessary, and that talk could wait. He gave Eleanor a brief kiss of greeting on her cheek at the same time as he placed his hand on Harry's shoulder. "I can't believe you're here," he beamed. "It's so lovely that you came. You must be finished?"

"It's been a long day … a long couple of days actually."

"I can only imagine. Come on," he added quickly, "let's pick up your bags and get out of here – out of the noise. I bet your suitcase is the heaviest, Harry?" Harry shook his head shyly.

"Do we need a taxi?"

"No, I have a car – till Monday when we hit the road."

That implied a change on Monday, but explanation could wait. Eleanor was struck by heat and heady scent as she walked, hand in hand with Harry, to Quince's car, and lights hurt as they drove, mainly in silence, into town. The motel comprised individual units, and their entrances were flanked by scarlet and yellow hibiscus bushes. She looked forward to seeing them in natural light.

"There's some macaroni and cheese, as well as a pizza, in the fridge if you're hungry. I turned on the air-conditioner before I left. They do have microwaves if you want the food heated."

"Thank you, Quince. I'll be more alive tomorrow."

"You can come alive whenever you like," he laughed. "Give me a shout next door, room eleven, when you're ready for breakfast."

"We will. Goodnight."

"Night."

Eleanor woke several times through the night, twice due to Harry's restless murmuring, but she fell into a deeper sleep after dawn – after watching a slice of red then orange sun slant in and onto a section of her wall, and after noticing, for the first time, an empty beer bottle on their coffee table primed with three sprigs of frangipani – their petals fashioned out of soft ivory.

––––––

The fun they had the next day was unanticipated. She was aware that Darwin was in the tropical north with water that no one could swim in because of box jellyfish, sharks, sea snakes and gigantic crocodiles. She'd learned of the Second World War bombings, of the cyclone in the seventies, and of Arnhem Land that lay to its east; but she did not know that it also had a saltwater wave pool. Quince did, and when Eleanor and Harry emerged from their air-conditioned motel room to find him sipping coffee at a small table in the shade of a poinciana tree, she was astonished to have him announce that they'd be surfing as soon as they'd had breakfast.

"Are you mad?" Eleanor laughed. "From what I've heard you can't even stand at the water's edge here, let alone surf."

"Yes, you can," he replied quickly.

"Can't."

"Can." Harry looked from one to the other expectantly. "You'd be game for a swim – a surf – wouldn't you, Harry?" Harry glanced hesitantly at his mother. "Grab your swimming togs, your hats, your sunscreen and let's go."

"Quince!" Eleanor said slowly, cocking her head and smiling. "You're up to something. I see mischief in your eyes."

"Trust me."

"Mm," she replied, before straightening her head and adding, "but we haven't got togs. Never thought to put them in."

"Easily fixed. There's a shop just around the corner – just beyond our breakfast stop."

"Okay then! This guy's crazy, Harry. We'll send him in before us, as bait. But first," she added, "I need an ATM."

They had breakfast in an outdoor garden restaurant with rough-hewn rocks as tables. Quince had egg, avocado and chips, Eleanor a Mexican omelette, while Harry had tomato sauce, fish fingers and baked beans, as well as half of Quince's chips. "They're called 'cheeps' here, Harry, and they're compulsory with every meal – even porridge. Lucky you had some of mine." Harry looked across at him with a half-smile. "I'm serious. You have to pay extra if you don't have them."

"But Mum didn't have any."

"And as a consequence, Mum, I'm afraid, will be paying five dollars extra for her omelette." Harry giggled. "And the same goes for mango smoothies," he added as the waitress approached.

"Mango smoothies?"

"Yip. Mango smoothies are compulsory too."

"Quince, I really couldn't."

Quince looked across at Eleanor in mock annoyance: "Can't sip ours."

"I wouldn't dare."

"Okay then," turning to the waitress, "just two, please. Coffee?"

"Definitely a coffee – a flat white."

"A coffee too, please."

Quince got up, ostensibly to go to the toilet, but Eleanor was not to be outwitted. "Quince," she said, looking directly at him, "I'm paying for this." He started to remonstrate: "No, I'm paying for breakfast. Beyond that we need to work out how we're going to do this … the motel, the vehicle hire … all the 'cheeps' that we're going to be feasting on."

He looked at her with a tenderness that she found both comforting and disconcerting. "I don't think that we will ever argue about money," he said quietly.

"I don't think so either."

"Good. Okay. I'll go to the toilet then. The smoothies – Harry's and mine – are not to be touched until I get back. You keep guard, Harry. Okay?"

"Yip."

"And then it will time to hit the wild surf."

"After we've visited the beachwear shop."

Quince waited outside while Eleanor and Harry went in. They emerged after just ten minutes with their togs wrapped in towels imprinted with bright green, yellow and blue parrots. "Now we're talking," he quipped. "The crocs will run a mile when they spot those colours."

"That's a relief!"

But they were more astounded than relieved when Quince led them out and onto the waterfront to reveal a huge, wave-generating saltwater pool. Harry stood staring. "Can we get in, Ma?" he finally managed to say.

"Of course … but you'll … we'll need to put our togs on."

"The changing rooms are through the turnstiles."

"Wait for me. Don't get in until I've changed."

Eleanor had never seen Harry more animated as he ran ahead of Quince into the men's changing room, and tears began to stream down her cheeks as she went in to change. He was waiting impatiently when she emerged, tugging at the top and bottom of her purple one-piece.

"Come on, Ma. You take for ever. Let's get in."

She felt self-conscious and 'noticed' when they joined Quince, who was waiting at the water's edge. Her legs were white as glazed porcelain, and the tropical light made them look unfamiliar – appendages of an older woman.

Eleanor was not a natural swimmer, and she was not confident about taking Harry out into the deeper and rougher water, but Quince reassured her that the artificially generated rollers were predictable in their size and sequence and that he was happy to stay close. Harry could swim, and Peter had taken him into the sea several times in Queensland, but she remained watchful, at least initially, as the two moved beyond the shallows. Soon though, with Harry attached to Quince like a baby lemur, she allowed herself to flop forward into an approaching wave, and float face-down, allowing warm saltwater to wash through her nose, mouth, and sinuses like a cleansing spirit. When she rose another wave hit, and then another, and another, interspersed with a period of subsidence and pause, when she could turn onto her back and float – gazing up at the agapanthus blue of the clear, clear sky.

"You okay, Mum?" Harry had returned to the shallows and was standing next to Quince and grinning.

"Absolutely! You boys must be battling though."

"No way! You have to dive through the waves, Quince said, or swim fast to catch them. Quince said he'd teach me."

"He did, did he? Well, I'll show you and Mr Teacher a thing or two!" she shouted, before starting to splash them.

They stayed in the water for almost an hour, and then, after a quick break, Quince hired a small boogie board for Harry, and Eleanor, lying prone and propped up on her elbows in the shade, watched her son battle away, wave after wave, until he finally caught one from break to beach. He stood, looked up towards her, and beamed – hardly able to believe what he had achieved; and she stood too, clapping her hands above her head.

They carried on, Quince and Harry, for another half hour, but were finally enticed from the water by barramundi burgers. A pair of tall, awkward-looking white birds with long curved beaks were pecking away at the grass close by. "Ibis," Quince pointed out. "They're all over Darwin. They were named after a hotel chain."

Eleanor laughed. "Don't listen to a word he says, Harry."

"Can we get back in?"

"Probably better to stay in the shade for a bit. The sun's fierce."

"Maaa! Will you take me, Quince?"

"Harry, I said …"

"Your mum's right, Harry. We've got a lot of swimming to do this holiday, and we don't want the sun to spoil it. I learned my lesson a hundred years ago."

"You're not a hundred?"

"Almost."

"Is he, Ma?"

"Almost," she laughed.

And then, almost on cue, a tennis ball ran over Quince's leg. Young boys were playing cricket in the shade of a tall hardwood. Quince tossed the ball to Harry. "Take it back to them, Harry, and ask if you can play."

"Will you play too?"

"No, I'm too old."

He looked from Quince to his mother, and then, hesitantly, took up a position two metres from a confident, zinc-painted little batter. Harry was ignored until he took a fine catch, and then the game was on.

"He has his moments, I'm afraid," Eleanor said quietly, as they watched the game progress.

"That was hardly a moment," Quince laughed. "What kid doesn't? Only now matters – at least until they're about twelve. I've seen it with my nieces and nephews. Wonderful to watch."

"What do you mean?"

"We look and plan for pleasure in the future, but they only know now." He paused for a minute, and then continued, "That's why stopping is always a disappointment."

"And that's why parents are the perennial spoilers?"

"I'm afraid so."

"Mm! A few minutes ago I was happy that he had had a happy swim; then I was unhappy because I had deprived him of a second happy swim; then I was worried that I'd turned him into a spoilt brat; then I became anxious that he was facing rejection from his peers!"

"And now you're hoping that he'll hit a six?"

"My happiness depends upon it."

"It's a lot less complicated being an uncle."

"I'm sure it is."

"Purple is your colour."

Eleanor laughed. "Quite a contrast to the white of my legs."

"I didn't think that I should comment on your legs."

Instead of tents they settled on a campervan with a side that came down in sections to form a room designed to frustrate everything from ants to spiders, to snakes, to mosquitoes. It was where Quince slept. Their first stop on the Arnhem Highway was at the Aurora camp in the South Alligator region, a region named after a river that accommodated every predator except alligators. This, and other Kakadu rivers, were named by an American explorer; and the Australians, because their concerns were centred more on survival than semantics, never sought a change.

Harry was impatient to see a crocodile, and so they set off after lunch on a circular three-kilometre walk through monsoon forest to a nearby billabong that was reputed to be teeming with them. Starting from a giant banyan tree with boughs that sprung roots, it was obvious early in their walk that it was not a well-worn track and should, really, have been avoided. If fact there was barely a track at all, and their progress, despite Harry's initial impatience, was slow. The forest was dense, damp, devoid of human sound, and vine-tangled, necessitating that they crawl at times to avoid being strangled. They could hear birds, hear scurrying and rustling, see bleeding bark, see webs the size of sails dangling black and yellow spiders two fingers from their faces … and then they came upon a sign: *Beware of Crocodiles*. It was old and in a partial clearing that edged onto an expanse of lily-layered water. Just that morning Quince had read and related to Eleanor a disturbing story featured in *The Northern Territory News* that reported a rise in fatal crocodile attacks mounted from land as well as water in the Kakadu and its surrounds. '*Since culling has been outlawed, numbers have escalated*', the article explained, '*and crocs are on the lookout for flesh in any form.*' '*Salties aren't stupid*', it went on, '*or they wouldn't have remained unchanged for 200 million years!*'

"We should walk quickly," Quince whispered. "We must be near the end by now."

Eleanor nodded, her face flushed from the heat and humidity. "Hold my hand, love."

"Are we okay, Mum?"

"'Course we are."

Quince broke off a large stick before moving forward, and he used it to open a path by parting vines and webs, looking left and right, until, after an interminable ten minutes, they emerged at the entrance to a protected walkway that led them out and onto an observation platform over the billabong.

"That was exciting!" Quince commented.

"Mm!"

"Time to stake out the wildlife."

"Definitely."

The sun, now unimpeded, beat down on their hats, and geese (they thought that they must be geese) lifted off with an almighty effort to their left. Little else moved. Most of the water surrounding the platform was covered by lotus lilies with pink flowers, and it was so still that they didn't even sway.

"Will we see a crocodile, Ma?" Harry whispered.

"Maybe."

"Watch for their eyes," Quince said quietly. "I was told that sometimes that's all you see."

"Can they see us?"

"I'm sure they can, Harry."

"Can they jump?"

"They can, but not up here."

"Sure?"

"Absolutely."

Eleanor was between the two 'boys', and she took each by the hand. "That was quite an adventure, that walk."

"It was," Quince smiled.

"Maybe our next one will be on a path well-worn and high above water?"

"That might be wise."

"Just as well I had my brave son with me."

"Just as well."

"And just as well you had a stick, Quince," Harry commented. "Maybe a crocodile saw your stick."

"Maybe."

No one spoke for a while after that. The exhausted peace fashioned by excitement and relief made speech superfluous, and they became absorbed by the flight of dragonflies and more geese, as well as by the slow movement of a water buffalo on the far side. Eleanor reached into a pocket for her camera, and then withdrew. She'd taken photographs, some close-ups, of the peeling, variegated, weeping bark of forest trees on the walk, knowing that she would paint their pain; but this was serenity of the sort that constellations engendered – serenity of primeval and enormous power. 'Just let it be,' she thought, 'we three will never forget this.'

And then, as if in confirmation, a long and elegant bird with eyes at the base of its beak landed on a bank nearby. It was enormous, about a metre tall and dull grey, with legs that articulated like tin stilts. Later, after searching through Quince's pocket guide to Australian wildlife, they agreed that it was a great-billed heron— a rare sighting of a shy, coastal bird.

Africa was always going to intrude, but its juxtaposition with the wilderness of Kakadu was never more poignant than at Ubirr. Eleanor had long been intrigued, and at times startled, by the Aboriginal paintings that she had seen in books and Australian art galleries. They had featured mesmerising arrays of earthy dots, rods, squiggles, circles and snakes that bore an uncanny resemblance to the images revealed by electron microscopes. She had identified bacteria (cocci, bacilli, and spirochetes); viruses in filamentous form; as well as whole human cells, complete with nuclei, mitochondria, Golgi bodies – even microtubules – contained by wavy walls. 'Dreaming' featured in many of their titles, like the painting she'd never forgotten by Jimija Jungarrayi Spencer, called *Wallaby Dreaming*; as well as another (although she'd forgotten the artist), called *Medicine Dreaming*, featured in the same Victorian gallery. The concept of *dreaming* was beyond her but appeared to represent a spiritual fusion with interplay of the animate, the inanimate, and all that came before. She suspected but knew of no parallel in Africa; but these rock paintings, set high above the East Alligator floodplains, were imminently comparable to those that Aaron had taken her to in the granite outcrops of south-western Bwazi. His knowledge, his pride, his reverence – his voice – came surging back, but the sting was not as sharp.

Like their African cousins, the peoples of Kakadu had discovered natural pigments that could defy the elements, endure, and record in outdoor galleries of breathtaking splendour the animals and spirits that sustained them. The Tasmanian tiger, extinct on the Australian mainland for two to three thousand years, was provided a lasting view over Arnhem Land; turtles, fish and kangaroos eight thousand years old featured in X-ray paintings; spirit images, much older still, were imprinted on inaccessible ledges; and the Rainbow Serpent – the primeval ancestor, creator, protector and punisher – had a rockface all to herself.

From Eleanor's elevated outcrop observation post the landscape had no end, no time, and she tried to visualise the scene in other seasons. Their Aboriginal ranger on the East Alligator River that morning had described six – from the present cool of May/June to the pre-monsoon of October/December, to the fruiting time of March/April, as well as to the others in between. She felt herself transported from the present – but only momentarily! Harry was hungry, and it was time to eat their egg sandwiches.

A few hours earlier he had seen his first crocodile in the murky green waters of the river. It looked like a floating log, and they would have missed it had the ranger, a young, thin man in khaki and a red cap, not pointed and said, "Who wannu tackle him?" When he was met with a nervous chuckle from the eight or so passengers on board he added, looking at Harry, "What 'bout you, young fella? You strong. You want to bite ees tail?" Harry smiled broadly and shook his head. The ranger steered their aluminium boat closer to the crocodile, close enough for them to see its entire length. "This fella got big teeth and bad eyes – like Donald Trump." He tried to steer the boat closer still, but the croc objected, twisting suddenly in a corkscrew turn, and disappearing in an instant, leaving them hanging on to their cameras and hushed. "He under us now," he said with big eyes. "Wanna bump us inna water." The ranger's poise was held for a few seconds, and then he burst out laughing, captivating them all with his good humour and by the commentary that followed. First, he drew their attention to the palm-like pandanus tree that lined the river's edge, explaining its historic importance as both a food source as well as a material for the weaving of containers, personal adornments, and shrouds for the dead. It was also, he told them, a hiding place for the file snake

– a hideous-looking constrictor that insinuated itself in the tree's roots, where it waited to catch and strangle unsuspecting fish.

"He stay under water forty minutes if he want," he explained to his enthralled audience, "but our little fellas catch him." There was a pause as they tried to process what he had said. "Him taste good. Little fellas, they jump in water while woman watch for croc. Them feel, feel, feel … grab him, then chuck him onna bank. Woman cook him nice. Good as barramundi," he added. "You wanna catch 'im?" he asked Harry.

"No way!" Harry answered, laughing again.

"Okay, we catch him later. You watch for big fella croc."

They saw several more crocs, some nudging the side of the boat, but they also saw a pair of splendid fairywrens performing ballet. Cerulean in colour and minuscule in size, they were Eleanor's favourite. The ranger went on to couple truth, myth, and mischief with respect to other birds that they saw, and merged them with surrounding plants, with nipping insects, with hidden fish, as well as with the unfolding landscape upstream.

It was upstream on the river's eastern bank and at the foot of a small sandstone outcrop in Arnhem Land that their excursion group had permission to beach and explore. A privilege in an area reserved, exclusively, for Aboriginals. The stop offered an opportunity for them all, even Harry, to sit in silence on the rocks and be subsumed by time immemorial.

Before returning to the boat, however, the ranger treated them to a demonstration of spear throwing that sent long poles zinging high and far towards the opposite bank. "Now you gotta fetchim," he said, turning to Harry.

And Harry was as happy as Eleanor had ever seen him. Would he have been as happy in Africa? She wasn't sure.

It was customary for the comfortably retired perennial roamers of Australia, collectively named the Grey Nomads, to occupy the prime campervan sites at tourist campgrounds, and the Kakadu was no different. They were the 'Aussie Battlers' who'd never battled, and any alien or other daring to encroach upon their lot would find themselves repelled – not by overt hostility, but by obstacles imposed. Tokens might not be available at the laundry, pool loungers might be occupied in advance, adaptors for older models at effluent disposal sites might go missing, and an effective phalanx might be formed at the bar when 'happy hour' was in play. They shared a common heritage of effortless wealth accumulation in a period without war, their children were off their hands, extensions to their city and beach houses had reached capacity, and overseas travel had lost its charm because of the hordes unleashed by new-found Chinese prosperity. They needed a fill-in for life's remaining third, and so they lumbered, endlessly and in long trains, up, down and across their great continent – constrained only by the time that they had to set aside for skin grafts and funerals. Their mobile home was their castle, and each was equipped with every accessory spied in the homes of others. At a minimum this included two satellite TVs for footy and Fox, laminar flow air-con, surround-sound Bluetooth for radio talkback, GPS accessibility in the Pilbara, and toilet floors that flush-washed automatically.

Eleanor and Quince were in the pool with one of the afore-mentioned couples but without Harry, who had found a friend, and they suspected that his absence had facilitated a thaw. Bernie, the man, had a belly with an inverted umbilicus, while Sue, the woman, had been mummified by the North Queensland sun.

"So you're from Kayway, mate? Thought you might be Victorian."

"Yes, we're from New Zealand," Quince responded. "Cambridge – the North Island. And you and your wife?"

"Queensland, mate. Always were, an' always will be. You can take a Queenslander outta Queensland," he added for emphasis, "but you can't take Queensland outta a Queenslander."

"Good beaches, Queensland."

"Good sheilas too, mate," he chuckled, affectionately kneading his wife's shoulder with his knuckle, "an' look at the beaut I landed."

Sue disposed of the compliment with a cackle of her own. "Your man this cheeky?" she asked of Eleanor, but Eleanor was fortunately left with no time to respond before Sue continued a conversational tandem with her husband: "But jokes aside, we had a lotta good, clean fun back in the day, didn't we, Bernie?"

"Did we ever! Not like today's mob."

"No."

"It's all about sex today."

"Can't turn on the TV without it."

"It's in your face."

"All paint and polish."

"Especially in Victoria."

"S'malians have taken over in Victoria."

"Really?" Quince asked weakly.

"Can't touch the bastards. They can rape, steal or wreck houses, and you know what they get?"

Eleanor and Quince shook their heads.

"Slap on the wrist and a bigga slice of the pie." Bernie waited for this to sink in before continuing, "Your pie. My pie."

"And you know what else?" Sue whispered conspiratorially.

Eleanor and Quince shook their heads again.

"They're all bloody Muslins."

"Muslims?"

"Every last one of them. You wanna get into this country? Just say you're a Muslin."

Just then the pool gate creaked. It was Harry, looking dusty and happy, with his friend Nathan.

———————

That evening they decided not to eat at the limited restaurant, and instead invited Nathan to join them for spaghetti Bolognese, which Eleanor prepared outdoors on one of the camp's barbecues. It was Harry's favourite meal on a Friday evening at home, partly because it was delicious, but also because it was the one meal when manners were not observed.

"Watch this, Nathe," he shouted, leaning over his plate, and sucking up swivelling strands of mince-flicking spaghetti. "You're allowed."

Quince feigned shock and horror, and this added to the boys' delight. Tomato sauce and generous sprinkles of Cheddar were added as toppings for both their first and second helpings, while their side plate salads were allowed to be left untouched. The finale, prepared by Quince, was lychees and ice cream with an experimental pawpaw smoothie. After that Harry made a half-hearted attempt to prolong the evening with more of the bagatelle that they had played earlier, but both he and Nathan were played out, and, since they were going their separate ways in the morning, it was time for the boys to say goodbye.

It could have been Harry's ensuing tears that had subdued her. It might have been Bernie and his wife. But it was an uncharacteristically quiet and sad-looking Quince that she found sitting in the awning enclosure after she had settled Harry that made her heart contract. He was the sweetest-natured person that she had ever met – always cheerful, teasing, playful, and … considerate. Yes, he was considerate. But was he considerate to a fault? Could anyone be too considerate? There had appeared to be no friction in this their first week together, but was it wearing thin? Was doubt setting in?

There was a hint of formality when she enquired, "Would you like some tea?"

"Tea?" he answered with a smile that required effort. "Would you?"

"I'm having tea, yes."

"I'll make it."

"No," she snapped, and then added, "Black?"

He nodded, and they were silent as the gas and kettle combined to crackle, hiss, and spit, and the silence continued through their sipping. Finally Eleanor spoke: "Have you had enough?" Quince turned to her in the half-light with a pained and puzzled look, before she continued, "I'm sorry, but Harry can be a little difficult at times."

"Eleanor, I ..."

"This is an imposition, I know that. You have no obligation to ..."

"Obligation! What on earth are you talking about?"

"Well, Harry ... and me. It was a big ask. Selfish really."

His eyes, she recognised now, were wounded, and confused. "How can you say that? You are a gift, both you and Harry – a glorious gift. Too good to be true."

"But you look miserable tonight, Quince, and I can only imagine why."

He dropped his head and hesitated, before continuing, "It's me, not you."

"What do you mean?" she asked tensely.

"Substance," he said quietly, pointing to his chest. "There's not much to me, Eleanor. I'm a shell – a facade. I really am. No better than those awful people in the pool."

"Nonsense, you ..." she began, but he looked up again and interrupted.

"Not in their attitudes, of course not, but, like them, I've always taken the easy road … done nothing really … and tonight," he continued, "this beautiful night with the boys … thinking about the beautiful week we've had … you, a successful doctor … I got frightened." He looked away briefly, before turning back and adding, "Or terrified – maybe 'terrified' would be a better word."

Up to this point there'd been no physical intimacy between them apart from touching hands and the odd perfunctory peck, and Eleanor had appreciated his hesitancy and 'consideration', but now, as she turned off the light and kissed his eyes, his neck – his mouth – he responded, and an unanticipated sense of calm guided them.

Later, with only the sound of a barking owl as background, they began to talk. They talked about Frank and his provocation, how he had recognised a sterility of purpose and an absence of challenge, separately, in each of their lives. He could never have anticipated the connection that would follow, yet his instinct was to insist that they take on the risk that made it possible.

"And your decision to grow mushrooms? Was that Frank's idea too?"

"Yes and no. I knew, deep down, that meaningful, challenging, purposeful work was missing, and he was unsparing in pointing that out, but it was the sunflower, El." He paused for the owl. "The look that it gave me after I'd fallen – that was my epiphany." Eleanor remained silent as he continued. "I was drawn in and entered the aperture of the eye that afternoon: The sequence of seeds swirling in the centre – obeying Fibonacci; the darker, pollen-tipped anthers further out; the dishevelled, yellow petals wet and dripping!" He paused again. "I thought the moment ineffable, but that night I met you." 'Woo-woof', woo-woof' came the haunting call.

"Have you met the woman since?"

"No, but I will. I must. Maybe she could help me with my mushrooms," he added, chuckling.

"Maybe."

They were up, whispering, well before dawn for their excursion to the Yellow Water wetlands, and were ushered onto their boat by torch light. Eleanor was prepared for a bird show, but she hadn't anticipated the volume, variety, cadence and cackle pre-dawn; nor was she prepared for the Delacroix-red of the rising sun. She forgot to breathe as it was captured on her retina, frame by frame, like photographs from space, and she had, eventually, to be nudged hard by Harry to look left at an amber-eyed four-metre croc that had sidled up alongside.

They were in an opening of lotus lilies, idling, with flocks of geese flying, and entered endless more. Each on board was pointing: "An Australian darter," the guide would say, "good spotting, matey. He's caught his feed already. Look at that fish flap," or, to a young girl, after she'd spotted a perching Brahminy kite, "Well done, darlin'. Your blood's worth bottlin'." They came up close to a blue-winged kookaburra, as well as to figbirds and finches; they drifted past thousands of noisy nesting ducks and nearly missed an osprey; storks stood their ground, and egrets too! "A bird's beak will tell you what she's partial to," their guide explained after he had spotted a paperback flycatcher on a bush nearby. "She's a little beauty, this one. Look at the long delicate curve of her beak. Beats a parrot's seed-eating secateurs. But wait … listen. You hear that?" The call, more a cry than a call, came again, and he followed it to the top of a distant, dead tree – to the outline of what could have been mistaken for caught cloth. "You see him?" he whispered. "A sea-eagle. He's a raptor and a half, that one. Can rip up a barramundi in five minutes flat. Smaller than a wedge-tail," he added, "but you can't beat that call."

Eleanor's favourite, though, the bird that the three of them would never forget, was the comical jacana, with its comb of vermilion, squat backside and cartoon toes – toes modified to walk on water lilies but dragged behind like kite tails in flight.

Would Aaron have loved this experience as much as she did? she wondered, as they returned to the jetty. As much as Quince? Could Aaron have avoided comparison? 'My birds are less abundant, but more varied – more likely to surprise. Mine are dry, while these are wet. Mine,' he could finally have argued, 'live closer to death.' But is it necessary to compare beauty? To choose one over the other. Is it even possible?

She was so absorbed by her musings and the hot, high sun that she was oblivious of the present as they disembarked, and Harry's cry caught her by surprise. "Harry?"

"Ow! Ow … Ow!" he yelled, leaping off a bench where they were to wait for their camp bus to arrive.

Her first thought (a thought common to New Zealanders when confronted by similar cries coming from the Australian bush) was … SNAKE. Western brown? King brown? Taipan, God forbid? But it was an ant! An ant with a green bum. In fact there was a nest of them in the tree above. They were common in the Kakadu, it was explained, and tasted delicious – "Like citrus. You can eat them live if you don't mind them biting your lip," the guide continued. "You okay, little fellow?" Harry nodded with tears in his eyes. "Good man, you've earned your stripes. Just rub on some vinegar when you get back to camp."

The next day, at a demonstration given by a Bininj woman at the nearby cultural centre, they were given the very ants to try. They featured on her 60,000-year-old menu, which included tastings of smoked kangaroo, pickled crocodile, and Eleanor's favourite, black bream stuffed with native lemongrass wrapped in paperbark and pandanus leaves before being charred on wood coals. Cheeky yam hummus was offered as a side dish, and Kakadu plum tart completed the meal. Harry was half-hoping for file snake, but never spoke out.

A child, and what would interest or not interest him or her, has to be the priority in holiday planning, and long-distance travel is something that any discerning parent would seek to avoid. Quince had, at the beginning of their holiday, spoken enthusiastically of the Red Centre – of Uluru, Alice Springs, the MacDonnell Ranges – and of the strip of Stuart Highway that would lead them there. "We can stop under the endless sky and boil tea along the way… call in to filling stations guarded by dusty dogs for ice cream. I did that in Western Australia. It was magical." So Eleanor was surprised when he suggested that they scrap that excursion, and instead complete a much shorter circle that included a few more days in their current camp, a trip down the Katherine Gorge, a visit to the Litchfield National Park, and a return to Darwin. "Another time, perhaps," he said.

"But why, Quince?"

"It's too far, El. Look at Harry when he's in a pool … when he's kicking a ball around … when he's spotting crocs. It's a full three-day drive, and an eleven-kilometre walk around a rock won't be his idea of fun."

"But …"

"It'll spoil what we've got."

"But it's your holiday."

"It's ours, El. Yours, Harry's and mine. It's the best I've ever had."

And so they spent three nights in Katherine, two in Litchfield, and a week in a motor camp in Darwin, drawing closer and ever more comfortable. They made a study of magnetic ants that aligned their mounds like ziggurats to the sun; they swam in cool, croc-free rock-pools; they slid down water slides; they 'surfed'; they attended a rerun of *The Lion King*; they played Monopoly and children's Scrabble; and they finally saw a snake in the wild.

Eleanor and Harry did spend a few days with Peter on the Sunshine Coast before heading home, while Quince flew back via Sydney. Her life, she realised, had been transformed. Frank had been right! She felt more complete, confident, and serene than she had been a mere three weeks before. Africa had transformed her also, but through thrilling agitation and excitement. This was different – preordained – as if Quince were meant to be.

PART IV

FRANK

Frank decided that he needed to broaden his mind, and *Ulysses* was where he started. In preparation he downloaded an eleven-page Wikipedia summary of the novel's plot and its linkage to the *Odyssey*. A small locational map of Bloom's Dublin was also included, and he hoped that the two references would help dispel some of the book's obscurity. He had considered a pre-reading of Joyce's biography, as well as (perhaps) of the classic poem itself, but his patient, Evelyn, a retired English lecturer, told him to 'Just get on with it. Read what makes sense and what you enjoy. Skip the rest, otherwise you'll never get through my list.'

'My list' had been compiled by Evelyn at Frank's request, and it provided him with what she had termed 'a small menu of musts'. Amongst them, of course, was *Ulysses*. "Not my favourite, Frank," she'd said with her head cocked to one side, "but one that rocked writers." Among others on the list were: *Little Dorrit, Moby Dick, Middlemarch, The Histories of Herodotus, Don Quixote, The Leopard* ("Perfect for you at your age, Frank"), *The Brothers Karamazov*, and, of course, several of Shakespeare's plays, including *Antony and Cleopatra* – "For its poetry. But if you want something more contemporary try Philip Roth, Saul Bellow, Patrick White – and if you really want to impress your daughter, Jonathan Safran Foer.'"

"Funny name!"

"Funny guy."

Ulysses was the first that he found in the second-hand book shop on Victoria Street, and so *Ulysses* it was!

>>Part I: Telemachia

Episode 1, *Telemachus* (alias Stephen Dedalus)

Episode 2, *Nestor* (Stephen teaching)

Episode 3, *Proteus* … trying, with great difficulty, to follow Stephen's 'stream of consciousness'.

And then, the breakthrough in Episode 4, *Calypso*, at the start of Part II when Frank was drawn in, enthralled, and astounded by the audacity and freshness of the language. He had never read anything like it! The cat *'blinked up out of her avid shameclosing eyes, mewing plaintively and long, showing him her milkwhite teeth.'* … *'the dark eyeslits narrowing with greed'* as Bloom *'ate with relish the inner organs of beasts and fowls.'*

He was away, sort of, often in the dark and only making sense of snippets, but away – relishing the provocation, the pathos, the characters, and, above all, the humour. It had to be the funniest book that he had ever read. He kept interrupting Milly with, "Listen to this, Mil, *'Kicked about like snuff at a wake'*. Have you ever heard anything like it?" and "Sorry, but this simile – it's amazing, *'With a belly on him like a poisoned pup.'*" and "Mil, Mil, sorry … listen to this description, *'The loose flesh of his neck shook like a cock's wattles.'* Perfect! Just perfect!" Milly hadn't seen him this animated in years, and she chuckled inside while feigning irritation.

Frank was quick to realise that he would never 'understand' the novel – the difficulties posed by the literary, parochial, biblical, mythical and classical references alone were bewildering, as was the impish obfuscation and word deconstruction – but he was able to glimpse the greatness, the originality – the layering and laying out of complex and conscious experience with unflinching accuracy and honesty. As he ploughed through episode after episode – the coarse, anti-Semitic and anti-immigrant tirade against Bloom in Barney Kiernan's bar, the edgy and sad *Nausicaa* that had attracted such notoriety, the central episodes of 'father/son', and, finally, the intimate entre into Molly's gyrating mind – he felt exhausted but exhilarated at the same time, as if new, intoxicating dimensions had been discovered – as if he were under the influence of his walnut's nocino.

Frank's effort at literary expansion preceded then overlapped Eleanor's absence, and, in retrospect, added to his realisation that something had to be done. He had anticipated as inevitable that he would tire while she was away, and he did, but it was the difficulties that he had in holding steady that unnerved him. Patient enrolments had increased markedly over the previous year, and he found both he and Edith booked days in advance. This posed difficulties when urgent cases demanded immediate intervention. Frank would be in consultation with a young man concerned about a testicular lump when two 'doubles' (in a different colour) would pop up on his appointment screen; he would be reviewing a twenty-four-hour blood pressure print-out with an anxious immigrant when the phone would ring: 'A doctor from the hospital for you, Frank'; behind schedule by forty minutes he would be hurriedly scanning the medical history of an elderly diabetic patient about to enter for a driving medical – one that he might have to fail – while noticing two, then three, messages appearing in his task bar; and then there were the rest-home patients to service – also Joan, dying at home and needing daily review – as well as endless results and 'paperwork'.

There were days when his chest moved up to his throat, and

there were moments when his tongue stuck fast to his palate. He carried many unresolved problems home, and their fragments swirled around in his fleeting and fitful sleep like crystals in a faulty kaleidoscope. There was a risk, a considerable risk, that he would miss something. Had he reached the stage when he was not safe? Was it time to read full-time?

Edith, he realised later, felt much the same, and he sensed that the practice was in peril; but Eleanor returned looking radiant, and she came to their rescue.

"We need another doctor, maybe two."

"But how will we find them, Eleanor?"

"By putting out feelers, Edith. I have contacts. We could employ GPEP 2 doctors – even GPEP 1."

"GPEP?" Frank interjected.

"Trainee GPs, Frank, on the education programme. They need placements in practices with fellows who will provide oversight, and we have three. Overseas doctors too, from the UK, India, South Africa, Iraq, Texas, Pakistan – they're all escapees of one sort or another."

"But Hamilton?"

"You and Edith have created something special here, Frank. A busy and efficient practice with a huge heart and the capacity to grow. We have patients banging on the door, for goodness' sake. It really is the envy of the town."

"I wouldn't go that far," Edith scoffed.

Eleanor laughed as she placed her hand on her colleague's shoulder. "But it is, Edith. It really is. I was so lucky to get a job here."

"Mm," Frank murmured, "we could argue that we were the lucky ones, couldn't we, Edith?"

"We could, but, Eleanor, these doctors – don't they all want part-time work these days? Bits and pieces? Would they carry out palliative care? Continue rest-home visits?"

"We'd only employ those that would, and part-time? Yes, most would want that, but so should we – especially you. I'm happy to continue with a 9/10 commitment for the next year or so, but beyond that I'd like to drop another session – spend it with my mother, pick up Harry from school." She paused then, Frank noticed, and looked at both him and Edith with a tenderness that made him want to cry, before continuing, "And you two can't go on like this. It's wearing you out and will make you sick."

"Yes," said Frank, speaking softly, "it might be time to ... you know, to stop as it were. To get the young ones in." But when he looked across at Eleanor, he was surprised to find that she was smiling.

"Nonsense, Frank. That's not what I was implying. You and Edith have only just peaked."

"No, seriously, Eleanor, it's a safety issue."

"But I'm talking about safety, Frank. Patients are safe with you, and they know it. You and Edith take every opportunity to maintain and extend your knowledge and skill, you have eons of experience, and you care. What more could anyone want? You mustn't stop. You don't need to – not yet – not when you're too exhausted to decide." She paused before continuing, "You sent me away to recharge and I'm half your age!" She paused again, then quietly added, "It must have been hell! It would have been hell for anyone, but I would urge you both to wait, to give me a chance to come up with something. If I'm successful in recruitment over the next six months you could reduce your sessions, and reduce them further over time, both of you. You could do more teaching, whittle down ownership as the others step up, have more time to mull over complex and perplexing cases – live a little."

"Would I have time to read *The Brothers Karamazov*?"

"The what?"

"It's a long story."

"Absolutely, Frank! You could even join an over-fifty fitness group and jump around in bright Lycra while we're slaving away here."

"Now you're talking! But only if Edith joins me."

"Tempting, Frank, tempting! But getting back to Karamazov. Did you know that Karamazov means 'black stain' or 'smear'?"

"Really?"

"Yes. Sort of like original sin."

"How on earth did you know that, Edith?"

"Just one of the useless bits of information I picked up from my father."

"Have you read the novel?"

"No, but my father went on and on about Dostoevsky when I was young, and that, to my shame, made me more determined than ever not to read him."

"Maybe you could tackle him now that Eleanor's letting us slack off."

"Maybe. Dostoevsky was an epileptic, of course … and, um, we'll see. I, I must get back to work."

<hr>

Eleanor insisted that Edith and Frank take off consecutive Fridays in the two weeks after her return, and, on impulse, Frank decided to make the most of her generosity. While keeping Milly completely in the dark he booked accommodation for three nights in an old but comfortable hotel set high above Auckland harbour in Parnell – a hotel that they had stayed in often but many years prior, when Jane was still at university. He arranged for them to drive up on the Thursday evening after work with Milly knowing only that they were setting off on their forty-fifth honeymoon.

Frank was careful to select a fourth-floor room with a kitchenette and a view to die for, but he also, unbeknown to Milly, booked a second room, one two doors down the corridor, for Jane and her husband Phil. They would arrive a day later, after flying up from Wellington early on the Friday evening, and the surprise would be complete.

As soon as they turned off the Khyber Pass off-ramp into Newmarket, Milly guessed where they were going. She touched his arm as they drove along Broadway and into Parnell Road, gripped it as they turned right onto St Stephens Avenue and then left into Gladstone, and gave him a peck as he pulled up just beyond reception.

"I did suspect, Frank. I hoped actually," she added. "Have we got the same room?"

"I think so. It might have been spruced up a bit though."

It could have been the same room, they weren't quite sure, but the city lights looked brighter, and those moving in the port below made more noise. Rangitoto was black and blocked out parts of the North Shore, but the Harbour Bridge was alive with lit ants.

"It's beautiful, Frank! Even better than I remember. Thank you."

Leaning hard against his left shoulder and beaming, Milly lifted her head and kissed him, and they stood there linked by a lifetime.

"Do you remember bringing Jane up here? The savoury snacks that we'd have before going out to dinner?"

"What was the name of the expensive Italian delicatessen? She went berserk in there – the prosciutto, salami, black olives, …"

"Sun-dried tomatoes …"

"And the mozzarella! That was to die for."

"On poppy-seed biscuits."

"Weren't the thicker, black pepper ones her favourites?"

"No, definitely the poppy-seed."

"And then we would walk up to Parnell Village and choose – Thai, Italian – never French, and later Chinese."

"Oh, Frank," Milly said laughing, "what about the champagne?"

"Don't remind me."

"It was after her graduation ceremony and David was with her – better not mention him …"

"And I'd set out our crystal glasses smuggled up from home, but the bloody stuff wouldn't pour."

"You'd frozen it – expensive French champagne!"

"What an idiot!"

"And the final straw was you and David trying to scoop out bits with a teaspoon."

"But we ended up having a good night."

"We did, Frank, we had many a good night here."

"We should see if we can find that delicatessen again tomorrow. Get a few bits and pieces for old times' sake."

"That would be nice. Pity Jane and Phil won't be here to share them with us."

"We could give them a call."

"We could.

They were tired that night and ate just a small pub meal before turning in early. Milly, he could see in her weariness, was deeply affected. She was pressed against his side and asleep within minutes of switching off her bedside lamp, and, with the curtains open and allowing in the distant city light, he was able to watch as well as listen as her breathing pattern mirrored transition through the planes of sleep. No one he knew was as appreciative of directed kindness as Milly. Each gesture was received with surprise and joy, as if it were rare and undeserved, and each time he succeeded in making her happy, such as now, he regretted not doing more, and more often. She was so easy to please, yet he had allowed a hundred thousand trivialities to intervene, to miscon-strue – to lower expectations and disappoint.

He looked down at the side of her unguarded face, listening for the start of dream, and determined that he would do more. Frank's focus over the previous year, he realised, had been upon himself – his paranoia about decrepitude – and Milly's concerns had largely passed him by. Had she had her November mammogram? He couldn't remember … would ask in the morning. He would also suggest more travel, perhaps to Africa this time, or Portugal, and drop her off in Ponsonby to shop – she always seemed to find something there. But no … not tomorrow, not without Jane. It would have to wait till Saturday … the two of them could spend the morning scooting from Ponsonby to Newmarket, to the city centre … that road off Queen Street with the coffee shops. He and Phil could meet them there, and in the afternoon they could all go for a drive. 'Devonport's nice,' he thought, looking across the water, 'Phil would love that book shop and we could climb the hill with the guns, but, no … no, we should skip the North Shore and head straight up to Puhoi. Jane and Milly would go silly in the cheese shop … buy presents for everyone. And the village? The village is exquisite.'

Frank couldn't wait for the tap on the door, for the moment when he could whip out his four crystal glasses – for the chatter and snacks. He couldn't wait. But where would they eat? The Persian restaurant up the road? Jane loved Turkish … not sure about Phil. 'I'll make a provisional booking,' he decided. 'Four for seven-thirty? No, four for eight?' It would give them more time on the balcony.

He leaned over to his right, to his bedside table, and tried to prise two Mylanta tablets out of their aluminium foil without disturbing Milly. She didn't budge, so he snapped off a couple of paracetamols as well.

Driving to work on a Monday in early July, Frank was as close to content as the absence of worry would allow. No one he loved was unhappy or ill, and help was on its way at work. In all probability he would be able to reduce his weekly commitment to just six sessions by the middle of August. It had also been agreed that neither he nor Edith would accept ownership of new patients – they would instead be allocated to those younger – and this would limit and inevitably reduce his burden of continuous care.

His walnut still had half its leaves, but he noticed as he drove that most other trees were bare. The nuts, though, had been collected and stored in large, aerated baskets, and each night while watching television he would continue the process of cracking and shelling – placing every third nut into a bag for freezing. The other two had to be handed in sequence to Milly and Emma. As a young dog Emma had been able to crack open the nuts herself, but her teeth were no longer up to it. Most years Frank froze two to three kilograms of walnuts, with the rest, unshelled, taken to work, or left in baskets on the road for passers-by.

He smiled as he reflected on his good fortune as he entered this the next phase in his life, as he entered … what should he call it? … early old age. The barriers that he had had to overcome, barriers that he had recognised in so many patients over the years, included fears of imminent ill-health – even demise – but also, and especially, of becoming useless. His work had defined him – 'I am a doctor', he could say – and, when this affirmation of usefulness had been threatened, he had wilted. But Eleanor had thrown him a lifeline – had illuminated a phase of transition that would allow him to adjust with dignity. He could continue his career without being dangerously overwhelmed, but at the same time find purpose in other pursuits. His smile broadened as he thought of her – thought of how she had been transformed by her holiday. Although she'd not spoken of it in any detail, he was aware that the Bwazian option had been shelved in favour of Australia, and that Quince had come into the picture. He would never have thought to match them, but now, as he pulled into his practice car park and reflected on how well he knew them both, he could see them as the perfect fit.

With doctor's bag in hand, Frank was about to enter through a side door, when Geraldine burst out: "Thank God you're here, Frank. I've been trying to call you."

"Really! I might have inadvertently …"

"You need to hurry. He might be dead."

"Who?"

"Kevin Burton."

"Kevin? The stroke?"

"Must be, yes. His wife has just called, Frank. She sounded frantic. Said he'd stopped breathing."

Age-old instincts turned a switch in his brain. "Send an ambulance, Gerry."

"I tried to tell her to do that, but she put down the phone."

"That's okay. Phone now. Tell them to hurry."

"Do you want their address?"

"No, I know where they live," Frank replied sharply as he ran inside and past her. "I need the defib."

He was in his car and speeding towards the Hillcrest home within minutes – his mind assembling all that he could remember of the patient's profile. 'Stroke, yes, but also heart … diabetes, hypertension, sleep apnoea. Could be heart … likely to be heart, but …', and this is when he felt his tongue shrivel, 'His wife. What was her name? Karen? Colleen? Could she … had she?' He tried to dismiss the thought, but, while waiting impatiently for a traffic light to change, images of the son and his concerns, of the visit to the house – of the patient's drab bedroom – swirled in front of him. 'Stopped breathing! She could have interfered with his CPAP machine … administered more insulin than she should.' It was approaching peak traffic in the Hillcrest area with students and school children spilling out of buses and SUVs. One, fawn, and occupied by a mother, was blocking his lane, and Frank momentarily considered mounting the pavement to pass her. He was checked, however, by a sober realisation – it would, in all probability, be too late: *The most successful intervention is immediate* – with retrieval rates falling off exponentially when measured against time. 'And if he is dead? Could I in all conscience sign a death certificate? Register a *Direct cause of death*? *Antecedent* and *Underlying*, yes, but *Direct*? Could I, *to the best of my knowledge and belief*, confirm that I have not omitted *other information pertinent to the death*?' And the cremation form, he knew only too well, was even more explicit:

15. Do you know, or have you any reason to suspect, that the death of the deceased was due directly or indirectly to:

(a) Violence. Yes/No

(b) Poison. Yes/No

(c) Privation or neglect. Yes/No

(d) Illegal operation. Yes/No

The implications if he reported the death to the coroner – if he refused to sign a death certificate and insisted on a postmortem – would be horrendous. 'The police will get involved, and Kevin's wife – Carol? Yes, Carol will be interrogated, poor woman. They could even charge her with … manslaughter? … murder? I would have to hand over notes … give evidence. Edith and Eleanor might be called in too.' His heart was racing as he made the final turn off Hillcrest Road and into her street. 'What a mess! What a mess! Terrible too, for the family – especially for the son who reported her.' The garden gate was closed so Frank pulled up sharply on the kerb, reaching for his bag with one hand and his defibrillator with the other. "But if I don't report this? If I don't …?" he murmured out aloud, as the gate squeaked shut, a dog barked, and he strode towards the open front door on a driveway flanked by flowers.

ELEANOR

For those who had known and grown to love Eleanor in more recent years it seemed she was transformed by her holiday, and different; but for those who had known her for many, like Mary or her mother, her old self had reappeared. Her endearing qualities of sensibility, kindness, warmth, and empathy – her ability to calm and make better – were undiminished; but a sparkle had returned. It was apparent in her step – the purposeful clopping of her heels as she hurried out to welcome patients; it was apparent in the engagement of her eyes; it was apparent in the energy of her ideas; but it was most apparent in the frequent eruptions of her infectious, rejuvenating laugh.

Her colleagues were the immediate beneficiaries of the change, as were her friends, family, and patients, but it was the promise of a new phase and fuller life for Eleanor herself that offered most. She was her former self, but also older and aware that happiness had its reciprocal – that it could be flipped. Eight years she had been healing in hibernation and incubating Harry, blunted by the consequence of risk and averse to more, but her holiday with

Quince, as brief as it was, had let light in, and there was no turning back.

The paradox, however, was that although the days flew by they offered more time: time to expand her interests and activities at work; time to become a member of the primary school's Parent Teacher Association; time to run, have her hair cut, resume reading before bed; time to visit Quince, or he her, most days of the week; and time to buy oils, charcoal, brushes, canvas and sweet-smelling vegetable turpentine so she could recreate, in abstract, the swirling colours of Kakadu bark. She had last painted in Africa, and her 'canvas' had been Ted's urn. Dear Ted! It was he, despite his illness, who had urged her to paint again (for the first time since leaving school), and it was he who was on her mind when her studio took shape.

The study appeared at first to be the obvious space, but it had become her 'medical room' – the place where she could log into patient files to check on results and hospital summaries, to write referrals and read journals – the place where she thought like a doctor. The spare bedroom was an option. Eleanor had intended furnishing it for guests but never had, and it had defaulted into a repository for overflow. Harry played in there, however, when he had friends visit, and Bonny suggested that it be formally converted into his space. "He wouldn't mess up his own bedroom then, Eleanor, and he could build giant things with Lego. It would be perfect for sleepovers too," she added mischievously. Harry, of course, was very enthusiastic about the idea, and it was not long before the junk had been cleared out and painted crates installed – one for sporting paraphernalia, one for electronic toys, and one for bits and pieces. The Lego had a place of its own in a side cupboard, and his books were stacked on shelves assembled by Quince. Once new racing car curtains were hung the room was complete, and Harry was in seventh heaven. Eleanor's art equipment, however, remained in boxes with nowhere to go – nowhere to go, that is, until Marion came up with the perfect solution: "Why not use the garage?"

"The garage? But the car's in the garage."

"I know, dear, but it doesn't have to be. It is in shade, and a car port could be attached in no time. Remember the one Dad put up?" she added helpfully.

"Mm! I do, Mum. That might be a solution."

"It might, dear."

"It wouldn't bother you though … the smell of turps … with you next door?"

"Not at all."

And, within a weekend, an old table had been purchased, shelves, heaters, pots, and lights had been installed, and it was time to begin.

First the pencil sketch on scrap paper – the scaffold; but before that the image – the idea; and before that the silence of insect zinging, the fwop-fwop-fwop of wing, and the web floss sticking. Eleanor flicked back through her camera app, back to before the billabong but after setting off, to the series on bark. Several caught her eye – whole trunks bleeding or peeling, some dead – but there! That was what she wanted! White winding streaks like spliced strips of chromosome intersecting a central smudge of variegated burnt red, and in-between grey grains, fawn dots, and a moose-like form in pale yellow.

Eleanor's creative hand and brain had laid dormant for so long that her pencil wasted page after page before a template took shape, but she could sense an awakening as she added shade to outline to capture the forest thrill. Next, she needed to stretch her canvas and begin, first with charcoal for line, then diluted base, and, finally, into chromatic mixing and application, revision and review – standing back and tweaking, blobbing, smearing, dabbing – confecting towards finality.

Eleanor was aware that the process could send her elsewhere, that she might resent Harry's interruptions and snap – that it might temporarily detach her from her son. But it was Whitey, with his scratching, snoring, and pawing at the door that was the irritant. Harry, she found, would linger to watch after entering, forgetting what he had entered for. He would finger and smell the crumpled, oozing tubes, tempted to lick them – intrigued by his mother's apron and easel. Soon he could identify the Cadmium Red or Alizarin Crimson, the Burnt Sienna and Titanium White, and watch, intrigued, as she softened her green by adding more yellow to blue.

The painting puzzled him. "I like it, Ma, but it doesn't look like anything. What is it?"

"This," she said, after scrolling through her Kakadu film. "The bark. Do you remember when we …?"

"But it's just bark!"

"But beautiful, love … the colours, the patterns, the textures … and oils help with the textures."

"The textures?"

"The feel."

He looked perplexed. "You should paint a croc, or a jacana."

"Maybe next time."

"Maybe I could?"

"Absolutely! Why don't you?"

"With your paints?"

"No, not with these, but you could get your own. Besides, you might find others easier."

"What others?"

"Water paints … acrylics, crayons … coloured pencils."

"What are these that you have?"

"Oils. Oil paints."

"Why d'you use them?"

"They take longer to dry – amongst other things."

"Why's that good, Ma?"

"It gives you more time to change the picture – to hide mistakes," she answered smiling, "but the real reason I prefer them is the smell."

"I like the smell too."

"But it's not good to breathe in too much. That's why I keep the windows open – even now that it's getting colder."

As the weeks went by, he learned why she chose linen canvas rather that cotton – why her palette was the shape it was. She pointed out the difference between sable and bristle brushes and explained why she needed knives and nails at times.

"I saw you use your finger yesterday, Ma."

"Yes, I use that too, love. Painters use anything that works."

"Even their feet?"

"Absolutely! Some people paint with their toes."

"Really!"

"Mouths too."

"Why?"

"Because they don't have arms."

"Why?"

"They're born like that."

"Why?"

"You'll have to ask your doctor!"

These exchanges were as happy as those that she had had while helping her father fashion rudimentary garden furniture out of offcuts – even driftwood. Some they would adorn with pine kernels, some with shells, small rocks, or pumice stone, and once a year at the Spring Fair they would set up a stand to sell. Eleanor, acting as treasurer, would prepare a coin and note float, and it was she who would split their profits at the end – three ways. One third for her, one third for Peter (which she felt was unfair at the time since he was too small to participate), and one third for the Sisters of Mercy (whom she never met). They would be provided with free donated tea and cupcakes at ten, and they once featured in a photograph on the front page of *The Volcanic Gazette* – a copy of which her mother had framed.

At the age of eleven, however, in her father's words, she grew 'too big' to participate, and she was well into her teenage years before she re-entered his shed. A friend's snigger had shown her the light.

Looking across at Harry, Eleanor realised that she needed to steel herself for the inevitable – for the necessary. Change … confidence, assertiveness … was already apparent. Was recalcitrance, even insolence, to follow? Whether it was the holiday, or whether it was the influence of Quince – even Bonny – she was not sure, but Harry was 'older'. Whereas he had previously been reluctant to entertain friends for example, he now had one, sometimes two, come over to play after school, and he would grumble when they were sent home to dinner.

Eleanor was surprised at the ease with which her relationship with Quince settled and advanced. The holiday had dispensed with second guessing, with doubt, and it was as if they were married but apart. He had his mushrooms to grow and she her practice and son. They messaged, FaceTimed, and met after work when they could. Weekends they would meet at one house or another – sometimes drive east to the Coromandel. There was no talk of commitment or 'moving in' because it was inevitable that it would happen. Inevitable too that he became another whose preoccupations, whereabouts and wellbeing were a part of her roving concern, another in her inner circle whose happiness was linked to her own. "Have you found Baker, Quince? Was he with Bonny?"

"How did the contractors' meeting go?" "Are you wearing a mask? A hat?" And Quince, for his part, reciprocated in kind, but by teasing, by touching – by showing Harry how to bowl a googly or have her mother laugh.

Each, in essence and at this early stage, put the other first, and for those not closely acquainted with their characters, the relationship appeared unsustainable and naive, but for those who knew them intimately, like Marion, Pansy – even Frank – they were made for one another.

———

"Joey. Joey Burton?" she called, and a mother with a small child stood up confidently and smiled. "Mrs Burton?"

"Angela."

"Hi, Angela, I'm Eleanor. Good to meet you. Come on in, second door on your left. Let me carry the car seat. Amazing how heavy they are."

Once seated Eleanor glanced at her computer and then back at Angela. "Joey's first visit, I see, and you're joining our practice too."

"And Evan."

"Your husband? Oh, good … well, welcome."

"Thank you."

"Now, Joey, you've had happier days I see."

"Yes, it's probably just a virus, but we're driving up to Northland tomorrow."

"Of course, Angela. If you wouldn't mind holding her sideways on your lap, like … ah, I see you've done this before."

Angela smiled. "I have a huge extended family up north, and I have worked in paediatrics."

"Paeds? Are you a doctor? Nurse?"

"A nurse, but I haven't started back yet."

"It's difficult, isn't it? Are you still breast-feeding?"

"Less and less. Might stop while we're up north … with my mother's help," she added laughing.

"Will you be away long?"

"No, just a few days."

Eleanor was about to mention her own mother's role in raising Harry when Joey coughed. "Whoops! Sorry, Joey. We'd better get started."

A brief history was taken before the examination began. Joey would have been a picture of health if she had not had a streaming nose, red eyes and a nasty cough. She was undressed and held firmly but comfortably by her mother as Eleanor checked her temperature, ears, tongue, neck, eyes, throat (plus swab), chest, skin, and abdomen, then took her weight, before writing up brief notes:

O/H 2-day history of fever, congestion, and cough. Taking feeds, but reluctantly. Nappies wet. Crying ++. No D/V. Fully immunised. Travelling north for a few days.

O/E T38.1 Wt. 9.1 kg. No rash/neck stiffness. Cap. filling time 1 sec. Tongue moist. No cervical lymph nodes. Ears clear. Throat clear. RR 22. No s/c recession/nasal flare. Chest clear with good air entry. Oxygen sat 97%. Abd soft and non-tender (but wriggling++). Urine not checked.

Diagnosis: Likely viral upper respiratory tract infection.

Management: 1. swab 2. fluids and paracetamol 3. Copy of clinical notes provided. Will text mother the swab result if +ve for strep (Amoxil Rx on hold).

"I agree, Angela, there's no sign of a secondary infection, but she'll be miserable for a couple more days, I'm afraid. Our nurse will contact you if the swab's positive."

"Mum will sort her out. She has a way with kids."

"I'm sure she does, but you do too," she added. "It's obvious."

"Thank you, Eleanor."

"Pity you don't have your mother close by."

"I do have my mother-in-law."

"Oh, really?"

"Yes, she's a patient of yours – Carol Burton. She recommended you."

"Carol? Oh, my goodness, I should have worked that out. Of course – you live on the same property, don't you?"

"Yes, the house has been subdivided."

"Has that worked out okay? She does seem happier."

Angela got up to leave. "She loves her garden … her dog, Alice – Joey of course … and she's very good to me."

"I saw her not that long ago. Wasn't she going to Australia, to visit her other son?"

"Yes, she got back last week."

"And it went well?"

"Not really, no."

"I'm sorry, I was hoping …"

Angela turned at the door. "We were hoping too, Evan and I, but Evan is considering staying home."

"Why?"

"It might be better for his dad."

QUINCE

Quince had completed his eight-part online course before travelling to Australia. He had also formulated a plan for construction, but now that he was home and looking down onto the steep, pegged slope that would be transformed into 'the site', he took fright. What, really, did he know about mushrooms? About greenhouse production? About marketing? Especially marketing! What did he know about anything?! The digger was due in the morning, weather permitting, and then there was no turning back.

Mulling over his plan while driving out of the Kakadu it had all seemed so easy. He had the capital, he had the land, he had the crop that never stopped growing; and he had Eleanor curled and confidently asleep on the seat next to him. The night before she had listened, advised, and endorsed, but mainly endorsed. She had also talked about her own work, workplace, and colleagues, about the changes that she envisaged; and she had sought his advice – his endorsement!

But that was the Kakadu. He looked down at a panting Pound and swallowed.

The truck straining up his long driveway housed two men in its cab and a medium-sized digger on its deck. One man had the belly of a Buddha, while the other was smoked thin. Both wore helmets and dusty visibility vests.

"Coffee, guys? Toast?"

"No, thanks, mate," the smoker replied. "Can we stop here? Need to be on the flat."

"Sure. Of course. Let me know if there's anything you need or want."

Large was a man of few words and wasted none on Quince, but he appeared to be the principal operator. Quince watched, intrigued, as they let down and released the digger, with Smoky sucking desperately through his teeth at air, but Large remaining laconic about breathing – hardly bothering at all. Quince worried that the bold splashes of fluorescent paint that demarcated power lines and water pipes might not be bright enough for a soul like Large, who was certain to suffer from sleep apnoea; but he could do little but admire the men as they got down to business.

First a claw was fitted to the digger to gouge out the earth, then a bucket to scoop and shift soil, and, finally, towards the end of the afternoon when rain was threatening, a blade to level the ground. They had regular breaks through the day, at ten, one and three, when Large consumed Coke and biscuits by the bottle and packet-ful, and Smoky smoked cigarette after cigarette with his black coffee.

Just before they were due to finish and while Quince was sending a picture of proceedings through to Eleanor, Terry drove up. "Hey, Quincy my boy, now we're talking! You need a hand?"

"No, thanks, Terry. They're almost done for the day."

"Are you sure the pads are big enough?"

"They were measured."

"Look small though."

"We'll see."

"We will, Quincy. We will indeed. Can always get these blokes back. What's happening tomorrow?"

"Nothing tomorrow, but the foundations, plumbing, power access and concrete slabs start going down next week."

"And then construction?"

"Construction, water connections, power, …"

"Three-phase?"

"Absolutely!"

"Things never work out as planned."

"We'll see."

"Always someone sick or sorry for himself, late with another job … fight with the missus."

"I've factored that in … weather too."

"That's a must."

With the smell of turned soil and possible rain, and after the noise and diesel of the digger, Quince longed for peace and solitude, but he wasn't unhappy to see Pansy and Bonny waving as they walked across the paddocks towards him. Pound bounded down to greet them, sniffing and play-fighting with Bill. He knew better than to mess with Bottom.

"Yahoo, Q, all this in one day!"

"Afraid so. Hi, Pans, hi, gorgeous."

"Hi, Uncle D. Hi, Dad."

"You want a wine, beer – tea?"

"French champagne more like it, Quincy, but no, a beer would hit the spot. Not one of those wimpy ones though."

"Sure, Terry. And a Pinot for you, Pans?"

"Midweek?"

"Why not?"

She chuckled. "Okay then, just one."

"And Bon?"

"I'll help myself."

"Good girl. I have some Phoenix Cola, but don't tell your mum."

"Secret's safe, Uncle L."

Once the drinks were poured, they clinked glasses and raised them to the levelled earth. "A new beginning, Q," Pansy said quietly, "I'm so pleased," and then added, "Is Eleanor coming out this evening, to have a look?"

"Not tonight, no. She's working late, but I have sent pics. I'll phone later. Might go across."

"I'm so pleased," Pansy repeated.

"And we'd like the lot of you to come for lunch on Saturday."

"We?"

"A combined effort – Eleanor, her mother Marion, and me."

<hr>

He had made a list: carrots, fish stock, celery, washed potatoes, tomatoes (not the best at this time of year) and fish. He had onions and garlic, and his lemon tree was loaded. Chillies? No, he had plenty in the freezer, and he'd have to go easy on those – 'Can't spoil it for the kids. Terry too'. Ginger, though, he needed fresh ginger. Still had some parsley in the garden.

The usual, older, lady was busy snapping at her underlings at the packing counter, and it took several minutes before one was dispatched to serve Quince. Wearing a hygiene hat like a new nurse, she approached cautiously, almost sorrowfully, and attempted to don fresh gloves with wet hands – her acne untreated and raw.

"Hello, hi, sorry – could I have a few pieces of gurnard? About three hundred grams?" She glanced back at her boss before making further vain attempts at housing her hands.

"What did you want?"

"Gurnard, please, just a few pieces. It looks lovely and fresh. You must have been up early to catch them?"

A hint of a smile crossed her lips as she peered at him through a tuft of escaped hair. "You said three hundred grams?"

"Yes, please."

"Big fillets – or small?"

"Any, thanks, I'm making a soup … or a stew … not sure which. Thick soup/thin stew, same difference."

She giggled as she meticulously, and with a degree of difficulty (due to the ongoing repulsive forces that separated her digits from her gloves), lifted first one strip and then another, and finally a further two, onto greaseproof paper. This was then transferred to the scale, and *'the man in the blue corner, weighing in at threeee hundred and ten grrrrams'.* "Is that okay?" she asked slyly.

"Show off!" Quince exclaimed. "I've never had anyone get that close before, not even her," he whispered, gesturing towards her boss lady. "You're born for the job."

"Hope so."

"You'll be in charge before your next birthday."

"Hope so," she giggled. "Have a nice day."

"You, too."

The key was to chop the ingredients up fine, first the onion, garlic, ginger, and solitary chilli, which required brief frying at medium heat ensuring not to brown, and then the carrot, potato, and celery. He had to remember to keep the fingers on his left hand flexed, especially when cutting the carrots! After softening the onions he added fish stock and stirred, then some hot water, then more. As soon as the pot came to the boil he threw in handfuls of the chopped vegetables, added the juice of a squeezed lemon, and stirred again. The only ingredient left partially whole was the tomato, but that would go in later. The fish, chopped into chunks, would be added minutes before the dish was served, and Bonny, if she was still a vegetarian, could have hers without. And bread! Ah, yes, Eleanor was going to pick up a couple of sourdough loaves on the way over. He needed to remind her.

The wind was nippy, and Quince decided that they would eat inside. It would be cramped but cosy with the fire going, and he could play some background blues. He turned the gas down to minimum and replaced the lid. The soup could be left to bubble on its own now.

Taking a dishcloth through to the laundry he noticed that Baker still hadn't eaten his food. In fact he hadn't been seen since the day of the diggers. He had had a habit of taking off, sometimes for a full week, but he was older now and Quince was concerned. 'I need to check the roads – ask Pansy to keep a look-out.'

Quince sat down and placed one hand on Pound's head, kneading him behind the ear. The lunch was going to be casual, he tried to convince himself, but of course it wasn't. Pansy and Terry had yet to meet Eleanor – Marion and Harry too – and tension was inevitable. He had thought to try to get Rose down from Auckland as well – the three of them hadn't been together for months – but then thought better of it. His sisters had been plotting to have him hitched for most of his adult life and an invitation to both might have raised expectations.

Quince looked over at his dining room table with its improvised seven-person place settings – its central jug of hellebores – and visualised again, as he had a thousand times before, the commotion: Baker, the vase breaking, the flower and the bird.

"Who would have thought, Pound?" Thump. "Who would have thought?" Thump, thump.

And who would have thought that a sparrow could salvage a lunch!

It was not going well in the early cheese and olive phase, and all that was being exchanged was politeness; but then Quince, because he was on edge and because Baker was on his mind, mentioned 'bells', and Terry immediately pounced: "What's that, Quincy? You mentioned 'bells'?"

"Bells?" Quince stared at him from the stove, "Oh … yes, I was just thinking about Baker for some reason … he's been missing … just for a couple of days. Not with you, Pans?"

"No, no, he's not, Q."

"He'll turn up. Probably with the ladies."

"But the 'bells'?"

"Cat bells, Terry. Won't keep them on. Keeps catching sparrows," he added forlornly while continuing to stir in the fish."

"Is Baker Chinese?"

"What?"

"Sparrows? You seen the doco on sparrows?"

"Sparrows?" Marion, who was sitting next to Terry, repeated.

"They killed more than forty million people."

"Sparrows, Terry?"

"Not sparrows, Marion, but not having sparrows." Eleanor looked across at Terry and her mouth twitched. "In China." Awkward pause. "You saw it with me, love, didn't you, or Bon? You might've been too young. It was years ago, on the History Channel, or National Geographic … probably the History Channel."

"Not sure, love. Doesn't ring a bell."

"Baker's bell?" Bonny quipped, and they all laughed.

"Anyway …"

"You mean the thing in China?" Marion interrupted.

"That's right, Marion, when Mao ordered them to kill sparrows."

"That was sickening."

"It was, wasn't it?"

"Beating pots and pans to stop them from roosting in the trees till they dropped out of the sky exhausted."

"Destroyed their nests too, and eggs and chicks."

"They ran around with nets … killed them in their thousands … millions probably."

"Yes, millions."

"But why, Dad?"

"They thought they were eating all the food, Bon, because Mao said so."

Marion turned to Bonny and Harry: "Those who killed the most got prizes, and those who refused were punished."

"But were sparrows eating all the food?"

"No, Bon, they were saving food."

"Saving?"

"By eating the insects that ate the food … locusts and things."

"So what happened?"

"Millions of people died of starvation."

"Forty million?"

"Thereabouts or more."

"Are they still starving?"

"No, they stopped starving after they stopped killing the sparrows."

"Why?"

"Because the insects stopped eating the rice."

Quince paused while Terry and Marion exchanged triumphant glances, and then he winked at Eleanor before serving up the soup.

"It was down this road and on the right."

"Are you sure?"

"Pretty much, but winter changes things."

"There won't be any sunflowers."

"True."

It was a cold Sunday, and quiet. Years ago there would have been smoke, but gas had replaced wood and the view west almost reached Raglan – would have if it were not for Pirongia. Quince had purposefully chosen a weekend because it was more likely that the woman would be home, and having Eleanor accompany him was a huge comfort.

"What should I take? Chocolates? A fuchsia? Something in a pot?"

"What a about a vase, Quince? The Heritage Gallery has some beautiful stuff." And there was one in the window that immediately caught his eye – a pottery vase in variegated blue with a deep base that would hold long stems.

"This is it," he said finally, as the car pulled up by a picket fence. "I'm sure this is it."

"She'll be thrilled, Quince. Who wouldn't? What was her name again? Do you remember?"

He was about to reply when a medium-sized dog of no discernible breed came bounding up to them barking joyfully. Violets and violas were already blooming in beds beside the driveway, and Quince noticed newly planted seedlings too – poppies mostly and cosmos. "Look at the conservatory, El," he whispered. "Isn't it lovely?"

"Begonias, I think, and the ferns ..." Her voice tailed off when she noticed someone stir in the conservatory.

"Excuse me," Quince called, "I'm sorry to disturb you, I ..."

"Doctor?"

"Sorry, I ..."

A woman slowly emerged from the side door of the conservatory, causing more excitement for the dog. "Stop, Alice. *Stop*. Sit. *Sit*."

"Carol!" Eleanor exclaimed in astonishment, while Quince

gripped his wrapped vase.

"He's inside if you want to see him – in his room," Carol said sulkily.

"Who?"

It was Carol's turn to be perplexed. "Kevin. You do want to see him, don't you? Everyone wants to see him."

"Is Kevin your husband?" Eleanor asked with a dry mouth.

Carol stared at Eleanor, then turned to look at Quince, at the parcel he was carrying. "I'm sorry, am I missing something? You aren't … um … selling or converting or something?"

"No, no, Carol, I'm sorry, I had absolutely no idea that you were the lady that my friend here …" but Eleanor was stopped mid-sentence by Quince's baffled expression. "Quince," she explained, turning to address him, "Carol is one of my patients."

A faint smile edged his lips. "I see."

"Carol, this is my friend, Quince. You were extremely kind to him some months ago – you gave him a flower – and, and he wanted to bring across a small gift to say thank you." There was a moment of silence with even Alice quiet, then Eleanor added, smiling, "He's spoken of you often, Carol, of your generosity, but I had no idea that you were you."

"I'm Quince," holding out his free hand, and offering his gift with the other. "You gave me a sunflower in the summer. It was magnificent."

Carol's face softened somewhat. "I do remember. You look younger though!"

"I am," he replied, laughing. "Eleanor has a potion that works wonders."

"She hasn't given it to me."

"She will, I'm sure. Lovely garden you have," he added.

"Needs a bit of work – pruning, planting – that sort of thing. You want a cup a tea, doctor?"

"Eleanor, please, Carol. No more 'doctor'. Okay?"

"Okay."

"We don't want to keep you though."

"No trouble at all. Make yourselves comfortable in the conservatory."

"Can I help you with the tea?"

"No," she answered sharply, and then softened again, "just make yourselves comfortable, but don't get too pally with Alice or you won't get a moment's peace."

Carol was thrilled with the vase, they could see that, and with Quince's recounting of the 'sunflower episode'. He proceeded to tell her about his mushroom venture without explaining the link and invited her to come out to visit. "Maybe you could give me a hand," he added, laughing.

"That would be lovely. Not sure though, I do work."

"Carol works at the local pharmacy, Quince."

"And there's my grandchild – she's away for a few days – and my garden … Alice."

There was no rush to get home as Harry was out for the day with a friend, so they took a drive out to Raglan where they ate calamari and chips on the cliffs.

"You mentioned a husband, El. What's the story there? I was surprised that he never came out to meet us."

"It's a long story."

CAROL

He was calling or coughing, she wasn't sure which … but there was phlegm. There definitely was phlegm. They'd talked about it at the hospital – what to do if it changed colour. He'd been given a 'back pocket prescription', as they called it, for turning brown – green too. To be honest Carol wasn't sure whether the colour had changed. She hadn't cared to look. They'd also provided a copy of his 'Compliance Report' at the Apnoea Clinic – she had it right here below her mirror. It had been compiled in the previous months through remote monitoring and offered detailed analysis of *Usage (hours)*, *Leaks (L/min)*, *Pressure (cmH$_2$O)*, and the one that she was most interested in and concerned about, *AHI (events/hour)*. This, it had been explained, pinpointed to the minute times when he effectively stopped breathing. Leakage was a problem for Kevin because of his facial hair, and this too could be detected by the monitor. In close proximity it was obvious: a good seal swished, and a bad seal farted.

Neither swish nor fart emanated from his bedroom and she assumed that he had removed his mask himself as she refocused attention to her hair (short and stiff after the expensive cut in Tristram Street), her forehead (recovering from the sun's exfoliation), her eyes (so similar to her father's), and her mouth – especially her mouth. It was taut with added crenulations that to an onlooker might have hinted at the sucking of an unripe plum pip, but to Carol it offered proof of defiance – of compliance with her covenant. Since her return from Australia she had determined that her mouth would not open and speak to Kevin, not when they were alone. She would nod, point, stare – possibly even construct a smile – but she would not speak.

With Evan, Angela, and Joey up north she could be less guarded. She had worried that they would get wind of her silent treatment – that it would cause further consternation for Evan and stop him from going. Her covenant, she found, did not extend to those that she was fond of, and, notwithstanding the hurt perpetrated by her son in Australia, she regretted that she had taken it out on the other.

"Joyce hasn't seen Joey for a couple of months, Mum, and there's the wider family too. I tried to get him into respite, I really did."

"Well, take him with you?"

"What?"

"The 'wider family' could dab the dribble on his chin."

"That's horrible, Mum!"

"No, Evan, he's horrible."

Evan looked at his mother despairingly. "He can hear you."

"I don't care."

Evan came over before work the next morning to say that he would not go away, and that Angela would go without him. It was obvious that he had had a wretched night, and Carol, if she were honest, had not slept well either.

"Nonsense, Evan, I ..."

"No, I should have waited until he could go into respite."

"Don't be silly, go. I can cope. Of course I can cope. I was just joking," she added unconvincingly.

"We'll talk later, when I get back this evening."

"No need. I'll be fine," and then she added after a pause, "and so will your father."

Evan was about to leave when he turned sharply. "Can you give Dad his meds this morning?"

"Of course."

"Joey's not well."

"Not well?"

"A cold or something."

"Can I help?"

"No."

"I can, Evan, I only go into work …"

"No … thank you. Angela's taking her to the doctor, to your doctor, this morning. Should be fine."

"Okay, well, I'm available if need be."

"Thank you."

It was so hard to do the right thing.

Evan did go, leaving early on the Saturday morning, with Carol making amends by wrapping up a hamper of boiled egg sandwiches and kissing them all goodbye. She had even mashed up Kevin's lunch-time potato with added butter and salt as if they were watching.

The weekend in fact had not been unpleasant with Saturday spent gardening, and Sunday … Sunday marked by that unexpected visit. Carol was still curious. The sunflower man she had not forgotten, but for him to arrive out of the blue with Eleanor Hutton! Very strange. Hard to fathom. Hard to believe that it was a mere coincidence after the house call from Dr Edge … yet Eleanor had seemed genuinely surprised … even embarrassed.

"He was nice though," she mused, speaking softly and still looking at the mirror in the morning light, "and he mentioned mushrooms. Wants me to visit. May even want help." She paused. "Now that would be something … growing mushrooms. Not that I like the ugly things," she added after scratching at a scaly blemish on her left temple that looked as if it was on her right, "not the way Mum fried them in inches of farm butter. Too rich. Made me vomit in the dahlias." A gurgle from next door distracted her momentarily, and then she continued. "Might spend a few days in Taranaki … see the old house … the club. Stay in New Plymouth. Would you like that?" she asked her eyes. "Might try and meet up with Stephanie. Married Steve, apparently. Wonder if she's still going."

It was after eight and she could see reflected behind her the Monday morning light catching Pirongia. The mountain looked larger than normal and she wondered whether it was the mirror's fault – whether it was curved one way or the other. She remembered that her uncle in Auckland had one that curved in and made the face look huge.

It was time to dress – she worked Mondays – but first she needed to give Kevin his porridge and pills – tidy his room before the personal care nurse arrived. Carol did not want tales of neglect getting back to Evan.

Alice, who had been scratching in the passage, started whimpering. "Don't you start! One whiner is quite enough for one house, thank you very much." Carol had opened the front door for her earlier, so it couldn't be that.

But Alice was not in the passage, she was in Kevin's room, and he was going blue.

It was compulsory for all employees of the pharmacy to complete a biannual Basic Life Support course, and Carol, who had completed one just six weeks prior, sprang into action:

D – Dangers? She swept the room with her outstretched arm. "All clear," she shouted, "No approaching vehicles."

R – Responsive? "Kevin, are you there?" No response. Listen for air… no air. Feel for pulse … not sure where.

S – Send for help. She ran back into her bedroom and lunged for her phone, fumbling to open the cover. First, she unlocked it, 1234; then pressed 1 on the way to pressing 111 – but it immediately started ringing (Evan, she vaguely remembered, had programmed in shortcuts for her 'contacts'). "Hello, Geraldine speaking, Edge Medical Centre. How can I help you?"

"He's stopped breathing."

"Who?"

"Kevin. Kevin's blue."

"Who's speaking? Address?"

"Carol Burton."

"Call an …" Click.

First Responder runs back into Subject's room wearing white nightie:

A – Open Airway? Not sure. Mouth shut. Pulls jaw back.

B – Normal Breathing? No. *Any Breathing?* Not sure – no hand mirror to catch condensate.

C – Start CPR. First Responder, with dog yapping, drags low, hard table to bedside, kneels on it and begins compressions using butts of hands with elbows extended: "1, 2, 3, 4, 5, 6, 7, 8, 9, 10, 11, 12, 13, 14, 15"; attempts breath administration covering Subject's mouth, but Subject's mouth remains closed and moustache tickles First Responder's upper lip; covers Subject's nostrils with mouth and exhales as if blowing up new balloon; moustache tickling First Responder's lower lip; begins further compression with dog bark at edge of upper scale; "1, 2, 3, 4, 5, 6, 7, 8, 9, 10, 11, 12, 13, 14, 15";

further vigorous and prolonged exhalation into Subject's nostrils while glancing sideways at Subject's chest to confirm chest wall response. No response. "1, 2, 3, 4, 5, 6, 7, 8, 9, 10, 11, 12, 13, 14, 15". First Responder's knees need repositioning. Quick breath (First Responder's chest bursting), then "1, 2, 3, 4, 5, 6, 7, 8, 9, 10, 11, 12, 13, 14, 15". Hot sweat of First Responder mingling with cold sweat of Subject causing "15" to slip and be ineffective. "15" repeated. First Responder not sure whether she can sustain another prolonged exhalation over Subject's nostril. Shifts knees and is about to try when Subject stirs ... twitches ... coughs coarsely, causing mucoidal filaments to collect at mouth corner and moustache. Brown? Green? Not really ... more like partially congealed clear jelly.

Carol stared at Kevin, and he stared back – his one eye more open than the other. For the first time she noticed his mask. It was at his side, his good side, and still hissing. She tried to hold it over his face, but he coughed, then coughed again more vigorously, and there was no seal to speak of. Switching off the machine she slowly eased first one of her bare feet and then the other onto the floor. He was not quite as blue – more mottled – but spluttering. *Recovery Position*, "Yes, recovery position." But he was so heavy, and the sheets were so wet. She pushed the table aside and positioned herself with one hand under his right shoulder and the other over the top of his left, and attempted rotation. *Put one leg over the other and the body will follow*, the manual had advised, but his leg was too heavy to lift. Carol managed in a fashion, however, to partially rotate Kevin, and as soon as he was on his side his colour improved. He fortunately had a rail on his bad side to stop him falling out, but she placed a pillow in his crutch, just in case, and was about to place another when Alice barked loudly, and she heard a voice:

"Carol – Mrs Burton," and in barged Dr Edge. He was carrying what looked like a toolbox in one hand and a square case in the other. "Is he … is he breathing?" he asked as he unfolded his stethoscope and leant over the bed. Carol, drab in her old white nightie and drenched in secretions remained mute. He listened over Kevin's chest and then felt for a pulse in his neck. "Good, Kevin, you're doing well. Just want to make you a bit more comfortable. Ambulance is coming. You're okay. You'll be okay." The doctor hurried round to the other side of the bed and gripped Kevin's jaw, easing it back a fraction. "Could we pull him over just a bit, Carol? That's it … a bit more. Excellent! Well done."

They could hear a siren approaching. "Did he complain of chest pain? Headache?" Carol shook her head. "Any cough, shortness of breath?" Carol nodded faintly. "Through the night?"

"Always," she finally managed to say, but barely above a whisper. "He always coughs."

"Was he restless last night? Did he use his machine?"

"Don't know."

The ambulance was pulling up outside. "Did he stop breathing?" She nodded. "But then got started again?"

"I started him."

"You did?"

She nodded, "With CPR … fifteen-to-one."

Frank stared at her as the ambulance officers came striding in with their equipment. He turned to the first who entered: "Possible MI … may be underlying pneumonia. Could have aspirated. Wife administered immediate CPR … got him going again. History of previous CVA, ischaemic heart disease and diabetes … on CPAP."

After inserting an IV line and nasal prongs for oxygen, the older officer applied leads to Kevin's chest, leg and arm, then peered at the first tracing that emerged. "Multiple ventricular ectopics and peaked T waves in V1 and V2. Probable septal MI." This information was then transmitted by radio to the receiving hospital registrar. "Code 1. I repeat, code 1. Two puffs of nitro already on board. No pain, no. Yeah, saturation improved with the oxygen on board – marginal though, just 91. Okay, yeah. We're on our way." And within minutes the ambulance was wailing off to Waikato Hospital without another word spoken.

Carol cut a forlorn figure with her bedraggled hair, smudged eyeliner, and soiled nightie. Her lips were trembling. Frank put his arm around her. "You go and have a shower while I make some tea. You did well, Carol. You really did. Can I call anyone?" he added, "Your son? A friend?"

"My son's up north."

"You need him here." Carol started weeping softly – something that she had not done for as long as she could remember. "Is there anyone who could drive you to the hospital?"

Carol sniffed and shook her head. "No, I'll be fine."

"You sure?" She nodded. "No neighbour I could call?"

She shook her head again and half-smiled. "No, I'll be fine. Got Alice," she added, patting the dog.

"Okay, you get spruced up while I put the kettle on."

"What about work?"

"Work can wait, and I need tea even more than you do."

"Thank you, doctor."

"Frank, please."

"You're like Dr Hutton."

"Eleanor?"

"Yes, she also wants me to call her by her first name. She's also kind. She was here yesterday," Carol added after a pause.

"Eleanor?"

"Yes."

"Were you ill?"

"No, she didn't know it was me."

"What do you mean?"

"She came with the man."

"What man?"

"The one who told me about the sunflower and the sparrow."

ABOUT THE AUTHOR

Fred Simpson was raised in a small village in southern Zimbabwe. In the 1970s he taught English in Bulawayo, worked illegally as a London labourer, failed as a cookware salesman in Germany, then studied medicine in Cape Town. He worked in rural general practice in South Africa before emigrating with his family to New Zealand in 1987. He currently lives in the North Island town of Cambridge with his wife and one cat.

He continues to work as a medical practitioner, but his 'secret love' is writing. His poetry has featured in New Zealand, Australian and South African literary magazines, and his first novel, *Ted's Urn*, was published in 2015.